the M & M Boys

LARA REZNIK

VIOLET
CROWN
Publishers

Austin, TX USA

Julie —

I hope you enjoy this book. Very different from the other. Check for my new one Bagels & Salsa do out Jan 2.

www.LaraReznik.com

Publisher's Note

All rights reserved under International and American Copyright Conventions. Published in the United States by Violet Crown Publishers, LLC. No part of these pages, either text or image may be used for any purpose other than personal use. Therefore, reproduction, modification, storage in a retrieval system or retransmission, in any form or by any means, electronic, mechanical or otherwise, for reasons other than personal use, is strictly prohibited without prior written permission.

This is a work of fiction. Names, characters, places, and incidents are either the product of the author's imagination, or are used fictitiously. Any resemblance to actual persons, living or dead, business establishments, events, or locales is entirely coincidental.

*This book is dedicated to my father
William Resnick,
my beloved hero and Pop.
Family man first, NYC fireman, WW II veteran,
and ... a devoted Yankee fan from the time
of Babe Ruth to the end.
On October 13, 2011, hours before he died
at age 95, the hospice doctor came to check on my father
in his bed at home. "Mr. Resnick, how are you
feeling?" he asked.
My Pop responded, "I'd feel a lot better if
the Yankees had made the playoffs."*

Contents

AUTHOR'S NOTE

Mixing real people, places, and events into a novel is tricky business. While this is a coming-of-age story about a fictional character, Marshall Elliot, it also depicts the real life struggles of two very renowned baseball heroes, Roger Maris and Mickey Mantle.

Die-hard Yankee fans beware. While this author has done extensive research and tried to capture many true-to-life events, at times I have had to rearrange schedules, batting orders, and game statistics when the story justified doing so. One important fact that I have taken literary license with in this book is depicting Roger getting to the Yankees from Kansas City in 1961. In reality Roger Maris was traded to the Yankees in 1960. He won MVP that season, a full year ahead of his home run chase. So much for those who say he was a "one season wonder."

On the other hand, this book contains rare quotes from Big Julie Issaacson, Tony Kubek, Bob Cerv, and others who hung out in the Queens apartment that summer with Mickey and Roger. Conversations have carefully been reconstructed based on research that include quotes from their memories of the events.

This novel is based on a screenplay, *The M&M Boys,* that I wrote and registered with the U.S. Copyright Office on April 22, 1999. The screenplay was optioned twice and considered for representation by the William Morris Agency in New York. Any likeness to an HBO film written by Hank Greenburg, and directed by Billy Crystal that aired on HBO on April 28, 2001, is purely coincidental.

One last note. For those of you who are fans of my novel, *The Girl From Long Guyland*, *The M&M Boys* portrays a glimpse at a young Laila the summer of 1961 when she spent the summer living with her grandmother in Queens after her father had a car accident.

LARA REZNIK

In the summer of 1961, while John F. Kennedy played hardball with the Russians, Roger Maris and Mickey Mantle battled to break Babe Ruth's single-season home run record, which had stood at 60 for 34 years. They became known as "The M&M Boys," locked in a battle of home run one-upmanship.

CHAPTER ONE

America's Favorite Pastime

MARSHALL

There were days I felt like killing my father. Well, maybe just whacking him over the head with my Little League bat. But even when I had such terrible thoughts, what I wanted most was for him to notice me. Baseball used to be the ticket to his attention. Most Saturday mornings we'd drive over to Hudson Park where we'd spend hours on batting and field practice.

"You work hard, you play hard, and you win," Dad often said. "No boy of mine is gonna be a loser."

Dad had been a star shortstop in high school and often bragged about how he'd gotten a full baseball scholarship to Binghamton University but turned it down to marry my mother and take care of me. He also boasted about *my* stats to the other dads. I could hear him from the dugout and it made my stomach knot up.

When Dad wasn't around, I spent most of my free time rolling balls off of our garage's pitched roof, or bouncing them off the curb for grounders. Sometimes, I took an old bat and launched rocks in the air imagining them flying out of the park at Yankee Stadium.

At eleven years old, all my hard work had paid off. Or so I thought. Kids on my Little League team had nicknamed me The Home Run King. I'd finally discovered my sweet spot and had hit five or six balls out of the park. After every ballgame, Dad would pat my head and we'd go get ice cream.

Life revolved around baseball. If I wasn't practicing or playing, I was watching the Yankees on TV with Dad, or trading baseball cards with my cousin Bobby. Like most of my friends, I dreamed that someday I'd be the next Mickey Mantle.

Everything changed after my last Flushing Bears' Little League game in 1960. Angry gray clouds threatened to cancel the game with our rivals from Forest Hills. But the fat raindrops stopped as quickly as they'd started, and the sun poked out in time for the game.

Dad chose that day to drag me over to the dugout where my coach sat working on the lineup. "How about giving Marshall a shot at shortstop?" Dad didn't say hello or nothing to Coach Lee, just got to the point. Besides, I was happy playing in the outfield.

Coach Lee glanced up from his clipboard. "Right now Marshall's doing a heck-of-a job in right field. And Mike Bernstein has the best arm on the team."

"My kid's better than that Jew boy. Maybe not as tall, but every bit as quick, and his arm is plenty strong."

I winced and prayed no one else had heard Dad talking.

Coach Lee locked his jaw. "Let me coach my team, Edmund."

Dad stormed off to the bleachers.

A few minutes later, a school bus roared into Hudson Park

and screeched to a halt. As the boys from Forest Hills filed out, our team stood bug-eyed on the field. "Oh, my God," whispered my cousin, Bobby, who played catcher for our team. "Those guys are monsters."

I had a horrible day at the plate and went 0 for 4. Worst of all, I struck out in the last inning with two outs, and the winning run on base. It cost my team the game and me a spot on the All-Star team. I'd felt bad enough with all the sad-sack looks from my teammates, but then Dad gave me a scalding look and steamed off to the car.

On the drive home, he muttered something under his breath about losers, then didn't say another word. Ma sat in the backseat like she always did when we drove to my games. She leaned forward and whispered in my ear, "Don't worry, sweetheart, there's always another season."

Dad switched on the radio to the Yankee game.

"This is Mel Allen with Phil Rizzuto bringing you the top of the ninth inning of the Yankee-Red Sox game from Fenway Park. Mantle's coming to the plate for the fourth time with runners on first and second. There's two outs. Boston is leading 5 to 3. The Mick may be the Yankee's last hope."

"That's right, Mel. The Red Sox have walked him three times today. He needs a hit."

"Here's the wind up ... the pitch to Mickey ... way outside, ball one. Brewer winds up again ... low, ball two. It sure doesn't look like they're going to give Mick anything to hit, Phil."

"They're certainly not gonna chance it now with the game on the line, Mel. We've seen this all year long. Mickey's been walked thirty times so far, almost every fifth time at bat. The Yanks sure need another power hitter behind the Mick so they can't pitch around him."

"Mantle's back at the plate. Here comes the third pitch. It's high and tight and almost hit the Mick. Fourth pitch is on the way. Outside and high. Mickey lunges and hits the pitch way out of the strike zone deep to left field towards the foul line. Holy Cow! It's outta here!"

When the Yankee game shifted to a Brylcream commercial, Dad broke the silence. "Mantle doesn't let his team down."

"Don't be so hard on the boy, Edmund," Ma said. "Can't you see he feels bad enough?"

"Shush your mouth. What do you know about baseball, anyways?"

I swallowed. "I-I just couldn't—"

"Don't give me any lip. You screwed up the last game of the season, and you'll never live it down."

No one said another word the rest of the drive home.

Later that night, Dad appeared in the doorway of my bedroom with a tumbler of whiskey in his hand. "You embarrassed me out on the field today, boy."

A swell of shame washed over me. "I'm sorry, Dad. I'll do better next time."

"Next time, my ass. Maybe you should take up the piano."

CHAPTER TWO

White Buckskins

March 1, 1961

The phrase "affirmative action" was first used to refer to a governmental requirement to promote equal opportunity by giving preferences in order to remedy prior discrimination. President Kennedy used the term with the issuance of Executive Order 10925. (1)

BIG JULIE

Casey Stengel and me was having a few at the Ritz. Casey killed a double-shot of Jack Daniels and glanced up at me with bloodshot eyes. "I need a favor, Jules."

"I'm all ears," I said.

"Can ya drive over to La Guardia to pick up our new boy, Roger Maris? He's flying in from Kansas City."

I smiled. "Ain't that where Dorothy from *The Wizard of Oz* came from?"

"You think that place's Hicksville? This fella grew up in Fargo, North Dakota, which makes Kansas City seem like Chicago. But the kid's produced a .278 batting average, 80 RBIs, and 28 homers. I'm expecting big things from him."

The answer to the Yankees' prayers. A power bat to complement Mickey so the pitchers would stop pitching around him. Casey couldn't afford another bad year. "I hope he's your man."

"The plane's due in at four-thirty," he said.

I checked my watch. "I dunno. The wife expects me home for dinner." Selma was gonna be pissed. Friday was the night of holy obligation for our weekly *Shabbos* dinner. And tonight her parents were taking the train in from Long Island.

But I owed Casey a lot. A few years back, I'd been taking bets on some boxers I managed and playing the horses more than I shoulda. I'd come close to losing the wife and kid over my gambling debts. I loved those two more than life itself. Casey got me a union job, plus hired me to handle special assignments for the Yankees, and I left my bookie career behind.

Casey poured himself another shot from the bottle on the table, grabbed some bills from his wallet, and handed them to me. "Work it out, Jules. You can count on me to make it worth your while."

ROGER

"NOW BOARDING AT gate 24, American Airlines flight 423 to New York City," wailed through the loud speakers in the Kansas City airport. I bit my lip so hard that I tasted the metallic flavor of blood just like the time I'd been hit in the mouth with a ground ball.

My wife Pat opened her big canvas purse that served double-duty as a diaper bag. She pulled out a washcloth and dabbed my mouth. "Ya can't be going to the Big Apple looking like ya just got in a brawl, now can ya?" Her eyes brimmed with tears.

"I'd stay here in Kansas City. I swear I would, if I'd known you and the kids weren't coming."

Pat pursed her lips. "We've talked about it enough, honey."

I glanced over at our three children dressed in their Sunday best. My oldest, Susan, was four and Pat had just enrolled her in ballet lessons. She was a real daddy's girl and followed me around the house asking tough questions all the time. "What is air made of, Daddy?" or "Where does God live?"

Roger Jr., dark and slender like Pat, was an active toddler and already liked to play Wiffle ball until I was plumb tuckered out. Baby Kevin, barely six months, cooed at me as he clung to his teddy bear. Would he even remember his daddy the next time he saw me? And when would that be?

I looked at Pat. "Honey, I know we agreed on this arrangement, but it just doesn't feel right now that I'm going. I bet if I call Casey Stengel they'd figure out a way and—"

"Don't start acting like a dumb hick on me, Rog. Playing for the Yankees is the chance of a lifetime. We've got three college tuitions to think about in the future. Well, four, if you count…" Her voice trailed off.

My heart felt like a grenade exploding. "Jesus, Mary, and Joseph. Have we got another one in the oven, honey?"

Pat blushed and gave me the same sweet smile she'd had when we met at a Fargo High School basketball game. Something about that smile of hers made me want to hold her in my arms forever.

"That settles it," I said. "I'm not gettin' on that plane."

"Stop your silliness. I'll be flying to visit you in New York whenever I can get Mama to stay with the kids."

The final boarding announcement ended our conversation. In my heart, I knew she was right. Best for everyone I go to New York. Make a chunk of money while the going's good.

I hugged each of my kiddos in turn, doing my best to hold back the waterworks. But when Roger Junior said, "Love do, Dada," hot tears formed in my eyes. I wiped them away with my jacket sleeve.

One last kiss from Pat, then I moved in line with the other passengers boarding the flight to LaGuardia. Cold rain mixed with sleet fell as I hurried onto the turboprop. I pulled my boarding pass from my coat pocket. Casey Stengel had sent me a first class ticket. Five years as a player for Cleveland and Kansas City we'd always flown coach.

As I entered the plane, I raked my fingers through my hair slick from the rain. I'd worn it in a crew cut my whole life, same as my brother Rudy. He had been my daddy's favorite, and the better athlete, but he'd contracted polio when he turned eighteen, which dashed all hopes of playing ball. I often felt guilty I was living his dream.

I handed my ticket to the tall blonde stewardess at the door.

She smiled at me revealing perfect Chiclet teeth. I always noticed a good set of choppers since kids in high school had teased me about my crooked ones. I'd be damned if I didn't make sure that all my kids got braces.

The stewardess touched my arm. "Would you like a cocktail before we take off, Mr. Maris?"

"No thanks, Miss—"

"Call me Betty."

The stewardess snatched my hand and squeezed it. "You have a good flight, now you hear? And don't hesitate to press the call button if you need anything." She winked. "And I mean *anything*."

I never knew how to handle women who flirted with me. Sure it was flattering, but it made me real uncomfortable. But no matter, Pat's always been the only gal for me.

As I shuffled down the aisle to my seat in 2A, someone was shouting at the stewardess. I turned around to see what the ruckus was about. A tiny old woman with frizzy orange hair had just boarded the plane. "I can't sit there, I tell you."

"You're going to have to," said the stewardess who'd been so friendly to me moments before.

"I get sick in the back of a plane. I'll throw up my lunch. Brisket, baked beans and green Jell-O all over everything. Not a pretty sight."

The stewardess placed her hand on the woman's shoulder. "The flight's sold out. There's nowhere else to seat you, ma'am."

The old woman's face puffed up like a donut rising in the pan. "Stop pushing me."

Everyone in the plane stared at them.

"You either take that seat or leave the plane. It's up to you, ma'am."

The poor old woman began to sob. "I can't sit there, I won't."

I squeezed through the line of boarding passengers toward the stewardess and the old lady. Not an easy feat. "Miss, ah, Betty, I'll be glad to change seats with this woman."

"I wouldn't hear of it, Mr. Maris. Go back to first class."

I produced my best crooked Fargo smile. "Honest, Miss. I like the back of the plane better."

The stewardess snatched my ticket from my coat pocket

and handed it to the woman. "Well, if you insist."

"First class! Wait until I tell my sister. You're my hero, young man." The old lady kissed my cheek.

I didn't feel like much of a hero as I endured a roller coaster of endless turbulence perched in the last row. Lightning bolts flashed in the sky, and thunder rumbled so loud I feared the plane might explode. A young couple across the aisle clasped their white-knuckled hands. Their faces looked pale as my wife's talcum powder.

Grasping the arm of my seat as the plane bucked and rolled, I tried to recall if I'd paid the last premium on my life insurance policy.

BIG JULIE

WHEN I ARRIVED at La Guardia, I learned that Flight 423 was running late. I sat on a cracked plastic chair in the waiting area and read the *New York Post* from cover to cover. Over an hour passed, and still no update on the plane's arrival time.

I schlepped over to the American Airlines counter clerk, an old army buddy of mine.

He smiled at me. "What's going on, Jules? You got a tip for me?"

"Sorry can't help you there no more, bud." In the past, I could make a quick buck just scribbling down the name of a horse to play. "Hey, what's the story on the flight from Kansas City?"

He gestured for me to move closer. "Control center's not posted a time for the plane's arrival. Rumor is they hit a shitload of turbulence."

I pictured the poor kid up there chewing his nails and kissing his crucifix. My buddy's left eye twitched. "So who the hell you waiting for?"

"Roger Maris."

"Never heard of the guy."

"You will."

I wandered through the airport to a wall of phone booths to call Selma and let her know I'd be late. She wasn't gonna be happy. But that's the way it was these days, checking in with the woman like a private to his sergeant. She had me by the balls, and to tell you the truth, I liked it that way. It kept me out of trouble. At least most of the time.

The plane had landed by the time I returned to the gate. I caught a glimpse of passengers as they teetered down the steps. Mostly businessmen in sport jackets and suits. A few minutes later, a little old lady and a young couple followed. All looked green at the gills. Then a couple of hot stewardesses with great gams paraded by. I just loved those tight uniforms they wore.

Where was the kid? I was screwed if he'd missed the flight. Selma would chew my head off if I came home any later than I'd already told her. Finally, this six-foot guy with a sandy crew cut and barn-broad shoulders straggled out dressed in a polo shirt under a seersucker jacket. Jesus, didn't he know that Yankees were supposed to look sharp in public? Navy sport coat, tie, starched white shirt with cufflinks.

When he passed through the door to the terminal, I greeted him with a stiff handshake. "Jules Isaacson. Everybody calls me Big Julie." I patted my stomach, which my darling Selma says resembles a basketball.

Roger half-smiled and apologized for keeping me waiting.

He had a soft Midwestern drawl.

"Ain't your fault the plane was late," I said. "Hope you don't mind me coming instead of Casey. So, how was the flight? Like riding a buckboard I heard. You must be starving. How 'bout a hot pastrami sandwich? I know a kosher deli not too far from here."

Roger squinted but didn't speak.

"Hey, if you don't like pastrami, we can get some Italian. You like lasagna, pizza, maybe? I know a place—"

"No disrespect Mr. Isaacson, but you sure talk a lot."

That shut me up for a full ten-seconds. "Well, are you hungry?"

"Nah. Just want to git settled in the hotel so I can call Pat. She always worries when I fly."

"No problem." I reached for my wallet to retrieve some of the dough Casey had handed me. When I looked down, Roger's shoes glared at me. White bucks. "You gotta get rid of them shoes."

"What's wrong with them?"

"Jesus, you can't wear Pat Boone shoes in New York," I said. "The seersucker's bad enough. Let's go shopping for some new clothes."

"I like the ones I got on."

The kid was serious. Minutes later, we were driving on the Grand Central in my new white Lincoln. Roger leaned back in the plush cherry-red leather seat. "Nice set of wheels."

"Just bought it last week. Maybe you'll get one someday."

"Cars really aren't my thing. I mean, I like to drive 'em okay. Just nothing fancy."

"What is your thing, kid?"

"Baseball."

"Besides baseball."

"I dunno."

"You gotta like something?"

He scratched his head. "Bowling, I guess."

"You're serious."

"The wife and I used to play in a Fargo couple's league every Friday night." He reached into his pocket and pulled out a snapshot of his family.

I glanced at the photo and handed it back to him. "Handsome brood. I got just my boy, Danny. You'll like my wife, Selma. We'll have you over for dinner some time soon."

"Thanks, that'll be swell."

Swell. Was he twelve? "So how 'bout getting some new duds?"

"Is there a Thom McAn's in this city?"

I let out my breath. "Now, you're talking. But let's go to Florsheims. That's where Mickey buys his shoes."

I swung by a small shopping center, but after circling for a while it didn't appear we'd find a parking spot anytime in the twentieth century. I handed Roger one of the hundred-dollar bills that Casey had given me. "Head over to Florsheims and buy some Wingtips. If you don't like them, get you a pair of good loafers."

Fifteen minutes later, Roger sauntered out from a store carrying two shoeboxes.

"Let me see what you got," I said.

He handed me the boxes.

When I opened them, there were two more pairs of white buckskins inside. I shook my head. "This town's gonna eat you alive, kid."

MICKEY

WHEN CASEY STENGEL first brought in Roger Maris from Kansas City, the kid pretty much stayed to himself and rarely broke a smile. It was rumored that Roger, a left-handed pull hitter, was my batting insurance. I tried not to think they were priming him to be the future heir to the Yankee dynasty like I'd been for DiMaggio.

We were playing an exhibition game in the Grapefruit League in Florida. It was the bottom of the ninth inning and we were down by one run, with two outs. I'd already hit one out of the park earlier in the game. I stepped up to the plate and hit a shot to the gap in left center for a double.

With first base open, they'd normally walk the cleanup hitter, but Roger was 0 for 3 that day. Casey had been all over his ass in the dugout. Exhibition game or not, this was Roger Maris's first chance to come through in the clutch for the Yankees.

As Roger approached the plate, Casey stood outside the dugout with a sour face and his arms crossed. Roger dug his back cleat into the dirt and readied himself for the first pitch. He swung hard and missed for a strike. Then Roger pulled the ball sharply down the right field foul line. He took the next pitch on the corner and fled into the dugout.

I could already see the headline in the morning papers:

"0 FOR 4 FOR THE YANK'S NEW POWER HITTER FROM KANSAS."

Later that night, the team hung out at Howard Johnson's

for dinner. Roger sat alone at a table eating fried fish and hush puppies. I slid into the vinyl booth without asking permission.

He raised his head as I sat down.

I snatched one of the hard rolls sitting in a wicker basket. "That was a helluva catch in deep right field. But nobody will print that."

Roger cracked a smile. "Thanks for noticing."

"Trust me, the game is already old news. I assume Casey chewed you out."

He swallowed a mouthful of hush puppies before responding. "We had some words. I told him he could send me back to Kansas City."

I laughed. "That's not how you deal with Casey. You want to grab a couple of beers? Treat's on me."

Roger flashed a wide, disarming grin. "Can't turn a deal like that down."

We drove to a local dive called Buster's. The joint was as dark as a cavern lessening the chance of us being recognized. I'd been there on more than one occasion with Whitey.

We both chugged down our share of whatever they had on tap. As straight an arrow as Roger appeared, he certainly could slam down a cold one. Four or five beers later, I realized there was a lot about Roger that reminded me of when I first arrived in New York in '51. That seemed liked a lifetime ago. "Everyone says you're homesick. Is that true?"

"Heck, my wife and kids are two thousand miles away. Sure, I'm torn up about it."

"My family's in Dallas. I haven't seen 'em in four months." I pulled out a snapshot of Merlyn and the boys.

"Handsome boys, and a pretty missus. Don't you miss them?"

I looked at him through bleary eyes. "I've been in New York almost ten years now. Came here straight out of high school. My life is complicated."

"Pat and I met in high school. We've only been apart when the A's went on the road. Back then, there was just my eldest Susan, and Pat'd often pack her up in the car and surprise me."

"I wouldn't like no surprises like that."

Roger squinted. "Guess not."

"You know, me and my wife, Merlyn, met in high school too. I played baseball at Commerce and she was the prettiest cheerleader at our rival, Picher High. The prettiest girl in Oklahoma, period." I'd screwed up bad when it came to my marriage. We'd started out two kids in love. My daddy had pressured me to marry her, thinking she'd settle my wild ass down. Unfortunately, fame and fortune had changed everything we both cared about. "Hey, you ready for another beer?"

"No thanks, I gotta get up early to take some extra batting practice."

"You're shitting me?"

"Nope. Tomorrow when we play Cincinnati, I'm gonna hit one out of the park. Show Casey what I can do. You be ready to run those bases."

"Not if I've already hit one out myself. I'll be waiting for you in the dugout."

Roger stuck his hand in his pocket and fished out a ten-dollar bill. "Wanna put your money where your mouth is?"

"You bet," I said.

The next day the Florida sun blazed bright in a cloudless sky. The stands were packed with locals and sunburned snowbirds from New York dressed in plaid shorts, T-shirts, and Yankee caps. A Good Humor Ice Cream truck was parked near the field. The owner was doing a brisk business.

As I sat in the dugout chewing some tobacco, I overheard Casey talking to Ralph Houk, one of the coaches. "Maris may have been a big mistake. It's one thing to be a stud for the A's, but that don't mean a guy can cut it with the Yankees."

Part of me felt relieved Roger wasn't living up to the potential Casey expected. Hell, I had enough problems without a serious competitor on my own team. But after hanging out with the guy, I felt sorry for him. Yankee management had forced him to leave his family behind. Now, before the season had even officially begun, Stengel was talking of canning him. Baseball was a business and you were only as valued as your last performance.

It was the bottom of the seventh and we were down by two runs. I headed to the plate and hit lefty. Bobby Richardson was on first base. The pitcher threw me an outside pitch and I hit a soft liner to left and took first base.

Roger was 0 for 2. He stepped up to the plate and took the first pitch for a strike. The next pitch was right in his wheelhouse, inside and low, and Roger pulled it deep for a home run.

The fans finally had something to cheer about.

When Roger crossed the plate, Casey ran up to him and slapped his back. Stengel had a lot riding on this kid from Kansas City. He was turning seventy and rumor had it that Yankee management wanted him to turn in his pinstripe uniform. We had to win the pennant this year or he was toast.

CHAPTER THREE

The Copa-Banana

April 16, 1961

At 01:00, the first group of a force of about 1,300 Cuban exiles of Brigade 2506 made an amphibious landing at Playa Girón, a beach at the Bahia de Cochinos ("Bay of Pigs") on the southern coast of Cuba. (2)

MARSHALL

Things between Dad and me were never the same after the 1960 Little League season. We rarely played catch or did batting practice anymore. As our front yard bloomed with my mother's beloved roses and tulips the following spring, Dad arrived home from work later and later. When he did get home, he argued with Ma about stupid stuff. "Damn it Marion," he might say, "look at all the grease on the countertops. And the linoleum is downright filthy." Complaining about the house was bad enough, but soon his comments became downright cruel.

There were times my mother fought back, resulting in ugly shouting matches. When the yelling got too loud, I'd head to my room, stuff cotton balls in my ears, and pull out my baseball card collection. Sometimes, I even hid in my closet.

One day, Ma spent the whole afternoon cooking lasagna, and baking Dad's favorite chocolate layer cake. The delicious smells filled the house and drew me to the kitchen where the table was set with my grandmother's china and silverware.

"What's going on? It ain't, I mean it *isn't* Christmas."

"It's our fifteenth wedding anniversary," Ma said. She smoothed down a crease in the tablecloth with the palm of her hand. "I want everything to be perfect."

Dad was late as usual, and shoveled down the lasagna without once mentioning anything about the anniversary.

"This is the best lasagna ever," I said. "Way better than Paisano's."

My mother smiled. "Thanks, honey." After we were done eating, she cleared the dinner plates and placed the chocolate cake on the table.

Dad looked down at the cake then glared at Ma. "You might cut down on the sweets, Marion. You're beginning to look like a baby elephant."

I cringed when he said it.

She flew up the stairs and slammed the door to her room. An hour later, I could still hear her weeping through her bedroom door.

A few nights later, Dad and I sat around eating popcorn as we watched *The Red Skelton Show*. It felt good to be hanging out with him, something that didn't happen that often anymore. After a commercial break, John Wayne, Dad's favorite actor, appeared as a surprise guest. By the stupefied pop-eyed look on Red's face, he was as stunned as the rest of the audience.

"Holy mackerel, it's the Duke!" Dad turned up the sound

on the television, sat back down, and grabbed a handful of pop-corn.

The TV screen suddenly turned to snow and made hissing sounds.

"Goddamn," Dad said, as he leaped up from the couch knocking the plastic bowl of popcorn off the coffee table. Kernels flew around like bullets in the air then landed on the shag carpet. Dad wiggled the rabbit ears on top of the television. When that didn't work, he banged on the console with his fists. "Can you believe this shit?"

My mother rushed in from the kitchen. "What's the matter, Edmond? That language is not—"

"Shush, Marion."

She began to pick up pieces of popcorn off the carpet.

Miraculously, the picture reappeared on the TV screen. The Duke busted up laughing when Red came out dressed in identical cowboy duds. Dad patted the couch and smiled at Mother. "Come sit down, honey."

When she did, he put his arm around her shoulders. I hadn't seen them together like that in a long time.

Just then, the phone rang. I raced into the kitchen and picked up the receiver.

"Hey, Marshall, get your mother, real quick," said Uncle George in a strange voice.

"Is something wrong?"

He took a deep breath. "Your aunt's on the way to the hospital in an ambulance."

"Ma!" I shouted. "Come here quick."

My mother raced into the kitchen and grabbed the phone from my hand. "Oh my God! I'll be waiting in the driveway."

She called out, "Edmund, they think Ethel's appendix burst. I have to go to the hospital."

Dad looked annoyed. "What about George?"

"He's a mess. I told him to pick me up on his way."

"You should have run that by me first."

My mother's eyes widened. "What for?"

"I had plans to meet Greeley to talk about our new project. He's probably on his way to the office as we speak."

Mother's lower lip trembled. "I need to be with my sister." The sound of a horn in the driveway interrupted the conversation.

"That's George." She grabbed her wool coat from the hall closet and said, "Don't you dare leave Marshall alone." Then she darted out the door.

"Damn!" Dad said to no one in particular.

"I'm fine," I said. "Go to work. Bobby stays by himself all the time."

Dad scratched his head. "Get on your jacket. You're coming with me."

Fifteen minutes later, Dad pulled the Galaxie into a crowded parking lot. A red neon sign said, COPA-BANANA.

"I thought we were going to your office."

"Sometimes guys do business over a beer. It builds relationships outside of work."

I followed him inside a dark room filled with men. The only ladies were three waitresses dressed in shorts and low-cut blouses like Daisy Mae from the comic strip. They waved friendly-like as if they knew us. One had white-blonde hair all teased up in curls on the top of her head. Another had long black hair down to the middle of her behind. One of her fake eyelashes had come unglued and was barely hanging on her eyelid. The third waitress had blood-orange hair and the biggest boobs I'd ever seen.

Dad smiled at the ladies, then waved at a tall guy in a booth in the back. "There's Greeley." We headed over to his booth and slipped inside. The vinyl seats were torn and the table was slick with spilt beer. "This is my son, Marshall," Dad said.

Mr. Greeley held out his hand to me. He was tall and muscular and looked younger than Dad, more like a college guy dressed in Wranglers and a black T-shirt. "I've heard a lot about you, Marshall."

I shook his hand, squeezing hard like Dad had taught me. "I've heard about you too."

Mr. Greeley pulled out a pack of Camels from his shirt pocket. "Oh, yeah. What did the old man say about me?"

The blonde waitress came up to the table. She had a plastic badge that said, CANDY COTTON. "Hey, Ed, what can I get ya?" She looked in my direction and smiled. "What a cutie patootie."

"That's my boy," Dad said.

She shouted across the crowded room. "Sweets, come over and meet Ed's kid."

The waitress with the long black hair strolled over to us. Her nametag read, SWEETIE POTATO. She winked at Dad then tousled my hair. "A chip off the old block."

Before long, the stacked waitress with orange hair joined the others at our table. The name on her tag was PEACH COBBLER.

For the next couple of hours, Dad and Greeley ordered shots of Schnapps which they chased down with glasses of draft beer. I listened to the ladies repeat the same line to all the guys. "Hey, big boy, wanna see a girl dance for a dollar?" Then they'd turn around and shake their fannies to whatever music was blasting from the jukebox. Dad, Mr. Greeley, and the others stuffed money in their shorts and patted their behinds.

The ladies kept bringing me free Coca-Colas. Dad offered to pay for them but they refused. Peach slid in the booth next to me. Her perfume was so strong I nearly gagged, and her boobs jiggled when she sat down. "What grade are you in, honey?"

I cleared my throat. "Sixth."

"I got me a little boy just about your age. Maybe you two can play together some time."

"Sure." Even though the ladies were nice to me, I just wanted to go home. Dad stared at them and spoke in a deep voice I didn't recognize.

Finally, the lights flickered on, and Dad stood up. The end of his nose was pink as my mother's roses. "Time for us to get going, son."

The Galaxie weaved all over the road on the ride home. Dad zoomed right through a red light and swerved just in time to avoid hitting a truck. I closed my eyes and gripped the leather seat. Then I started to silently pray.

When we pulled into the driveway, I said, "Thank you, Lord," out loud.

"Thank you, Lord, for what?" Dad said in a muffled voice. He turned off the car. "You don't say nothing to your mother about that bar, you hear me?"

"Yes, sir."

"We were at the office with Greeley working on a project, right?"

"I thought you told me never to lie."

He raised his hand at me.

I flinched.

A sheen of sweat coated his forehead. "Just keep your trap shut."

When we entered the house, there was no sign of Ma. "Guess she's still at the hospital," I said. "Hope Aunt Ethel is okay."

"We just got lucky. Now go to bed."

The next morning, Dad stumbled down the stairs in his boxers and a white undershirt and sat down in the kitchen. His face looked like a ripe pumpkin. He smelled of Schnapps. "Coffee, Marion. I got me a helluva headache."

My mother handed him a mug of black coffee and shook her head. You'd have to be dumb, deaf, and blind not to see his 'headache' was a major hangover.

I sat down at the table and looked up at my mother. "How's Aunt Ethel?"

"She's fine. Turned out she just had a bad stomach ache."

Dad shuffled the newspaper. "Speaking of ache, can you call work and tell them I'm sick. Say that I'm in bed with a fever."

My mother did as he asked. When she hung up the phone, she glared at Dad. "So what did you boys do last night?"

Dad peered down at me. His eyes reminded me to keep my lips zipped.

We all sat in silence.

"Is anyone going to answer my question?" My mother looked at me. "Marshall?"

"I, ah, got to meet Mr. Greeley." At least that was the truth.

"At the office," Dad added.

My mother was no idiot. I knew she sensed there was something fishy going on. Worse, she'd probably figured out I was now a part of Dad's lies.

I ran upstairs and returned to the kitchen with my schoolbooks. "Gotta go." I gave my mother a peck on the cheek, like I did every school morning.

Dad looked up from his newspaper. "Let's play some catch later, okay?"

Now he wanted to play catch? Was that my reward for deceiving my mother?

MICKEY

WHEN THE TEAM returned to New York, we wore our Florida tans and tried to stay out of trouble as we waited for the '61 season to start.

One night, Whitey Ford and I headed over to the Copacabana. The pretty blonde hostess, what's-her-name, seated us at my table. I'd say one thing for the Copa, they had class, keeping that spot available for me whenever I came in.

My favorite waitress, Darla, approached with two Johnny Walker's on ice like always. Bless her big-titted chest. Whitey and me had come in to let off some steam, and maybe catch us some snatch.

Two young sweeties approached us with their napkins held up. The redhead said, "Can we get your autographs, Mr. Mantle and Mr. Ford?"

"You bet." I scribbled my signature then handed the napkin

to Whitey.

"You're more handsome in person than on television, isn't he Mabel?" gushed the girl.

"And blonder too," said her friend.

I took the opportunity and patted Red's shapely ass.

Her cheeks resembled two candy apples. "Oh, Mr. Mantle."

"Mickey."

Whitey grabbed my arm. "Lookie over there." He pointed at the door where three reporters stood showing their press credentials to the bouncer. "Send those babes back to Romper Room."

"Ah, girls, Whitey and I need a little privacy now."

They scooted off giggling with the napkins tucked in their fists.

I shook my head. "Why can't they leave us in peace?"

All three of the news-hounds hustled up to our table flashing bulbs at us. It was a damn good thing that Whitey had seen them in time to get rid of the babes. I was already in the doghouse with Merlyn.

The shortest of the three reporters winked at his buddy. "Told you The Mick would be here." Then he took off his straw hat in some kind of gesture of respect. "Mr. Mantle, it's been a rather dismal exhibition season for the Yanks so far. Are things gonna improve with the addition of that new kid from Kansas City?"

I shrugged. "With another good hitter in the cleanup spot, they won't be able to pitch around me."

"Is it true you and Roger Maris don't like each other? That you told Casey you opposed adding him to the team?"

I laughed. "I barely know the fella." *Where the hell do they get this crap?* "Sit down, would you, bud? Let me buy you a drink."

I'd barely ordered the schmo a beer when one of the other reporters, a paunchy man with a neck like a turkey, started in on me. "So Mick, whaddaya think of the new kid from Kansas City?"

"Good night, guys. I'm heading home to my wife." I stood, grabbed my sport jacket, and nodded at Whitey. "Come on, Slick."

Whitey downed his drink and rose to his feet. "I'm right behind you, bud."

We left the reporters at the table and raced to the exit. As our feet hit the pavement of 60th Street, someone tapped my shoulder. I was tired, loaded, and had enough from these vultures for one night. As I spun around, I braced my fists ready for battle.

But to my delight, there before us stood Red, the gal with the nice ass. Her girlfriend was a few feet behind her. "Would you boys like a little company?"

CHAPTER FOUR

Everybody's Got *Tzuris*

May 15, 1961

On May 14, Mother's Day, in Anniston, a mob of Ku Klux Klans-men, some still in church attire, attacked the first of the two buses The driver tried to leave the station, but was blocked until KKK members slashed its tires. The mob forced the crippled bus to stop several miles outside of town and then firebombed it. (3)

MARSHALL

O ne sunny day in late spring, me and Bobby raced outside of PS 107 Elementary School carrying our books and matching Mickey Mantle lunch boxes. As we left the schoolyard, Bobby turned to me. "So whaddaya think of the Yankee's new hitter?"

"Roger Maris? He's no competition for the Mick."

"He didn't do that good in Florida," Bobby added.

I grabbed a broken branch from the ground, scooped up some rocks, and swung at them.

"Ow!" yelled Rocky Romano, the biggest kid in the sixth grade, who was walking ahead of us with his friend Frank

Caruso. One of the rocks had hit the back of his head. He spun around. "You're gonna pay, Marshmallow."

"It was an accident," I said, hating the nickname kids often teased me with.

Rocky rubbed his head with the palm of his hand. "Like hell it was. I'm gonna beat the crap outta you and your dumb-ass cousin."

Bobby and I raced down the street with Rocky and Frank in pursuit. Fortunately, they weren't near as fast as they were big. Three blocks later, we reached the Van Wyck Expressway and ran toward the overpass to the safety of Bobby's house on the other side.

Except that Bobby stepped in a pothole and fell face down on the pavement.

Rocky and Frank drew closer by the second.

"Get up Bobby," I shouted.

"I'm too dizzy…" He sat up but his brown eyes looked glassy. I tried to pull him to his feet, but he was too wobbly. I had two choices. Run to Bobby's house to get help, or stay and try and defend us. Little chance I could take on Rocky, let alone him and Frank. But no way would I leave my cousin wounded and helpless.

They arrived with vicious grins on their faces. "We got you now," said Rocky.

I stood between Rocky and Frank with my fists in front of me. "I don't wanna fight you, but I will if I have to." *Famous last words.*

Rocky wiped sweat from his forehead. "You two think you're such hot shit winning the game last summer."

Could I reason with them? "You got that all wrong."

"Why were you bragging and mouthing off at school then?"

We had beaten their team last season in the game before I had screwed up. It was a tie ballgame and we'd gone two extra innings when I hit the winning home run. Thinking back, maybe we boasted a little too much about our victory. I might have even said their team stunk. "I'm sorry, Rocky, if I hurt your feelings."

"Not as sorry as you're gonna be." Before I knew it, Rocky threw a haymaker right at my nose.

I staggered backwards blinded by the pain. I covered my mouth with my hand to keep from crying out. No way would I let them hear me whimper like a baby.

Frank headed over to Bobby, still on the ground and stunned by his fall.

Rocky pushed me hard knocking me flat on my butt. He dropped to his knees, raining down punches on me. Saliva dripped down his mouth to his chin then across my neck.

No time to wipe his disgusting spit off as I was too busy blocking his punches. I figured we were done for.

Then, miraculously, a Yellow Cab screeched up to the curb. The driver, Uncle George, honked at us, killed the engine, and stepped out of the car. My uncle, a really big guy and former Marine, peered down at us. "That's enough, boys."

Rocky and Frank took one look at my uncle towering over them, and scrambled back in the direction they'd come from.

I stood and wiped my nose with my sleeve.

Uncle George helped Bobby up. "You all right, boys?"

Bobby brushed the dirt off his clothes. His face had a few scrapes and his lip was busted. "I'm okay. But thank God you showed up when you did."

My uncle turned to me. "That's a lotta blood coming outta your nose."

"I'll be fine." I gulped.

Uncle George opened the trunk where he found some old rags. He handed one to each of us.

I wiped the dripping blood while Bobby dabbed at his bruised mouth.

Uncle George opened the passenger door. "Jump in the cab and I'll drive you two home."

"Don't you gotta go back to work?" Bobby said.

"I can take off for a while." Uncle George worked long hours in his Yellow Cab. Aunt Ethel also had a night job in a factory. My mother used to say it was the only way they could make ends meet.

"How's that nose doing, Marshall?"

"I think it looks worse than it is," I said. Blood had made its way down my neck and there were red splotches on my shirt, but it had finally stopped gushing.

"We're good to walk home, Pop. Don't think they're coming back," Bobby said.

"You sure? I can get Max to cover my shift."

"Honest, we're fine. See you at home later," Bobby said.

Uncle George stepped back into the cab, tooted the horn, then drove off.

Me and Bobby walked across the Van Wyck overpass which vibrated from the cars rushing by below us. On the other side, little kids splashed in water from an open fire hydrant. When we reached Bobby's house, Aunt Ethel opened the front door and stepped outside in her polka-dot apron. "Oh my God!

What happened?"

Bobby filled her in on our fight.

"Come inside and let me have a better look at both of you. Why don't you stay for dinner, Marshall?"

"Thanks, but I gotta go." Truth was I'd rather have hung out there where I felt safe. Uncle George made corny jokes at dinner and never raised his voice to Aunt Ethel. He even helped her with the dishes. Things had gotten worse around my house. Dad had a white-hot temper that flared up for no reason I could see. My mother spent hours scrubbing the floors and counter-tops so he wouldn't have something to yell at her about. We both tiptoed around the house when he was home which wasn't that often. Many nights he came home after I was asleep.

As I ran the five blocks home, I wondered what the odds were of Dad playing ball with me next weekend. He always had a lame excuse. Would he ever have faith in me again?

I was surprised to see Dad's Galaxie pulling into the drive-way. As he stepped out of the car he waved, then his eyebrows flew up. "What the hell happened to you?"

I told him that Rocky and Frank had come after us.

"Did you flatten those guys?" He seemed to like the idea.

"Sure I did. They ran home crying their eyes out."

Dad grinned. "That's my boy. Hey, you wanna play some catch before it gets dark?"

Wow! I couldn't believe my ears. He was obviously proud of me for fighting. "Sure. It'll take me no time to cleanup and change." I raced inside and ran up the steps.

"What's going on?" Ma yelled from the kitchen. "You might say hello."

I was thankful she didn't see my bloody face and clothes.

"Dad's home and we're gonna play catch."

"Really? That's great, honey."

I washed the caked blood off my face, peeled off my dirty clothes, and slipped into my baseball pants, a sweatshirt, and my Yankee's cap. When I got downstairs, Dad was sitting in his favorite new La-Z-Boy chair with a beer in his hand. Still dressed in his sports jacket and dress slacks, he didn't look like he was going to play catch anytime soon.

"Aren't you gonna change your clothes?"

He shook his head. "Have a seat. Walter Cronkite just announced that Yankee management fired Casey Stengel. The sports are coming on after the commercial."

"But what about playing catch?"

"This story is all they'll be talking about at work tomorrow."

I sank into the cushions on the coach, and quickly wiped a tear that had formed in my eye. Would I have to beat the crap out of some kid before he'd pay attention to me again?

MICKEY

AFTER TWELVE YEARS as the Yankee manager, Casey Stengel had been canned. They brought in Ralph Houk, the first-base coach and acting manager when Casey had been sidelined with an illness. Hell, Casey was a hard act to follow for anyone. That night, Whitey called me and suggested we get together for drinks.

We met at a quiet bar in the East Village that was patronized by hipsters and beatniks who didn't give a hoot about baseball and generally left us alone. Whitey seemed shook up about the whole thing and ordered himself a double shot of Johnny Walker Red.

For once, I decided I better not get too shit-faced, and ordered a Budweiser.

"Casey and I have certainly had our ups and downs," Whitey said. "But I'm not sure Houk can fill his shoes."

I signaled the waitress for another round. "Ya know, I always liked Casey until he jerked me out of that game last year in front of 50,000 fans for failing to run out the ball."

Whitey nodded. "Yeah, I remember."

Between my crippling bone disease, and my goddamn knees, I suffered from chronic pain. Regardless, I still played hurt and I played hard. My philosophy was that sometimes I deserved to take it easy.

Whitey slugged down his drink. "How do you know Ralph will be any different?"

"He understands me better. When he was acting manager, if I hit a fly ball to the outfield and didn't run hard to first base, he'd let it go. I've heard he's prone to pulled leg muscles himself."

"Time will tell," Whitey said. "So what do you think of Roger?"

"Is that a joke? You damn well know how tired I am of every stinking reporter asking that question."

"But you've never told me what you really think about the guy," he said.

"Okay. Here's what I *really* think about Roger Maris. He's the press's new whipping boy. The hick from the Midwest who doesn't appreciate the golden status of being a Yankee."

Whitey smiled. "Didn't you go through the same crap when

you arrived from Oklahoma in '51 and dared to challenge DiMaggio?"

"You betcha."

"So "Maris gets *you* off the hook."

I held up my Bud. "I'll drink to that."

He clinked his glass on my beer bottle. "They sure like to make you and Roger out to be enemies."

"Hell, it sells newspapers. But you know, if truth be told, I respect the guy 'cause he doesn't put on any airs, and you can count on him on the field."

"Yep. He's a first rate athlete," Whitey said.

"And he's a challenge for me which makes me play harder."

Whitey cocked an eyebrow. "So technically Roger Maris is helping you win the race?"

We both had a good laugh then chugged down our drinks. After a few more rounds, I left the restaurant and flagged a taxi. I sat back in the seat and thought how much we all had riding on the 1961 season. Everyone had big expectations of me. Would I play as good as I'd done in the past? Could I break Babe's home run record? Maybe, the kid from Kansas might actually beat me out. How long could I endure the severe pain of my injuries and hide it from the fans?

And Merlyn was threatening to leave me. Again.

ROGER

I HAD AN AWFUL start to the Yankee season and everyone was wondering if I could live up to my reputation as a power hitter capable of challenging Mickey Mantle.

My wife Pat was having a difficult pregnancy, which made

it hard for me to focus. But if I mentioned that fact to anyone, they'd say I was just using it for an excuse. So I kept my worries to myself.

In mid-May, a full month into the season, my bat remained ice-cold. I worried that with just a .200 batting average, I was playing myself off the team. The New York press crucified me, and I feared I'd never play baseball anywhere again if things didn't improve soon.

Casey Stengel had not minced words about my disappointing performance. He'd switched the batting order around placing me third and making Mick the cleanup hitter behind me.

When I took a shower, strands of my hair filled the drain. If it weren't for Big Julie, I'd probably have given it up and returned home to Kansas. I became a regular at his family's Friday night *Shabbos* dinners. His wife Selma made me feel right at home, and I loved the Jewish tradition of a weekly family supper with prayers, candles, and wine.

"Just ignore those schmucks," Julie said one Friday night as he poured me another glass of Manischewitz. "You need to relax and focus on the game and it will all work out. I feel it in my bones, Rog. This is gonna be your year."

I didn't have that feeling at all. "Don't deny Ralph thinks Casey made a big mistake recruiting me."

Jules cleared his throat. "Well, I, ah, do have something I need to share with you." He chugged down a whole glass of wine before continuing. "Ralph asked me to arrange for you to go see an optometrist. He thinks there may be something wrong with your eyes."

I slammed my fist on the table. "There's nothing wrong with my eyes. Tell Ralph to go ef himself."

"Ralph's got his own *tzuris*," Big Julie said.

"What's *suris*?"

"*Tzuris,* with a TZ. It's Yiddish for troubles."

It was true. As our losses mounted early in the season, the press ripped Houk good. All the New York editorials said that Yankee management should cut him loose and bring Casey back.

Big Julie refilled both our wine glasses. "Just go to the optometrist. I'll set you up an appointment and drive you there myself."

"I'll think about it," I said. But I had no intention of going to the doctor, even though I knew Houk would be royally pissed off. Maybe even give me the boot.

BIG JULIE

THE SEASON BEGAN on a grim note. The Yanks lost their home opener for the first time in seven years as only 14,000 fans showed up in the frigid weather to watch Minnesota beat them 10-6. The press blamed Ralph and almost universally said it'd been a big mistake to replace Casey. Bless the guy's heart, he remained optimistic and fired back by insisting the Yanks would win the pennant in November.

Bitter cold and rain delayed the ball club from playing again for five days. After that, Mick got on pace early with five home runs, eleven RBIs and was hitting .455.

Roger, on the other hand, started the season slowly, with a batting average of .161. My buddy was in a slump and even after Ralph threatened to can him, Roger flat out refused to get his eyes checked out. I finally bribed him with a good steak dinner.

He gave me a boyish grin. "Throw in a two pound lobster tail and I'll even go to a gynecologist."

But his eyes checked out fine. Something else was wrong. A full month into the season and Roger was batting a pathetic .208.

Then Houk acquired Roger's Kansas City teammate and good friend, Bob Cerv. Having Bob around helped Roger regain his confidence. Suddenly, his timing returned. I hung up a corkboard in the Yankee locker room and pinned the most positive newspaper articles to it.

May 17, 1961 - *The Chicago Post*:
"ROGER MARIS THRASHED HIS 4TH HOMER AGAINST WASHINGTON."

May 20, 1961 - *New England Weekly News*
"ROGER MARIS DRILLED HIS 5TH HOME RUN OFF THE INDIAN'S JIM PERRY."

May 23, 1961 - *The Cincinnati Daily World*
"MARIS HITS HIS 6TH HOMER OFF ONETIME TEAMMATE GARY BELL. LIKE A LONG-DORMANT VOLCANO, ROGER MARIS HAS BEGUN TO RUMBLE."

May 24, 1961 - *The Dallas Statesman*
"ROGER MARIS SMASHED HIS 7TH OFF BALTIMORE'S CHUCK ESTRADA. MARIS HAS ERUPTED."

With four homers in four games and a season total of seven, my boy Roger was out of his slump. In June, Roger caught on fire. In the next seventeen games, he hit .300 with twelve homers and twenty-five RBIs. Everyone joked it was the baloney and eggs that me and Rog ate for breakfast every morning at the Stage Deli.

The race was on! Now the fans were counting. That's about the time Ralph Houk asked me to approach Mick about living with Roger. "You think you can find those two an obscure place to live where the press won't hound them? Keep 'em out of trouble?"

One of Ralph's first orders of business as new Yankee Manager was to get Mantle and Maris in line. Mickey was out of control with the booze and ladies, while Roger pissed off the reporters every time they interviewed him. After six months in New York, the kid was still homesick as a new puppy.

It was a tall order. I had no idea how the hell I'd convince Mickey to agree to something like that. When I suggested it to him, he gave me his famous boyish grin. "You're shittin' me, Jules. Why would I want to move from a suite at the St. Moritz to shack up in Queens with two guys from Kansas?"

"*You* came from Oklahoma," I said.

"Give me a break. That was ten years ago. I'm a full-fledged New *Yorka* now."

"Ralph has his mind made up," I said. "He believes it will help…I, er, can't think of a delicate way to say this."

"Help keep me in line, right? Screw him. I rather bunk with Whitey."

"We both know that's not a good idea."

Mick crinkled up his piercing blue eyes. "What if I refuse?"

"Have you forgotten your recent escapade in the ER?" A few weeks earlier, the Mick had partied it up a little too much and the guys had taken him to the emergency room fearful he had alcohol poisoning. It took me a couple of bucks to keep the story out of the press, but somehow Ralph had gotten wind of it.

"Heck, I played the next day. Even hit a home run," Mickey said with a smirk.

"You're gonna kill yourself if you keep this shit up."

"I'll die young anyways."

"*Whaddaya* talking about?" I said. "You just need to straighten out your act."

Mick looked me dead in the eyes. He took a deep breath before speaking again. "My daddy, granddaddy and two uncles all died of Hodgkin's disease before they were forty. I figure I might as well make the best of the years I got left."

I didn't know what to say. It explained a lot about how Mick lived. "Do you wanna lose the race to Roger?"

"You'd like to see that, wouldn't you, Jules?"

"I'm probably the only one in the state of New York, but yeah, I don't deny that's true."

"Okay, I'll move in with the choir boys and I'll bet you five gees I win the race."

That set me back on my heels. "You're on."

CHAPTER FIVE

Magic in Baseball Hats

June 26, 1961

JERUSALEM *(Israeli Sector), Adolf Eichmann told his Israeli judges today that he "felt like Pontius Pilate" when the Nazis met in 1942 to plot the annihilation of European Jews. (4)*

MARSHALL

"**N**o more books, no more schnooks, no more ugly teachers' looks," sang Bobby and me on the last day of sixth grade as we shuffled down the street filled with kids from PS 107.

"Just think," Bobby said, "Next year we'll be in Junior High."

It was a swell afternoon, not a cloud in the sky. I didn't have a care in the world as I thought about the long lazy days of summer ahead of us. Well, except for making All-Stars. I was determined to make my dad proud of me again. Maybe, he wouldn't be so mad at me and Ma all the time. I turned to Bobby, "Wanna go hit?"

"Heck, I'd like to, but I'm going fishing with Pops tomorrow and I need to help him pack."

"I wish my dad would take me fishing. He thinks it's just a big waste of time."

"It's really fun. Especially the campfires and s'mores."

"Maybe someday he'll change his mind," I said, but doubted that would ever happen.

A couple doors down from Bobby's house an old woman pushed open her screen door and shouted, "Time to come wash up for dinner."

A young girl in the front yard slid off a tire swing. "I'm coming, Nanna."

Bobby waved at them. "Hey, Laila."

The girl smiled and waved back.

When we reached Bobby's house, Uncle George stood with a garden hose watering the patch of grass in their front yard. He shouted, "No more books, no more crooks—"

"We already sang it, Pop." Bobby said.

"Hey, Uncle George."

My uncle smiled. "Wanna come fishing with us, Marshall?"

"Thanks, but I'm not sure I could sleep in the woods. I gotta be in top shape for the game on Monday afternoon. Coach Lee is announcing the All-Star team afterwards."

Bobby gulped, "This Monday?"

"Remember, Coach told us last week."

"Geez, I totally forgot. Now *I* won't sleep out there." Bobby looked up at his father.

"How about we go next weekend instead?" Uncle George suggested.

"That would be swell, Pop. I sure hope I make it this year."

I patted his back. "Don't worry. No one is as good as you

behind the plate." Bobby hadn't made All-Stars last season either. But this year, things looked good for both of us. Me and Bobby had the highest batting averages on the team. We'd been playing our hearts out and going to the batting cage on our own.

"You think 'cause we're cousins there's less chance of us both making it?"

"Nah." I said, but thought he might be right. I was gonna feel terrible if *I* made the team and Bobby didn't. And I'd feel worse if *he* got chosen instead of me. Baseball was everything to both of us.

When I reached home, the next to last one on a dead-end street, I skipped up the porch steps and opened the screen door. "I'm home, Ma." The aroma of meatloaf lured me to the kitchen.

My mother wasn't there but a cloud of steam rose from a big cast iron pot and water bubbled down onto the stovetop. "Ma, where are you?" It wasn't like her not to be waiting for me. Usually with a glass of milk and my favorite oatmeal cookies.

I turned off the gas burner and the water stopped spilling over the sides of the pot which was filled with peeled potatoes. "Ma, you upstairs?"

Still no answer.

I climbed the staircase and peeked in the half-open door to my parents' bedroom. My mother was asleep on top of the covers. Her furry pink slippers lay next to the bed. Why was she still wearing her nightgown? She seemed so tired lately. Best to let her sleep.

With nothing better to do, I went outside, picked up an old rubber Spaldeen, and tossed it against the side brick wall of our house over and over again.

About an hour passed, when a shiny white Lincoln followed by a big red convertible halted at the shabby duplex next door to us. A cardboard FOR RENT sign had been planted out in that front yard for the past couple of months.

We didn't see fancy cars in the neighborhood very often. Couldn't really think of the last time one had come around. The three guys in the convertible wore Red Sox caps and T-shirts. Guess they were from out-of-state. No one in New York would be caught dead in them. They had big muscles and wore cool sunglasses. They sure looked familiar, but I couldn't say where I'd seen them before. Then it hit me, and my mouth fell open.

BIG JULIE

I STOPPED IN FRONT of this gawd-awful, run-down duplex in Flushing, got out of the car, and looked around the barren street. The boys pulled up behind me in Roger's new Buick convertible.

Sheltering my eyes with my hand from the bright sun, I took a survey of the dilapidated neighborhood. At least the dead end road appeared isolated. A sump pit and a power station took up most of the street. There was only one small house next door to the duplex with a kid in a Yankee's baseball cap throwing a rubber ball against the wall. I hoped he didn't recognize the new tenants though that seemed unlikely.

Mickey opened the door of the convertible, stepped out on the street, and took off his sunglasses. "This is a goddamn dump. You couldn't find something a little more upscale?"

"You wanted to get away from the press."

"How we gonna bring babes to this dive?" Mickey said.

Roger and Bob Cerv joined us. "We're not s'posed to bring babes here," Roger said.

"Okay, Saint Roger." Mickey craned his neck toward me. "Where can we get some beer?"

"I'll drive around and look for a liquor store," Bob said.

I shook my head. "You may be a new Yankee but your picture's all over the New York papers. That'll bring the bloodsucking reporters."

Just then, the kid next door bouncing his Spaldeen missed a shot. The ball rolled down the steps onto the sidewalk, inches from Roger. The boy ran over to retrieve it. So much for no one knowing where the guys were living.

Roger picked it up and handed it to him. "Here you go, kid."

The boy's eyes grew big as two giant meatballs while he studied Roger's face. Then he looked at Mickey.

"Yep, it's us," Roger said.

The kid stood there still as a corpse, gaping at every New York boy's heroes.

MARSHALL

I COULDN'T SWALLOW, and blinked a few times to make sure I wasn't dreaming. No, they were still there. The M&M boys. Mickey Mantle and Roger Maris. Magic in baseball hats. Every boy in New York would give their right arm to be in my shoes.

Mickey winked at me and wandered up the path to the

house with the other guy from the convertible. Was he Bob Cerv, the new outfielder from Kansas City? I'd check my baseball card collection when I got home.

Roger sat down on the steps of the porch with the fat guy who kept talking and waving his hands while Roger barely said a word.

I couldn't stop myself from staring at the new power hitter for the Yankees. He wore a checkered suit and a pair of real funny white shoes. I'd read he'd grown up in North Dakota and figured that's how they dressed out there. To my surprise, he stood and glanced in my direction. "Are you a Yankee fan, kid?"

"Yes, sir."

The big guy arched an eyebrow. "You play baseball?"

"Yes, sir."

He laughed. "Can you say something besides 'yes sir?' Everyone calls me Big Julie."

"Yes, sir. I mean, Big Julie. I'm in the little league majors. I hope to make All-Stars."

Roger walked toward my house. "What position do you play?"

"They stuck me out in right field," I said. "My dad wants me to play shortstop like he did when he was my age."

"What's wrong with right field?" Roger said. "That's my position, you know."

"Wow, that's right."

"Looks like we have something in common," Roger said.

Big Julie stepped down from the porch and waddled up to me and Roger. "But can you hit?"

"I-I need some help with my swing right now. But I've hit five home runs so far this year."

Roger smiled. "You sound like my kind of guy."

"Can I ask you something, Mr. Maris?"

"Shoot."

"I thought you and the Mick hated each other. I mean the paper and even TV—"

The screen door creaked opened and Mickey came outside smiling. "The newspaper likes to play that up."

"Mick and I are good friends," Roger said.

"And we'll still be buddies after I break the Babe's record." Roger winked at me. "You mean after I do."

"Maybe you'll both break the record," I said.

Everyone laughed. Even Big Julie. "You a politician, son?"

Roger scratched his head. Strands of hair came off in his hand. He looked annoyed but pulled out a wad of money from his pocket, peeled off a few bills, and handed them to me. "Is there a grocery store someplace around here, kid?"

"Gelaro's is just a couple of blocks away."

"Can you pick up some snacks, chips and pretzels and a carton of ice cream for us?"

"I'd sure like a couple of six packs," Mickey added.

The skin between Big Julie's eyebrows buckled. "Are you nuts? No one's gonna sell the kid beer."

"I know Mr. Gelaro real good," I said. "He'll give it to me."

"Well, in that case, my money's on the kid," Roger said.

Mickey slapped Roger's back. "Yeah? I'll bet he comes back empty-handed."

Roger took more money from his pocket. "Fifty says he brings it, and it's even cold."

Mickey cracked a smile. "You're on."

As I charged off toward Gelaro's Market, I heard someone

call out from behind me. "Hey kid, wait a minute."

I stopped running and turned around.

"What's your name, son?" Roger asked.

I told him.

"Hmm, Marshall. Nice strong name. You can call me Roger."

"Yes, ah, Rog."

He looked me in the eye. "I need to ask you a big favor, son. And, it's gonna be harder than you think."

"Anything, sir. I mean, Roger."

"I don't want you to tell anyone, and I mean no one, about us living here. You understand?"

"Yes, sir, I promise." I thought about Bobby. "Not even my cousin?"

Roger shook his head. "If you tell your cousin, then he'll tell a friend, and that friend will tell a friend. Get my drift?"

I nodded. Bobby was sure gonna be pissed when he eventually found out.

Roger put his arm around my shoulders. "I know half the fun of ya meetin' us is tellin' all your buddies, but we don't want this place filled with crowds of gawkers."

"I understand."

"We're s'posed to be here through the summer and we sure could use someone to run errands. Can we count on you, Marshall?"

Was this really happening to me? "You can count on me, sir."

"Okay then it's a deal. Let's shake on it."

I shook his hand.

"Now hurry up, and don't forget that beer. Busch's my favorite."

I ran the four blocks to Gelaro's Market. That's where my mother bought all our groceries. The knotty-pine door squealed like it always did when I pushed on it. The smell of the salamis that hung above the deli displays filled the room. I rushed past shelves crammed with bread, canned vegetables, and my favorite, Hostess Twinkies.

Mr. Gelaro stood at the soda fountain dressed in a white shirt, red bow tie, and navy pinstriped apron. His head had a full-moon bald spot surrounded by a circle of dark curly hair.

A thin girl with two thick braids and big green eyes sat on one of the vinyl stools. She smiled revealing dimples that looked liked two parenthesis on her cheeks. "You're Bobby's cousin, aren't you?"

I vaguely remembered her swinging on a big tire at the small brick house down the street from my cousin's. But I thought the place belonged to an old lady. "Do you live with Mrs. Levin?"

Her chin jutted out. "She's my Nanna. I live out on Long Island but my father got in a bad car accident so I'm staying with her until he's out of the hospital." She brushed away a tear from the corner of her eye.

"I'm sorry." I couldn't imagine how I'd feel if something happened to my dad. It was bad enough he was working all the time and hardly home these days. Buried in my brain I recalled hearing her name. The school assembly maybe? No, she was too young for the sixth grade. Then I remembered. Bobby had said hello to her when we'd moseyed by her house. "Laila, right?"

"Yes, and you're Marshall."

"That's me all right." I wondered how she knew *my* name

but suddenly remembered the urgency of my mission. "Maybe I'll see you around some time." I turned to Mr. Gelaro. "I need to get a couple of six packs of beer, and some chips and pretzels, right away."

Mr. Gelaro looked at me like I'd just arrived from Jupiter. "Hold on there, Marshall. I'm helping out this young lady right now."

Laila chewed her bottom lip. "I'd like a strawberry malted, no, change that to vanilla. And I could use a new Pez dispenser and maybe some candy buttons. No wait." She spilled some change on the counter and counted it.

Why couldn't she make up her mind? I headed over to a stand with baseball card packages while Mr. Gelaro made Laila her malted. It seemed like forever before she finally settled on some candy and paid Mr. Gelaro for everything.

While she sat sipping her malted, Mr. Gelaro headed my way. "Did I hear you say you want some beer?"

"It's not for me, I swear."

"I assumed that, Marshall. But it's against the law to sell beer to minors."

"You just gotta sell me some Busch. It's real important."

Mr. Gelaro raised an eyebrow. "Who's it for?"

"It's umm, a secret."

Laila interrupted. "I think I'll get that Pez dispenser." She handed Mr. Gelaro some change and headed to the exit swinging a paper bag.

Mr. Gelaro rubbed his hands together. "Okay, so, who's the beer for, son?"

"It's for Roger Maris and Mickey Mantle. They moved next door in the vacant—" I slapped my hand over my mouth. I had broken my promise already.

Mr. Gelaro smiled. "And I'm having dinner with Joe DiMaggio at the Waldorf tonight."

I faked a laugh. "I was just kidding, of course. It's really for my dad. He's having a poker game and—"

"Tell your father to come buy his own beer."

I grabbed a few bags of chips and pretzels from a shelf and tossed them on the counter.

Mr. Gelaro rung up the total on the cash register, and placed them in a sack. "Sorry I can't help you, kid."

"Dad asked my mother to buy the beer for his game. But she's kind of sick, throwing up and everything. He's gonna be *really* mad at her."

Mr. Gelaro shook his head. "Hmmm. Mrs. Gelaro, God bless her soul in heaven, would turn in her grave if she knew, but I'll make an exception this one time. Your mother's a nice lady and she sure looked pale as a ghost yesterday when she came in for a quart of milk."

He opened the wooden cooler, pulled out two six packs, placed them in a paper bag, and handed it to me.

After I paid him, I ran out the door and hightailed it home. I couldn't wait to see the expressions on Mickey and Roger's faces.

Then I heard someone yell my name and turned back around.

Laila smiled at me as she shuffled down the steps from Gelaro's Market. "Do you really know Roger Maris and Mickey Mantle?"

Oh my God, she'd been standing there all the time! Should I lie? I looked into her green eyes. "Well sorta."

Her eyes sparkled. "They live next door to you?"

"You didn't hear that. Promise me you won't tell no one."

She grinned. Again, her dimples punctuated her cheeks. "What's to tell? I didn't hear anything."

I brushed her forearm with my fingers. "You swear to God?"

"I'm Jewish. We don't swear. But I promise. Your secret's safe with me. Who do you think is going to win the race? I'm rooting for Roger."

"You're a baseball fan?"

"I'm a Yankees fan. That's different from being a baseball fan. Pop takes me…well, he used to bring me to all the games. He loves Mickey, but he thinks Roger's going to do it."

"I never met a girl who liked the Yankees before. Are you pulling my leg?"

"Why would I do that?"

I shrugged. "Prove you're a real Yankees fan?"

"I know every player on the team. Besides Mantle and Maris there's Yogi Berra, Whitey Ford, Bobby Richardson, Moose Skowron, Tony Kubek, Hector Lopez, Elston Howard—"

"Okay, I believe you."

"Want me to tell you their positions? Their stats?"

"No, it's fine."

Recently, Bobby and I had started talking about girls. Between us we knew jack about them. How did you talk to one? What did they do after school? And, of course, we wondered what they looked like without their clothes. We asked our first baseman David Gold if he would share his knowledge since he had a big sister who often accompanied his parents to our games. Both Bobby and I thought she was hot.

"They're not that different from us. Except, of course, they don't look the same without their clothes," he gushed.

He had our full attention but we were both tongue-tied.

After an awkward few moments of silence, Bobby finally croaked, "You've, ah, seen your sister naked?"

"I was just stating a fact. You think I'm a pervert or something?" David said.

Bobby had a crush on Rachel Lazar, a seventh grader with big bazoombas. My face felt red-hot just thinking about that.

I blinked my eyes and turned my attention back to Laila. "Gotta go. See you around the neighborhood." She was so cute. And surprisingly easy to talk to. I'd never felt like this about a girl before. But would she keep my secret?

MARSHALL

I BARRELED UP the steps of the duplex where I found Roger sitting on a folding chair reading the *Daily News*. "Well, if it isn't Mr. Marshall. Did you succeed at your first mission?"

I launched a big smile and took out a six-pack of Busch from the paper sack.

He placed his arm around my shoulder. "Let's bring this inside to Mick."

I followed him into the kitchen.

Two pretty women sat on red vinyl chairs sipping bottles of beer with Mickey as we entered the room. Three six-packs of Ballantine sat on the counter. At the sight of all that beer, my heart sank. "Guess you don't need this beer anymore."

Mickey grinned. "Are you kidding? We can always use more

beer. How'd you manage to get it?"

I half-smiled.

Roger whacked Mickey's shoulder. "Where's my fifty smackers?"

"Son-of-a—" Mickey blurted, but cut it short as Roger shot him a stern look.

Mickey pulled out his wallet and handed some bills to Roger, who tousled my hair and stuffed a five in my hand.

"Thank you sir," I said then glanced at clock on the wall. "Geez, it's six-thirty. My mother's gonna kill me!"

Roger said, "Stop by tomorrow, Marsh."

"Sure thing." I raced out the door.

My mother stood by the stove whipping up mashed potatoes. She'd combed her hair and put on a pink blouse and plaid pedal pushers. Her face still looked pasty as oatmeal but I was relieved she had gotten out of bed.

She glared at me. "Where have you been?"

"I was, playing with some guys. Guess I lost track of the time."

"It's not like I don't have enough worries with your father lately."

The table was set for three. "Is Dad coming home for dinner tonight?"

"This morning he said he'd be here. But that doesn't mean much anymore."

"I promise not to be late no more."

"You won't be late *any* more. Now go upstairs and wash your hands."

As I ran up the stairs, she yelled, "Who were those guys next door?"

Should I lie to my mother? But if I told her the truth, I'd break my promise to Roger. Both she and Dad had always told me never to lie. I stood on the staircase feeling torn. Fortunately, the phone rang. I walked into my parent's bedroom and picked up the baby-blue Princess phone the same time my mother answered the call in the kitchen. Before I had a chance to say hello, my mother did. Then Aunt Ethel said, "What did the doctor say, Marion?"

"I'm pregnant!" my mother said. "Just like we thought."

I carefully hung up the phone and sighed. For years I'd wished for a little brother or sister. By my tenth birthday, I'd pretty much lost hope of it ever happening. So I was thrilled my mother was pregnant. But my throat tightened up as I thought about what Dad was gonna say when he found out.

CHAPTER SIX

The Split

July 2, 1961

American novelist Ernest Hemingway committed suicide at his home in Ketchum, Idaho two days after returning home to Idaho from a course of treatment for depression at the Mayo Clinic. (5)

MARSHALL

For the next few days, I ran errands for my heroes next door. While they never asked me to buy beer again, I brought them Chinese takeout, pizza, bags of groceries, chips and pretzels, cleaning supplies, starched shirts from the dry cleaners, and other stuff. I mainly dealt with Roger, who often invited me to hang out with him on the porch. He always asked me about my Little League games and talked a lot about how much he missed his family. I rarely dealt with Mickey unless he needed me to fill a prescription at the drug store.

This summer was turning into the coolest time of my life. Not only did I have my heroes living next door, but that cute girl, Laila, with the big green eyes and dimples, had been waving and smiling at me every time I walked home from Bobby's. And

I had a real good shot at making All-Stars. Maybe, if I made it, Dad would start coming to my games again. I was so excited thinking about all of this one night, it took forever for me to fall asleep.

I had just barely closed my eyes, when I awoke to the sound of loud voices coming from my parents' bedroom. I'd been dreaming I'd just knocked a baseball out of the park and the crowds in the stands stood and cheered me on as I trotted around the bases. But as my parents continued shouting at each other, the dream faded, and I covered my head with a pillow.

Without warning, something crashed and my mother screamed.

I leaped from bed and raced into their bedroom. My father stood next to a shattered bedside lamp on the floor. Broken glass was scattered all over the shag carpet. Blood gushed out from an ugly gash on my mother's forehead.

"Oh my God! What happened?"

"It's not that bad, sweetheart. I, ah, knocked the lamp off the nightstand and some glass scratched my face." She grabbed some Kleenex from a box on her nightstand and pressed them to her forehead. Blood quickly soaked the tissues. She snatched a couple more from the box and replaced the old ones. Blood continued to gush out.

"You need stitches." I said. "We should go to the hospital." I'd gotten six stitches myself last year after a friend accidentally hit me with his father's golf club.

Dad eyeballed me. "She's fine."

I shook my head. "I-I'm not so sure."

"Get over here, boy!"

I moved closer to Dad and gagged from the powerful smell

of alcohol on his breath. He grabbed the back of my neck with his big freckled hand and shook me.

My knees buckled. I gasped for breath.

Ma clawed at his fingers. "Leave the boy alone!"

Dad let go. "Get the hell outta here before I—"

"Go back to your room now, Marshall," Ma said in a softer voice. "For me."

I hugged her, feeling angry and scared at the same time.

She stroked my cheek with the palm of her hand. Blue-black pouchy bags under her eyes made her look like she'd grown old since yesterday.

"Yeah, get the hell outta here," Dad shouted. "You're nothin' but a pussy. I always knew you was a mama's boy."

I looked up at him and muttered under my breath, "Well, what is a guy who hits his wife?" When I got back to my room, I burrowed under the covers like an earthworm from science class. I wanted to forget everything that had just happened in my parents' bedroom. Rewind back to this afternoon.

But I couldn't get the vision of my mother bleeding and Dad's bloated face out of my head. Did he really think I was a pussy? A tidal wave of fear, anger, and sadness made me gasp for air. I rubbed the back of my neck, which felt sore from Dad's fingers. How could I love him and hate him at the same time?

MARSHALL

EARLY THE NEXT morning, I awoke to the smell of bacon and eggs. I was tired and my head ached. "Wake up, sleepy-head," my mother shouted from downstairs. "Breakfast is on the table."

I could barely drag myself out of bed, but I stumbled down the stairs and into the kitchen in my Roy Rogers pajamas. Bright sunlight crept through the bay window. The coffee pot was percolating. Two slices of bread popped up from the toaster, which Ma smeared with butter. It felt like normal, as if the fight last night had been a bad dream.

Dad sat at the table reading the *New York Daily News* like always. He glanced up at me and smiled. "Morning, son." Then he lit a cigarette and turned his attention back to the business section.

"Sit down," Ma said. The white bandage on her forehead reminded me that last night was no dream. "I'll get you a plate and some OJ." She opened the freezer door and attempted to wrestle a can of frozen Birdseye orange juice out through all the built-up ice inside.

Dad puffed on his cigarette and glanced up at her. "Isn't the coffee ready yet?"

My mother stabbed the ice harder. "In a minute, dear. We really need a new fridge. I just defrosted this thing day before yesterday."

"Stop your yapping and get me a cuppa coffee. We can't afford anything new right now," Dad said. "Maybe when I get my bonus."

"With all the hours you've been putting in lately, we should be able to refurnish the entire house."

Dad clenched his fist like he was getting ready to punch her.

I could hardly breathe. *Please God, don't let him hit her.*

But then he unclenched his fist and handed me some of

the newspaper. "I'm done with the sports section if you want to read it."

I let out my breath. "Ah, sure." Maybe I'd been wrong about him balling up his fist at my mother. Maybe...

He looked up from the paper. "So what are you doing today? I remember that wonderful feeling of freedom after school let out."

"Could we play some catch? And I need help with batting practice real bad."

"Shoot. I'd really like to, but I promised Brooks I'd work on this project," Dad said.

My mother sighed. "On Saturday?"

"It don't have to be today," I said.

"It *doesn't* have to be today," my mother corrected.

I looked down at my corduroy slippers. It had taken all my nerve to even ask. I needed him to help me with batting practice or I'd never make All-Stars.

"Tell you what," Dad said. "We'll get up early before church tomorrow."

"Right."

"Don't get sassy with me, boy. I'm doing the best that I can to provide for you and your mother."

"You don't make time for me no more since I screwed up that game last year and embarrassed you." The words left my mouth before I could stop them.

He glanced up from the paper. "I've just been busy is all."

"They're announcing the All-Star team after our game on Monday night."

"I didn't realize the season was almost over."

"I got me a chance to make the team this year."

"Really? You bet I'll be there." He knitted his brow and looked at Ma. "I've been trying my darndest to get that manager's job. Greeley's got the inside track, always kissing-ass to Mr. Brooks."

I remembered Mr. Greeley from the night at the Copa-Banana.

My mother pursed her lips and took the frying pan off of the burner. "I don't like that language in my house, Edmond. Certainly not in front of Marshall."

Dad winked at me. "The kid's heard worse on the baseball field, haven't you, son?"

"Guys are like that, Ma."

"Well, there's two of you 'guys' and just one of me."

"Maybe the baby will be a girl. Then you'll have someone on your side," I said.

My mother dropped the frying pan. Eggs splattered on the floor. "How'd *you* know?"

"I heard you on the phone with Aunt Ethel."

Dad looked from me to Ma. "What baby?"

"I planned on telling you last night."

"What about the diaphragm?"

"Good lord, your son is in the room!" Ma shrieked.

"Go out on the porch. Your mother and I need to talk."

I'd just screwed up real bad. I ran to Ma and hugged her waist. "I'm sorry. I didn't mean for it to slip out."

She pulled me closer. "It's okay, honey. Best everyone learn the truth."

I raced outside too choked up to speak. Why did I have such a big mouth? I'd betrayed Roger and Mickey to Laila, and now I'd ratted out my mother. Maybe, she'd been waiting for him to be in a better mood. Maybe, if *I* hadn't been such a disappointment, he'd want to have another kid.

MARSHALL

SOME TIME LATER, Dad appeared on the porch. He'd changed his clothes and was wearing a pair of Wranglers and a blue-and-red striped T-shirt. "Gather up your baseball equipment and take it out to the car."

I couldn't imagine what made him change his mind. Hopefully, my mother had fixed the mess I'd made by surprising him about the baby. And just maybe, this was my chance to prove myself worthy of his time and attention.

We arrived at Hudson's Park with two baseball mitts, my bat, and a bucket of balls. A couple of boys chased their big green kites. Some little kids played on the swings and monkey bars while their parents held hands on a blanket. I couldn't remember the last time I'd seen my mother and father hold hands.

Dad threw me grounders for a while. Then suddenly, he glanced at his watch. "I've had enough, son."

"But you haven't thrown me any batting practice yet. I need to get my swing in the groove for Monday's game."

"I've got to go to work. Be thankful I took you out. With the new pressure from your mother…" He shook his head. "I can't believe she pulled this crap."

"What crap?"

He waved his hand. "Never you mind. Just get in the car now. I'm done here."

On the drive home, I sank into the soft leather seat of the

Galaxie. Dad spent hours waxing that car every weekend. He'd nicknamed it the White Diamond. Sometimes I felt like he cared more about the car than me.

It was stupid of me to think Dad was ever going to give me another chance. He had changed. The dad who used to play ball with me, and cuddle with Ma on the couch had turned into someone who hung out at a place like the Copa-Banana and came home smelling of whiskey most nights. And then there was the gash on Ma's forehead…

Dad brushed my shoulder with his hand. "Hey, how about we make a quick stop and get some ice cream?"

"Nah, let's just go home."

"Since when don't you like ice cream?"

"I'm just not hungry right now."

He made a left on Northern Boulevard in the direction of Gelaro's. "Well, we're going anyhow."

As we got closer to the market, I felt like a family of rattlesnakes had invaded my stomach. The odds that Mr. Gelaro would not bring up me buying the beer were less than zero. The last thing I needed right now was for Dad to find more reason to be angry with me.

As we entered the store, Mr. Gelaro was busy wiping dust from some shelves. An old woman with pink hair curlers limped toward the exit with a bag of groceries in her arms.

Dad held the door open for her.

I dawdled behind him as he headed up to the counter.

"Edmond, I haven't seen you in ages," said Mr. Gelaro. "How was your poker game?"

Boy, I was in for it now.

Dad cocked an eyebrow. "Poker game?"

"Didn't you have a poker game at your house a couple of nights ago? I sold Marshall some beer for it. Not a habit of mine to do something like that."

The room fell silent for a long moment. Dad's eyes looked like arrow slits. "Oh, sure, *that* game. Yeah, we had a lotta laughs. Why don't you give us a couple of chocolate cones with sprinkles?"

We walked out to the Galaxie in silence with our ice cream. Dad switched on the ignition and eased into traffic.

I finished the last of my ice cream cone then gnawed on my cuticles.

About a block from our house he said, "That's the last time I ever lie for you, kid."

"I can explain."

"You don't have to explain. I was a kid once myself. Although I was more like sixteen when I stared experimenting with booze."

"The beer wasn't for me."

"Don't you dare lie to me after I saved your ass in there! You act like a man and tell the truth."

"I'm *trying* to tell you the truth, but I promised—"

"Promised what?"

"The beer was for some older guys who hang out in the neighborhood."

"I bet they were impressed."

I shrugged. "Yeah, sure they were."

"I'm not certain how I should punish you, son. You do realize you're way too young to be drinking?"

"I didn't drink any."

"Stop your lying or—"

He made it impossible for me to stick to the truth. "I promise never to do it again. Are you gonna tell Ma?"

Dad maneuvered the car into our driveway. "Considering you kept my little secret about our, er, adventure to yourself, I'll do the same for you. Man-to-man."

Man-to-man, father-to-son. Like Bobby and Uncle George going fishing. He glared at me as I got out of the car holding the bag of equipment. Dad remained inside the Galaxie and kept the engine running. "If I hear you've done anything like this again, it's the belt. And I'll ground you from baseball too. Do you understand?"

"Yes, sir."

"I've gotta go to work now."

"It's Saturday. Who will be there?"

His eyebrows formed one grizzled line. "I'll be there is who. And maybe Greeley."

"You mean at the Copa-Banana."

"Are you looking for a whipping?"

I looked down at my high-top sneakers. The laces were frayed real bad. "No, sir."

"Go inside and tell your mother I'll see her later." He slipped the car in reverse, backed out of the driveway, and drove off.

I waved goodbye. When I entered the house, I heard the sound of the vacuum cleaner whirling around upstairs. As I opened the coat closet to put away the canvas bag of baseball equipment, I saw Dad's briefcase half-buried behind a blanket. He never went to work without it.

A few minutes later, the noise from the vacuum quit. "Edmond, Marshall, is that you? I made a nice lunch."

"It's just me. Dad left for work."

She lugged the vacuum down the stairs and served me grilled cheese sandwiches with sliced carrots. "All these years and he never worked one Saturday."

"He said something about meeting with Greeley." I kept my suspicions that the "meeting" might not be at the office to myself.

I spent most of the afternoon organizing my baseball cards on the floor of the living room while I watched *Mighty Joe Young* at least twice on Channel Nine's *Million Dollar Movie*. They played the same movie all day long on weekends. I never tired of seeing them over again. Often I memorized the dialogue and would say the actors' lines before they did.

My mother spent the day polishing furniture, scrubbing floors, washing clothes and cleaning the bathroom. The house smelled like Mr. Clean. The floors and tables sparkled. I was sure she'd destroyed every dust bunny who dared hang out in our home.

It was already dark and I was getting hungry when my mother entered the living room. "Did your dad say when he'd be home?"

I looked up from my cards scattered on the braided rug by the TV. "No."

She walked into the hallway lugging the vacuum cleaner and opened the closet.

"Hey, let me do that for you."

Suddenly, my mother doubled over moaning, "Oh, Lordy." Her face was death-pale.

"What's the matter?"

"Call your father."

My mother took a couple of deep breaths and told me to hurry. I raced to the phone in the kitchen and picked up the receiver. My finger shook so much I could barely dial.

I wasn't surprised when Dad didn't answer his office phone and quickly dialed Bobby's number.

Uncle George answered on the third ring. "I'm on my way."

When I got back to my mother, she was curled up in a ball on the floor. I pulled the old blanket from the open closet and covered her with it. Dad's briefcase tumbled out from inside.

She glanced at the briefcase and locked eyes with me. Then she passed out.

BIG JULIE

AFTER SUNDOWN ON Saturday, I drove the in-laws back to Long Island and made a pit stop at the duplex in Queens. I'd tried to explain to Selma how important my assignment was to keep Roger and Mickey out of trouble and incognito. Bottom line, it meant I'd be spending a lot of time with them in Flushing. With my history of playing the horses still fresh in her mind, I'm not sure she believed me.

As luck would have it, my boy Danny was in the kitchen while we bickered. He'd recently broke his femur roller skating down Flatbush Avenue, and had been homebound recovering for the last three weeks. His eyes lit up at the mention of the M&M Boys. "Do you really know the Mick too, Pop? Can you invite him home to meet me?"

He smiled for the first time in weeks. Poor kid had been moping around the house since his accident. He was behind in school and missing spring baseball. Worst of all, he'd also been forced to cancel his private bi-weekly *haftorah* classes with Rabbi Citrin, which meant we might have to postpone his Bar Mitzvah. My wife had already put down a deposit with the caterer at the Waldorf.

Selma, who had zero interest in baseball let alone the Yankees, suddenly insisted we extend an invitation to Mickey. Roger had already become part of the family. "And when you leave here, make sure you're dialing finger doesn't get broken. I don't want to get sick worrying about you."

Code for: Call me every couple of hours so I can keep tabs on you.

When I arrived at the duplex, I knocked a few times but didn't wait for anyone to answer before using my own key to unlock the front door. The pungent smell of fresh tomato sauce with garlic and oregano filled the house.

I waved at Mick, Bob, and Whitey in the living room then climbed up the staircase to the second floor. Roger and Bob were bunking together in a room with two twin beds covered with girly paisley bedspreads. I made a mental note to order them something more appropriate from Selma's JC Penney catalog. Mickey had settled into the master across the hall, which had a double bed and its own bathroom.

I walked back to the living room where the boys sat watching the movie *Mighty Joe Young* on the black-and-white TV. Mickey kept banging on the back of the box and moving the rabbit ears because the reception was so bad. I made another mental note to ask Houk to buy them a new color console. The gesture would go a long way with Mickey.

I found Roger in the kitchen wearing a red-and-white

checkered apron and bust out laughing. He opened the pantry, pulled out a matching apron, and handed it to me. "Be useful and put up some water for the spaghetti."

The apron ballooned out over my big belly and Roger chuckled when he glanced up at me. After I got the pot of water on the stove, I set up a small stereo on the counter and played one of the Yiddish records I had brought over. *Hava Nagila* blared through the speakers and I sang along to the music. Roger smiled and sang along.

Just then, Mickey, Bob, and Whitey ambled into the kitchen. Mickey glared at Roger in the checkered apron singing *Hava Nagila*. Then he playfully punched my arm. "For crissakes, Jules, you're turning Roger into a Jewish grandmother."

A few minutes later, Roger and I placed five plates of spaghetti and meatballs on the table. Mick, Bob, and Whitey sat down and began eating.

"Man, this is really good," Mickey said between bites. "Where did you learn to cook like this, Rog?"

"Cooking relaxes me. Pat really appreciates the help in the kitchen."

"Ain't that too sweet?" Mickey said. "Merlyn doesn't like me in the kitchen. Hell, Merlyn doesn't like me, period."

"Well, you and Bob have dishes duty," Roger said.

Mickey chuckled. "Why don't we just hire a maid?"

"Blonde, brunette, or redhead?" said Whitey.

"As long as she's got some big knockers," Mickey said.

Someone banging on the front door interrupted the conversation. I offered to answer it in case it was the press, but Mickey took off before I could stand up.

A minute later, he reappeared with a big grin, a blond on

one arm, and a brunette on the other. "Lookie, the maids have arrived."

"Hey you can't have babes in here," I said. Mick looked at me like I'd just escaped from Bellevue. Then, he and Whitey whisked the girls into the living room.

I returned to the kitchen to help Roger with the dishes. While I was doing my best with Mickey, I clearly couldn't control him. Houk would be on my ass if he found out what was going on here.

Roger filled the sink with soapy water and asked me about Danny's recovery. I had called him the night I'd taken my son to the emergency room. "The doctor says his femur's doing real good. We're just worried about him getting through his Bar Mitzvah in September."

"What's a Bar Mitzvah?"

"In the Jewish religion when a boy reaches the age of thirteen he's considered a man. He goes through a ceremony where he gets called to read from the Torah in front of the congregation."

Roger squinted. "What's a Torah?"

"Hell, weren't there any Jews in North Dakota?"

"I met Hank Greenberg a couple of times but I never knew him."

I patted his back. "You know one now. And it'd mean a lot to me and my boy if you and Pat would come to Danny's Bar Mitzvah."

"That'll be swell."

The moan of a siren halted our conversation. I glanced out the window and saw the flashing lights of an ambulance next door.

MARSHALL

UNCLE GEORGE'S YELLOW cab screeched up to the curb the same time as the ambulance. Four guys rushed inside the house and carried my mother out on a stretcher. Flashing lights and sounds of sirens filled the neighborhood.

Aunt Ethel squeezed my hand then got inside the ambulance with my mother.

Uncle George put his arm around my shoulder. "I'll drive you to our house. You can hang out with Bobby. And there's Aunt Ethel's fried chicken in the fridge."

I shook my head. "No, I want to be with my mother."

"The hospital's not a great place—"

"I'm going if I have to walk there." No way anyone was gonna keep me from seeing my mother.

"Okay, okay, get in the cab."

We drove to Flushing Hospital where we met Aunt Ethel in the waiting room. She explained that they'd taken my mother up for emergency surgery. The overcrowded room was hot and stunk of a combination of body odor and ammonia.

Uncle George pulled out a handkerchief and wiped sweat from his forehead. "You want some coffee, Ethel?"

"Yeah, sure."

He put his hand on my shoulder. "How about a Coca-Cola?"

"No, thanks. I'm gonna try my father again."

Aunt Ethel handed me some change from her pocketbook. "I can't understand why he doesn't answer his darn phone."

"Dad gets real busy when he works." Why was I defending him?

"Busy? That guy should—"

"Don't say nothing bad about Edmund to his boy," Uncle George said.

The last thing I wanted was for Uncle George to get mad at Aunt Ethel because of Dad. "I'll be right back." After locating a vacant phone booth, I stuck a dime inside the coin slot of the telephone, and dialed zero.

"Operator, how can I help you?"

"I need the phone number of the Copa-Banana," I said.

"You mean, Copacabana."

I explained the difference and a few minutes later she rattled out the number. "You want me to connect you?"

One of the ladies answered the phone on the first ring. "I don't know if you remember me. I'm Edmund Elliot's son, Marshall. I'm looking for my Dad. It's kind of an emergency."

"Oh, sweetie, of course I remember you." I couldn't tell if it was the blonde, brunette or redhead. "But I haven't seen your father in weeks."

If Dad wasn't at the Copa-Banana, and he wasn't at the office, where could he be?

I arrived back at the surgical waiting room just as a tall man dressed in scrubs walked up to Uncle George. "Mr. Elliot, I'm Dr. Reynolds. Your wife—"

"I'm, ah, her brother-in-law."

Aunt Ethel stood. "You can speak to me. I'm her sister."

The doctor looked confused. "Where's Mrs. Elliot's husband?"

I inched my way in front of Uncle George. "My father's at work."

Dr. Reynolds peered down at me. "Let's all step out of the room."

We followed him into the hallway. Aunt Ethel clutched my hand. "Oh dear, what is it?"

The doctor reached in his pocket and pulled out some coins. "Perhaps the young man can go buy some candy."

"Let the boy stay," Uncle George said. "He needs to know what's going on."

The doctor looked at my aunt. "There's no easy way to say this. Your sister's lost her baby."

I felt like someone had punched me in the gut. "How could that happen?"

Doctor Reynolds touched my shoulder. "I'm sorry, son." He turned to Aunt Ethel. "I need you to sign some papers."

"Yes, of course. Poor Marion. She wanted this baby real badly."

"She told me," Dr. Reynolds said. "At least she's still young. There'll be others."

Aunt Ethel pulled out a handkerchief from her pocketbook, and dabbed her eyes. "Can we see her?"

"She's still in recovery but they'll be taking her down to room 240. Give it about twenty minutes. And keep the visit short."

We walked over to the hospital gift shop where Uncle George purchased a small bouquet of daisies and handed them to me. "Give this to your mother. It will cheer her up."

Before heading over to room 240, we wasted some time looking at knick-knacks. When we entered the room, I blinked a few times. Was that really my mother all hooked up to tubes and wires in the hospital bed?

An old lady in the bed next to her had patches on her eyes. Her husband was feeding her soup with a spoon.

A faint smile formed on my mother's lips when she saw me. "Marshall."

I handed her the flowers. "These are for you."

Her eyes watered up. "There's no more baby."

I didn't know what to say. Should I tell her I already knew? Would it cheer her up to mention that Dr. Reynolds had said that she was still young and could have another one?

Aunt Ethel took her hand. "Everything's going to be okay, sweetheart. Maybe it's for the best."

My mother sat up and looked around the room. "Where's Edmond?"

"We haven't been able to reach him," Uncle George said.

"Take Marshall home, please, George."

"We'll take him to our house," Aunt Ethel said.

"No. I want him to go home!"

Aunt Ethel whispered something to Uncle George. He took my mother's hand in his. "The boy shouldn't be alone now."

"Edmond will show up. He always does," Ma said.

"I'll be fine." I looked up at Uncle George. "Please just take me home."

"I'd like to go to sleep now," my mother said. "Marshall, come give me a kiss."

I kissed her pale cheek and left the room with Uncle George. Aunt Ethel stayed with her a few more minutes and met us out in the hall.

No one talked much on the drive home. We turned onto our dead-end street, which was packed with cars. Music blared from the duplex next door.

Uncle George pulled the cab into our driveway. "What's all this?"

"Don't worry, it's just our new neighbors," I said.

Uncle George narrowed his eyes. "Who are they?"

I shrugged. "Just some guys."

Aunt Ethel turned to face me. "Come home with us."

I did my best to hold back tears. "Ma wants me to stay here. My dad will be home soon."

Uncle George touched Aunt Ethel's arm. "Let the boy do what makes him feel comfortable."

"Call anytime, day or night," Aunt Ethel said.

I opened the door and stepped out of the cab.

Aunt Ethel rolled down the passenger window. "We love you, sweetheart."

"Love you too." I walked to the front door, picked up the spare key my mother kept hidden under the mat, and unlocked the door.

Uncle George waited until I was inside the house before driving off. I waved back at him from the front window, then entered the living room and sank down on the couch. It felt strange sitting alone in the dark house, and I began to regret my decision not to go home with Uncle George and Aunt Ethel. I turned on the television and rotated the channel knob. *My Three Sons* with Fred McMurray, and a *Perry Mason* rerun. *The Ten Commandments* on Million Dollar Movie. Nothing that interested me at all.

Music blared through the open windows next door.

I dialed Dad's work number and listened to his office phone ring eight or nine times before hanging up. Maybe the lady at the Copa-Banana had lied about Dad being there. Yeah, he was probably there boozing it up with those barmaids.

I was done lying for him. When he came home, I'd tell him

his secret was no longer safe with me. I wouldn't let him hurt my mother anymore. My shirt was soaked in sweat. I went out to the porch, sat on the steps, and finally, let out the waterworks.

And then, someone tapped my shoulder.

ROGER

IT HAD BEEN a pretty miserable night. As I stepped outside and lit up a cigarette, I heard the sound of sniffles coming from the porch next door. That poor kid. Something was very wrong. I was about to check up on him, when two scantily clad ladies opened the screen door and dashed toward one of the cars parked outside. Mickey stumbled down the steps after them. "Hey where you two beauties off to? Don't you wanna go to the Copa with me?"

The girls giggled, got into their car, and drove off.

"Damn you, Roger," Mickey said. "What'd you say that made those dolls go home?"

"Beats me."

"Now what am I gonna do the rest of the night?"

"Let's play some poker," I said.

"Shoot. Who wants to play poker? I wanna get laid."

"Damn it, Mick. I'm sick and tired of you bringing girls here." I'd said it all before. He'd never change.

Mick shrugged and went back inside.

I sprinted over to the kid's house and tapped his shoulder.

He quickly wiped his cheeks with the sleeve of his shirt. "Ah, hi, Rog."

"What's the matter, son?"

"Nothing."

"Are your parents asleep?"

"Yeah…well, no."

I smiled. "Yeah, well, no. What does that mean?"

"My mother's in the hospital."

"Good lord, is she okay?"

He swallowed. "I-I don't know."

"Where's your father? Why don't you come over for a while? Are you hungry?"

"I guess. I only ate breakfast."

"You like spaghetti?"

"Sure, I do."

We went inside and I filled up a plate with my spaghetti and meatballs.

Marshall shoveled the food down like he hadn't eaten in days. His hair stood up in cowlicks, and his eyes were red-rimmed. The boy's parents' bedroom window was just a few feet from the room I shared with Bob. We often left the windows open, and I'd awake to the sound of them yelling at each other. Made me uneasy all over again. I was no stranger to living in a home where parents had knock-down-drag-out fights.

After Marshall finished eating, he insisted on washing all the dishes in the sink. Someone had taught the kid good manners. As he washed and I dried, he talked about his mother losing her baby. "And we couldn't find my father." he said in a choked up voice.

Tears formed in my eyes and I looked away. I always had a terrible fear whenever Pat was pregnant that something would go wrong. Especially now with me being so far away. What words of comfort could I offer this poor child? He was living my worst nightmare. "I'm truly sorry for your loss."

He shrugged.

"Why don't we see what the guys are up to?"

He followed me into the living room where Whitey, Bob, Mickey, and Big Julie were playing stud poker. Hank Williams blared from the stereo.

"Man, I hate that country sound," Big Julie said. "Everything sounds the same."

Both Mickey and I had grown up in the Midwest, and shared a love of country music.

Mickey dealt everyone cards. "No offense, city boy, but Roger and I ain't so crazy about those Yiddish records you're always playing."

"Speak for yourself," I said. "I'm starting to like that *Hava Nagila.*"

Mickey patted the seat next to him. "Why don't you *hava* over here and play some more poker?"

"Don't feel like it anymore."

"That's 'cause you're winning. Quit while you're ahead, heh?"

"Sometimes I wish I could quit."

The room fell silent. Everyone stared at me. They knew I wasn't talking about the cards. I tugged at my scalp and strands of hair ended up in my hand.

"What's with the hair?" Mickey said.

"I've had it with the pressure. It's making my damn hair fall out."

"Yeah, well I don't like it any better than you, bud." Mickey picked up his beer and headed upstairs to his bedroom.

"At least the fans love him," I said.

Big Julie scratched his stomach. "It wasn't always that way.

They used to boo Mick before you got here."

"Well, it's making me nuts." It was first time I'd brought the topic of the home run race up—the elephant in the room we'd all been dancing around.

"If you ask me those fans are dumb," Marshall said.

Bob put his arm around my shoulder. "The kid's right. You and that long ball formula of yours seem to be working."

Big Julie rippled a brow. "What formula?"

"Heck, it's no big secret. If I hit the ball an eighth-of-an-inch off center, it's gonna be a high fly, an eighth higher, a line drive. But right in between, that's my sweet spot."

"Not much wiggle room," Marshall said.

I winked at him.

Mickey reappeared dressed in a navy sport coat. "Who wants to go to the Copa? Drinks on me."

"Hell, I'll go," said Whitey. "How about you, Roger?"

I squinted. "Are you guys nuts? If Houk discovers you're going out this late—"

"Screw Houk." Mick said. "What's he gonna do, fire me?" He looked over at Whitey. "Who's pitching for Washington tomorrow?"

"Dick Donovan."

"I'll get one off that guy," Mickey said.

"Yeah, and I'll get two," I said. "What do you think, Marshall?"

We all looked his way. Marshall grinned.

Mickey turned to him. "I hear you're a ballplayer, kid."

"Yes, sir. Tomorrow night after our game I'll find out if I made the All-Star team."

I had an idea and smiled at the kid. "Why don't you show

us what you got? Whitey, would you have the honor of pitching to Marshall?"

Marshall's eyes sparkled. "You're serious?"

"Of course." I winked at Mick. "Our usual bet?"

Mickey reached in his pocket and pulled out some bills. "Fifty says he can't hit the ball."

"You're on." I grinned. "Go home and get your bat, kid."

As we all headed outside, Big Julie whispered in my ear, "Brilliant."

One thing I'd learned about the Mick. He was always up for a challenge.

BIG JULIE

I BREATHED A SIGH of relief. Roger had just saved my butt. This was the hardest job I'd ever done. Well, except for my marriage to Selma, God bless her. Ironically enough, an interesting balance existed between the two sluggers, and they helped each other out of trouble more often than not. Honestly, I never thought the living arrangement would work out. Pure genius on Ralph Houk's part.

Standing on the sidewalk that humid summer night, I watched the two most famous ballplayers in America share their love of the game with the Little Leaguer from next door.

Whitey threw a slow pitch out. Roger played catcher. The boy swung hard but couldn't connect with the ball. Next pitch he did the same thing. This went on for about three more throws.

"Time out." Roger said. "Give me that bat. Watch what I'm

doing. Get your back elbow up, head down. Start your swing earlier." He handed the bat back to the kid.

Marshall wiped the sweat above his lip, and followed Roger's instructions.

"Hold your elbow a little higher." Roger said.

When Whitey threw the next ball, the kid hit the damn thing over Whitey's head and down the street.

We all cheered and whistled. Roger hugged him.

Mick wiggled his eyebrows at Marshall and ponied up the bills to Roger. Marshall's face lit up.

Just then a white sedan rounded the corner.

The boy's face froze. "Gotta go." He bolted to his house and ran up the steps.

"Move the party back inside," I said. The last thing they needed was the kid's father to see them out there.

Mick and Roger entered first, followed by Bob and Whitey. As I dragged my big ass back up the porch steps, the car door opened and the kid's father said, "Marshall, what the hell is going on around here?"

From what I'd heard from Roger, the guy was a jackass. If he discovered who was living next door to him, no telling what he'd do. It could mean big *tzuris* for all of us.

MARSHALL

MY DAD DROPPED his keys on the hall table. "What were you doing outside so late?"

"Hitting the ball around with our new neighbors." I smiled. If he only knew who they were.

"At midnight you're playing stickball by streetlight? Who

are those people?"

"Just some guys," I said.

"How ridiculous for grown men to play in the street this late. I've seen them out there at all hours before. Don't they have jobs?"

"Sure they do," I said.

"Something's weird with those people if you ask me. You stay away from them."

I bit my lower lip but said nothing.

"And where's your mother?"

"Ma's—"

"Don't tell me. She's sleeping. Probably hasn't gotten outta bed all day."

I gulped. "She's at the hospital."

"What?"

"She lost the baby."

He sighed. "Oh, Christ."

"I called you like twenty times at work. Where were you?"

"I guess the phone at work was broke," he said.

"You're lying. I-I saw your briefcase in the closet."

He lifted his right hand and smacked me across the face.

My cheek stung but I choked back the tears. No way would I let him see me cry.

His voice softened. "Come here, Marshall. I didn't mean to hit you."

When I didn't move, he inched closer and gave me a stiff hug. "We'll go to the hospital in the morning. I'll buy your mother some yellow roses. They're her favorite."

Roses! Did he think that could make up for him not being around when my mother lost the baby? I felt sick inside every time I thought about the death of my baby sister or brother. In my mind it was all Dad's fault. My face still stung from the slap, and I feared that our family would never be the same.

MARSHALL

EARLY THE NEXT morning, Dad pulled the curtains open, and I squinted at the unwelcome light filling my bedroom. "Get up," Dad said in a husky voice. "We've got to get to the hospital right away."

I opened my eyes and yawned, not quite awake. Then panic sunk in. "Did something happen to Ma?"

"We need to get over there early. Don't dawdle now." He left the room.

I threw on a pair of shorts and a T-shirt, did my business in the bathroom, and met Dad in the hallway downstairs. We left right away without even eating breakfast.

Dad made a pit stop at a florist on Northern Boulevard. He arrived back into the car with a dozen yellow roses. He never seemed to notice all the work my mother did in her flower garden. "You could have cut some from the yard,"

"Now you tell me," Dad said.

When we entered my mother's hospital room, he kissed her forehead. "I'm sorry I wasn't here last night. Brooks—"

"I don't care to hear your excuses."

Dad's eyes twitched. "You don't understand what's happening at work."

My mother shot him a hard look. "I understand too well." Then she turned to me. "Are you okay, honey? Did you get something to eat last night?"

I started to tell her about Roger's spaghetti but decided it might flare up another argument. "I had a peanut-butter-and-jelly sandwich." How would I keep all these lies straight?

She looked back at Dad. "And breakfast?"

"We ate Cornflakes," Dad said. "Right, Marshall?"

"You mean Wheaties," I said. My mother knew I'd never eat Cornflakes. This lying business made me feel ashamed of myself.

We sat around her room for a few hours while nurses and other hospital staff checked on her before she could go home. Each one asked her a lot of the same questions.

"How are you feeling, Mrs. Elliot?"

"Have you eaten?"

"Have you gone to the restroom?"

"Do you have someone to take care of you when you get home?"

Dad kept checking his watch. "I can't believe how long it takes a person to get outta this joint."

Finally Dr. Reynolds showed up in his blue scrubs and bent over my mother's bed. "I'm sorry it's taken me so long to get here this morning, Mrs. Elliot. I just got out of a lengthy surgery. How do you feel?"

My mother said she felt better but I thought she was lying. She looked white as the bed sheets.

Dad introduced himself to the doctor and stuck out his hand.

Dr. Reynolds narrowed his eyes as he shook Dad's hand. "I need to do a quick examination and then you can take your wife home." He swished the curtain closed around her.

Me and Dad waited outside. After the doctor was done examining her, he pulled the curtain back open. "Let's go outside so your wife can get dressed." When we were in the hall, Dr. Reynolds patted my shoulder. "How are you doing this morning, son?"

I smiled, uncertain what to say. I felt tired and sick to my stomach. No way I was admitting that. "I'm okay." I finally said. "Just worried about my mother."

"She's going to be just fine." Dr. Reynolds turned to Dad. "It's very important your wife stays in bed for at least a week. She needs total bed rest. Are you able to take care of her, Mr. Elliot?"

"I can manage."

"Don't you worry, sir, I'll take good care of Ma," I said.

"You're a good boy," Dr. Reynolds said.

Dad put his arm around my shoulder. "He certainly is."

I didn't believe for one moment that Dad could be counted on. It was up to me to help my mother get through this. I made myself a promise that no matter what happened, I would be there for her.

CHAPTER SEVEN

The Competition

July 6, 1961

In Moscow, North Korea and the Soviet Union signed a "Treaty of Friendship, Cooperation and Mutual Assistance," providing that if one of the nations was in a state of war, the other one would extend military assistance." (6)

MARSHALL

Monday morning, I sat in the kitchen eating my Wheaties. I was so tired, I could barely hold my head up. If only I could stop thinking about my mother losing the baby. But I couldn't get it out of my mind. Tonight they would be picking the All-Star team. It was important to focus on getting some rest for this make-or-break chance to make the team.

Dad cooked some bacon in a pan. The grease splattered all over the stove and hit him in the eye. "Damn." He poured himself a cup of coffee from the electric pot, took a sip, and spit it back into the cup.

"You didn't wait until it finished percolating." I said. "Ma says it's not ready until the red light stops blinking."

"Okay, smart boy. Why don't you try and cook?"

I stood up. "I don't mind."

"Just sit down and shut up."

"Ma's gonna be in bed for a while. Someone's gotta do it."

I heard footsteps on the staircase. "Is everything going okay?" Ma said. "I'll be right there to help with breakfast." Seconds later, she appeared in her robe.

Dad put his arm around her waist. "Let's you and I go back upstairs."

"Me and Dad are doing just fine," I said. "The doctor said bed rest."

"*Dad and I* are doing just fine," she said pulling away from Dad. She eased over to the sink, grabbed a scouring pad, and began scrubbing the grease on the stove. "Who wants an omelet?"

Dad looked relieved. "Are you sure you can handle it?"

My mother suddenly clutched her stomach.

"Are you okay, Marion?"

She stood up a little straighter. "Guess I'll make those omelets tomorrow. Sorry, guys, you're on your own today."

Dad helped her back up the stairs then reappeared moments later. He glanced at the unwashed dishes and narrowed his eyes. "I'll be late if I don't leave now."

"Don't worry, I'll take care of things. Just don't forget my game," I said.

"When is it?"

"Geez, I can't believe you forgot."

"You know there's been other things on my mind around here lately. Like your mother for instance."

"It's at five o'clock sharp."

He held my chin in his hand. "Don't you worry, I'll be there, son."

If I made the team, maybe, he wouldn't spend so much time at work. Maybe he wouldn't be so mad at me and Ma all the time. This was my chance to turn things around.

MARSHALL

LATER THAT AFTERNOON, I put on my Bears uniform, heated up some leftover meatloaf and mashed potatoes from the fridge, and carried a tray up to my mother in her bedroom.

Ma glanced up at me. "You're the best son in the world." She looked so small in her pink nightgown curled up in the big bed.

I kissed her cheek. "Well, of course."

"I'm so sorry to miss your game."

"It's okay. Dad will be there. Now try to eat something."

"It looks terrific."

"I'll be home straight after the game. If you need anything, Aunt Ethel said she'd stop by."

A few minutes later, Uncle George pulled up in his Yellow Cab to drive Bobby and me to Hudson's Park. We were playing another game with the Tigers with both Rocky Romano and Frank Caruso psyched to destroy us. With everything else going on, I'd forgotten they were on the Tiger team.

A big crowd of parents and siblings filled the bleachers. The concession stand opened and kids lined up to buy corndogs, hamburgers, popcorn, sodas, peanuts, and cracker jacks.

The smell of meat on the grill made my mouth water.

The Tigers headed to the dugout. Rocky gave Bobby the finger when he darted by him at home plate.

My teammates circled Coach Lee, stacked hands, and chanted, "One-two-three, Bears." After trotting out to right field, I checked the bleachers for my father. Everyone else's parents were cheering them on.

The umpire moved behind the plate, raised his hand, and shouted, "Play ball."

Frank Caruso, the first batter, drew a walk. He threw down the bat and shot me a dirty look as he took his base. The second batter smacked the ball up the middle for a single, and Frank rounded second then slid into third. The next batter swung hard like he was going for a home run, and struck out after three good pitches. One, two, three.

Rocky, the cleanup-batter, stepped up to the plate. He nodded his head at the pitcher, then, spit on the ground. After two strikes, he eyeballed me in the outfield. On the next pitch, he whacked a line drive to right field.

I dove toward the ball, caught it in my glove, and hurled it to the first baseman for a double play ending the inning, and saving the run.

Rocky heaved the bat down then turned and shoved Bobby.

Bobby shoved him back, but Coach Lee was quick on the scene and stepped between them. Coach whispered something in Bobby's ear that caused him to march over to the dugout.

The Bear parents cheered as the side was retired. When I ran in from the outfield, I scanned the crowd in the stands again. Coach Lee and a couple of the players patted me on the back. Uncle George ran up to me. "Beautiful catch, and quick thinking on the throw to first base, Marshall."

"My dad's played a lot of catch with me," I said.

"Where's he tonight?"

I shrugged. "I'm sure he'll be here soon." But I wasn't.

"What a shame he missed that."

As my uncle headed back to his seat, I saw Laila, the girl at Gelaro's Market, smiling at me. She was hanging out with a group of her girlfriends from PS 107.

Next thing I knew, Laila was standing right next to me. "Great play, Marshall."

She was the cutest girl in the universe. Only problem was I didn't have a clue how to talk to a girl. "Ah, thanks. I'm glad you like baseball."

"I told you I like the Yankees. Little League is kind of boring."

I scratched my head. "Then why are you here?"

"Well, I hoped I might get to see you." She smiled and her cheeks turned quite red.

"Oh, ah—"

Before I could say another word, she raced back to her friends.

I was all mixed up. This was the first time a girl actually liked *me*. Wow!

The game evolved into a pitcher's duel with both sides making lots of good defensive plays. I walked up to the plate in the bottom of the final inning.

The Little League announcer sat in front of the crowd with a megaphone. "At the bottom of seven, it's a tied ballgame, with two outs. Bobby Cecchini is on first base. Batting for the Bears, right fielder, Marshall Elliot."

This was my last time at bat for the season. I checked out the stands once again, even though I knew it was hopeless. My throat burned as I dug my cleat into the dirt and readied myself into position.

The pitcher threw the first pitch, which I swung at and missed.

I wiped sweat from my brow then held my bat back for the next pitch. As the ball approached the plate, I swung hard, too hard, for strike two. I sucked in my breath as it dawned on me that I was only one strike away from repeating what I'd done last season.

Then I thought about Roger's batting advice. *Keep your elbow up and your head down.* I swung at the next pitch crushing a high fastball, and took off for first base.

"Long fly ball to left field," shouted the announcer as I roared off to first base. "The outfielder going back, way back. It's out of here for a home run!"

The Bear fans cheered as I rounded the bases.

I could hear Laila's voice above everyone else's shouting my name.

The announcer hollered, "And the Bears win the game, three to one."

When I crossed home plate, my whole team ran out on the field and gave me hugs and pats on the back. Mike Bernstein and Bobby lifted me up on their shoulders.

"You did it," said Bobby. "You're a shoo-in for the All-Star team."

Uncle George appeared at the dugout. "Great going, son. Your dad's gonna be real sorry he missed that."

Uncle George had no idea how crushed I was feeling.

After the crowd calmed down, Coach Lee called out the

names of those selected from the Bears for Flushing's All-Star team. "Bobby Cechinni, Mike Bernstein, and today's hero, Marshall Elliot."

Bobby hugged me then shook hands with the other kids who'd been chosen. I walked off by myself to the dugout and grabbed my bag. For years I had dreamed of making the All-Stars. Yet now, rather than being thrilled like everyone else, I just wanted to be alone.

Following Coach Lee's announcement, the Tiger coach, a fat guy with a hook nose, revealed the names of the players from his team who would be playing along side of us. No surprise that both Rocky Romano and Frank Caruso were selected. Rocky eyeballed me and Bobby, while Frank pretty much ignored our existence.

The kids who weren't chosen slumped off the field and piled into cars with their parents.

Coach Lee and the Tiger Coach asked the All-Star team to meet at the dugout. They brought us Cokes and boxes of Cracker Jacks. The parents of the newly selected All-Star team ran down from the stands and hugged their kids.

Uncle George had a big grin on his face. "Thank God, both you boys made it." We all feared that wouldn't happen.

"I knew all along," Aunt Ethel said. "Let's go celebrate with a pizza."

"I should go home." I said.

Uncle George unlocked the Yellow Cab doors. "Are you sure? Paisano's pepperoni and sausage. Your favorite."

"Thanks, but I've got a headache." It was true. My head was throbbing.

Aunt Ethel pressed her palm on my forehead. "You do

seem a little warm."

"Geez, Marsh. You look like someone ran over your dog, not like a kid who just made All-Stars," Bobby said.

MARSHALL

WHEN I GOT home, I ran up to my mother's room where I found her in bed reading a copy of *Life* Magazine. "Did you know Ernest Hemingway killed himself?" She pointed at the cover and shook her head.

I kissed her forehead. "Sorry about Mr. Hemingway. Was he an actor?"

"He was a great author." "Well, I have some good news. I made the team."

"That's great, honey." Her eyes filled with tears.

"No reason to cry."

"I'm sorry I wasn't there to cheer for you when they called your name."

"It's okay, Ma."

"No it's not. I've obviously been a terrible wife and now I'm a terrible mother."

"You're a great mother."

"Please leave now and close the door."

Something was really wrong with my mother and I didn't know how to help her. A lump formed in my throat and I felt like I was suffocating. I charged down the stairs and pushed open the screen door. I needed some fresh air.

Roger was just stepping inside his red convertible. He saw me and waved. "Hey, Marshman. What's up?"

I frowned.

"Problems at home again?"

"Yeah, kinda."

"Hey, how 'bout you come to Yankee batting practice with me tomorrow? I sure could use some company."

"Really? Sure."

"Be outside and ready to go at one o'clock sharp."

I thanked him and ran back inside to the kitchen where I made myself a peanut-butter-and-jelly sandwich. After I finished eating, I took a hot shower and put on my pajamas. I was more than ready to drift off to sleep. But part of me wanted to give my Dad a piece of my mind. Let him know it wasn't okay to hurt my mother and miss my All-Star game. I dragged myself down the stairs and switched on the television.

The next thing I knew static hissed from the old console and Dad was shaking me. I looked up at him. "You missed my game."

He shrugged. "Damn that Brooks. He wouldn't let me go until I finished this report."

"You been drinking while you were working so hard?"

"Are you calling your daddy a liar?"

Ma suddenly appeared in her ratty old nightgown. "You are a liar."

"So I worked late and then had a couple of beers with Greeley. That don't make me a liar."

My mother moved closer to him and sniffed his collar. "Does Greeley wear perfume?"

"What's that supposed to mean?"

"Who is it, Edmond? That new girl in the clerical pool? The floozy who wears dresses up to her navel?"

Dad slapped her across the face. "Who you calling a floozy?"

She gasped. A red imprint of his hand was framed on her cheek.

I rushed up to Dad and kicked his knee. Hard.

A vein on his neck bulged. "You son-of-a-bitch. I'll have your hide for this."

"Don't you ever hit my mother! Why don't you leave? We don't want you here anymore."

Dad limped toward the staircase and hobbled up the steps. "Good idea."

"No!" cried Ma. She raced up the stairs behind him grabbing the back of his jacket.

He shoved her off, nearly knocking her down the stairs.

What was she doing? I followed the both of them to their bedroom where Dad began to fill an overnight bag with clothes.

My mother's whole body was shaking. "The boy didn't mean it. Marshall, tell your father you want him to stay."

"Let him go, Ma," I said.

Dad's eyes watered up. "Someday you'll understand, son." He hurried down the stairs and out the door, slamming it behind him.

Between sobs, my mother said, "Why did you tell him to go?"

"He was gonna go anyway."

She looked at me with papery eyelids, and pupils that expanded like giant black marbles. "This is all your fault!"

I tore out of her bedroom toward mine. All I wanted was our family to be together. But instead, I had destroyed everyone's lives.

MARSHALL

THE NEXT AFTERNOON, the hot July breeze blew in our faces as me and Roger Maris drove down the Grand Central with the top down. Neither of us spoke much. He seemed absorbed in his own thoughts. Just sitting there beside him, made me feel great despite everything that had happened yesterday.

It surprised me that he hadn't asked me if I'd made the All-Star team and it felt awkward for me to bring it up. Had he forgotten about it like my dad?

When we reached the Whitestone Bridge, Roger cleared his throat. "So, son, did you make it?"

I grinned. "Yes, I'm an All-Star."

"I've been dying to ask you but you look like an ol' droopy-faced hound-dog. I assumed you hadn't made it."

"Yeah, well, my dad moved out."

He touched my hand. "Wish I could do something to make you feel better."

I pushed a lock of my hair out of my face as we drove across the bridge. "You already have."

"Now that you're an All-Star, it's really important that you get a lot of batting practice. Unlike a lot of my teammates, I really enjoy it."

"I like batting practice too. It's just—"

"What?"

"My Dad *used* to take me a lot."

"I'd take ya myself, but between all the double-headers, practice, and traveling to away games, I don't get much down-time."

"Don't worry, I'll figure it out."

"I have no doubt you will, son. I hope by the time my boys play ball, I'll be done with my major league career. I may even try my hand at coaching."

He pulled out a well-worn leather wallet and handed it to me. "Check out my family." Inside a plastic sleeve was a picture of his wife and three kids. Two boys, and a girl. The boys were still babies. They'd be playing baseball in five or six years.

I handed his wallet back to him. "You'd actually give up the Yankees to coach your kids?"

"You betcha. My daughter Susan's about to have her first ballet recital. It breaks me up thinking I won't be there."

"Really?"

"I'd quit tomorrow, but my wife won't hear of it."

Just knowing that someone like Roger existed in the world gave me a sense of faith.

When we arrived at Yankee stadium, Roger took me to meet up with Big Julie so he could escort me to my seat. Only a handful of people sat in the stands as workers in pinstripe shirts rolled out the batting cage. One of the coaches stood behind an L-shaped screen about halfway between the mound and the plate and threw straight pitches to the batters.

Big Julie pointed up at a seat above the dugout next to some guy wearing a hat. Roger winked at me whenever he got up to bat. It was a night I'll always remember. Roger was the man I wanted to be when I grew up. If only my mother had married someone like him.

ROGER

THE FOLLOWING NIGHT, the sunset at Yankee Stadium filled the west sky with streaks of red, yellow, and purple. Darn near as pretty as sunsets in Kansas. We were playing an early night game against the Washington Senators. The stadium was packed.

It was the bottom of the fourth inning. The first two batters struck out. Then Bobby Richardson followed with a double and slid into second base.

Everyone thought I was an imbecile for publicly saying in an interview I wanted to go back to Kansas City. There was even a cartoon in the *New York Daily News* with a tornado and a caricature of me carrying Toto from the movie, *The Wizard of Oz.*

But it was true. All I wanted was to return to Pat and the kids and live in the beautiful ranch house we'd bought last year in the suburbs. I resented every last minute I was away from them. Yeah, I cared about the money like the next guy, but I didn't know how much more I could take of being made to feel like a pariah.

As I approached the plate, the New York crowd booed. I tried to ignore them, but they'd penetrated my armor. With a knot in my gut, I spat in the dirt.

"Go back to Kansas and take Toto with you," shouted a fan above left field.

"We want Mick to win the race not you," yelled another.

I left the batter box to get some pine tar and gave serious thought to walking off the field and never coming back. To hell with them all. But then, I flashed on Marshall's ear-to-ear grin as he sat in the empty stands watching batting practice last night. What would he think of me if I quit? How would the kid deal with his own problems if he knew that I couldn't deal with mine?

I would show the hostile crowd the stuff I was made of. The next ball came in high and fast. I swung hard and heard the CRACK of the bat. You know right away when the bat sounds like that. It went straight down the right field line, high into the upper deck. I jogged around the bases with my head down.

The stadium announcer said, "Another home run for Roger Maris."

There was a pitiful amount of cheers, along with boos, as Mick headed to the plate.

"Batting for the Yankees, Number 7, Mickey Mantle."

The crowd cheered wildly. Mickey walked after four bad pitches.

Part of me was ready to slip inside the shiny red convertible that Jules had talked me into buying, and not stop until I hit Kansas. But I stayed for the kid.

CHAPTER EIGHT

Changing Times

July 10, 1961

The United Klans of America was created by the merger of several different racist groups meeting at Indian Springs, Georgia, seeking a revival of the Ku Klux Klan. (7)

MICKEY

O ne steamy, hot night, I left the duplex profusely sweating and swatting at the mosquitoes holding a party on my face. The shapely weather girl on TV had said the ninety-nine degree temperature was breaking all New York records.

I took the 7 Train to Manhattan. It was so hot I passed by some guy in a clown's suit on Forty-Sixth Street frying an egg on the sidewalk. Whitey and I began the evening in the bar at the Ritz, and ended up at some peep show on Forty-Second Street. The gal I was with wore a slinky red dress. She had asked me if I believed in having sex on the first date.

I smiled. "Hell, you can't have sex *before* the first date, now can ya?" Ha, ha, ha. I ordered us all another round.

She brought me home to some one-bedroom dive in the Village that smelled of garlic and sewage. The sex was kinky, even for me, and she burned my cheek with a cigarette. I don't remember much about the ride back to Queens other than Big Julie lifting me into his big white Lincoln and rolling his eyes.

The next morning, Roger turned up the stereo full blast with *Reveille* playing on some old scratched record. Where the hell did he buy a record like that? Then he and Bob started singing along with the bugle, *"You got to get up, you got to get up, you got to get up in the morning."*

It was Rog's idea of a joke.

I staggered into the kitchen and joined Bob at the table. He looked up from the newspaper. "What the hell happened to your face?"

"Beats me," I said.

Roger was whistling and flapping pancakes on the stove. "Want some breakfast, Scarface?"

"Do we have any Ginger Ale? My head feels like it's gonna explode."

Roger rubbed his neck. "Go to the fridge and check it out yourself."

I was embarrassed to admit that I could barely move, let alone stand up. My knees ached worse than usual. I'd been eating painkillers like candy buttons and had no idea how I would play baseball that afternoon. But somehow, I always managed to pull my body through.

Bob handed me the sports section. "Maybe this will cheer you up."

THE M&M TERRORS BLAST IN BACK-TO-BACK HOMERS
NUDGING DETROIT OUT OF FIRST PLACE.

It had become our pattern, Roger and me. Like some kind of magic dust that rubbed off of each other. When he'd hit one, I'd follow up at the plate and smack one out myself.

A few days later, I hit two out of the park and Rog poled one off the Orioles. After the game, all the guys left for the Copa to celebrate. I'd told everyone I'd meet them later. My knee was badly bruised from stealing second base, and the team physician sat with me in the locker room icing it down. "You have to rest those knees, Mick, or you're going to cripple yourself."

I squeezed my eyes shut. "Just give me some of that magic potion from your bag of tricks."

"I can't keep you on cortisone shots. They're not good for you."

"Then I'll have to get them somewhere else." Doc just didn't get it. Without painkillers and cortisone, I might as well have checked myself into a nursing home.

Just then a red-faced Roger entered the room and hurled a baseball at the lockers. I'd assumed he'd left with the rest of the team.

"The press get to you again?"

"Why can't they just let us play baseball?"

I shrugged.

"Thank God they don't know where we live," he said.

I smiled through the pain. "I'm glad Houk suggested I move in to that dump."

"He more like read you the riot act." Roger moved closer then gasped. "Holy shit. Your knee looks like an overripe cantaloupe."

I winced. "It looks worse than it is."

Doc turned to Roger. "If you have any influence on Mick, tell him to rest his knees for a couple of weeks. He's going to destroy them permanently if he doesn't."

Roger looked at me earnestly. "Mick, you ought to listen to the good Doc."

"Of course you do. Then you can just waltz off with the record."

"See, Doc, he thinks I have an ulterior motive."

I grinned. "Well, don't you?"

Roger smirked. "I'll beat you fair and square."

"Then tell the good Doc to give me one of his magic bullets."

"Forget it, Mick," Roger said. "Let's go join the guys at the Copa."

"I'm game." As I headed toward my locker, my knee gave out and I lay helplessly on the cold cement floor. I gritted my teeth to keep from screaming.

Doc yelled to Roger. "Call an ambulance."

"No, please," I groaned.

Roger's eyebrows drew together. "Is there another way?"

Doc shrugged. "I've done all I can. I won't take responsibility anymore. If you care about Mickey, call that ambulance now." He packed his black bag and was gone.

Roger lifted me onto a chair. "How 'bout I drive you to Flushing Memorial?"

"No, I won't...I can't go there."

The kid from Kansas City stood for a moment chewing his lower lip. I'd put him in a tough spot. I never doubted he wanted to do the right thing by me. He'd heard what the doctor said about my knees, but he also understood what it meant if I missed a few weeks of games. Finally he said, "I'll call Jules. He'll know what to do."

Less than an hour later, Jules arrived at the locker room with a physician buddy of his who owed him a favor.

MARSHALL

THE FLUSHING ALL-STAR TEAM sat on the dugout bench as we awaited our first big game against Jamaica.

I hadn't slept much last night. Even with both our bedroom doors shut, I could hear my mother sobbing. She'd stopped getting dressed and stayed in her nightgown all day.

We hadn't seen or heard from Dad for over a week. July 4th had come and gone without him. Normally, Dad took me to see the big fireworks display at Flushing stadium. It wasn't the same as I shot off firecrackers and twirled sparkers with Uncle George and Bobby in front of their house.

The bleachers filled with the players' families. When we finished warming up, Coach Lee said we could visit with our folks before the game. "Try not to eat anything too heavy or you'll get a stomach ache."

Mike Bernstein's mom slid open the concession stand window.

Kids holding change in their hands quickly formed a long line around the little cement block building.

I was dying for a hotdog with lots of mustard smeared on it. Did that count as something that would give me a stomachache? Probably. But I couldn't resist the aroma and the vision of the fat juicy dogs riding around on the spit.

Laila stood in the line with a couple of her girlfriends. When she saw me, she waved. "Marshall, over here."

I pulled a crumpled dollar bill from my pocket and ran over to her. Before I could speak, Laila squeezed my hand. "Good luck with your game."

I was so nervous my tongue felt like sandpaper. I could barely get out, "Can I buy you a hot dog?"

Her friend with the red ponytail giggled. "Is *he* your boyfriend?"

Laila ignored her. "I'd love a hot dog. Come get in line with me."

I hesitated for a minute then cut in front of her.

A few kids gave me dirty looks.

I stood there wordless with a smile pasted on my face. What do you say to girls? Then I remembered what she'd told me about her father and I asked her how he was doing.

"Much better. Mother says he's out of the wheelchair and using crutches."

"That's great."

"It's really nice of you to ask. He hopes to be walking by the end of the summer. Then we can all go home."

"We?"

"I have two sisters. They're staying with my Aunt Etta and Uncle Gene in the Bronx."

"I'm glad *you* were the one they sent to Flushing."

Laila's cheeks reddened. "Me too."

"I always wanted a brother or a sister," I said. My chest tightened up as I thought about the baby my mother had just lost.

Finally, we reached the front of the line and I ordered two

hotdogs. I put lots of mustard on mine while Laila splashed hers with ketchup. Mrs. Bernstein also handed us two cups of water. I wish I'd had enough money to buy us Dr. Peppers or Coca Colas.

Me and Laila found a spot under the bleachers where there was a patch of grass. The sky darkened as we sat eating the food and sipping cups of water through plastic straws. We didn't talk much.

Suddenly, the announcer said, "Fifteen minutes until game time." The umpire, a tubby man with a frog-like face, walked onto the field.

I picked up a napkin and wiped some ketchup off the corners of Laila's mouth.

She smiled. "Thank you. I guess you better get going."

I shot her a hard look. "Before I go, I need to ask you…

"Don't worry. I haven't said a word to anyone. Your secret is safe."

I let out my breath. "Thank you. See you after the game." Next thing I knew, she kissed my cheek.

With my hand pressed to my face feeling the slightly wet place where her mouth had touched it, I raced back to the dugout vowing not to ever wash that side of my face again.

Coach Lee prepared the batting order. "Just relax and play your best."

The players on the Jamaica All-Star team threw the ball around the field. They wore their hair greased back in ducktails. In contrast, we all had crew cuts or wore our hair like President Kennedy's son John-John.

I didn't bother to scan the stands for Dad since I hadn't told him about the game. Ma wasn't there either. She'd been asleep when Uncle George and Aunt Ethel arrived to pick us up. I sat next to Bobby talking about the new swing Roger had taught me.

"Who showed you that?" Before I could respond, he smacked my arm and pointed in the distance. "Look over there!"

A man in a business suit was headed for the dugout with a bat in his hand. His hair was slicked back and he had a big grin on his face.

At first, I didn't recognize him. Maybe because he was the last one in the world I'd expected to see there. As he moved closer, I realized it was Dad.

He held out the bat. "I thought you could use this for your first All-Star game."

My heart pumped so hard my ribs hurt. Did this mean he was back in my life? I thought about the last few days of mother lying in bed all day. "Thanks. I like the bat I got."

"Ah, c'mon, take it for luck." He nudged the bat at me.

I paused for a minute then took hold of it.

He smiled again. "This Louisville Slugger set me back fifteen smackers. Top of the line."

"You didn't have to buy it."

"I wanted to. You gonna hit one over the fence for me?"

Now I felt even more pressure.

He slapped my back. "Just give it your best, boy."

Uncle George headed down from the bleachers and walked up to Dad. "Long time no see, Edmund."

Dad extended his hand for a handshake. "Hello, George."

My uncle left Dad awkwardly standing with his hand held out. "Too bad you missed Marshall's home run last week."

"I've had a lot of pressure at work lately."

"Marion mentioned that. I hear you've been working day and night."

Dad stuck his face inches from Uncle George's. "I guess Yellow Cab doesn't put much pressure on their employees."

My uncle's face burned red as a brush fire. "Oh, Mr. Bigshot executive. Too good for us plain working folk now?"

Dad stepped back toward the stands.

Uncle George blocked him with his bulky body. "I was with your wife at the hospital."

"Get outta my way," Dad said.

Parents in the stands gawked at them. "What's wrong with you two?" one woman hollered.

I wanted to go home and hide under my bed.

Uncle George shouted, "Where were you that night, bud?" I'd never seen my uncle so mad.

"None of your damn business," Dad said.

"A man who leaves his family is a total loser in my book."

"Who you calling a loser? You're nothing but a two-bit cabbie. Always will be." Their voices grew louder.

Mike Bernstein, our shortstop, headed to the plate. He was built like a string bean but he could be counted on for a base hit. Mike peeked around his shoulder at the crowd shouting at Uncle George and Dad.

Meanwhile, the umpire huddled with both coaches. The Jamaica team readied themselves in the field. I kept looking back at Uncle George and Dad as their pitcher threw the ball to his infield players.

Aunt Ethel rushed down from her seat. "George, come back up to the bleachers."

Uncle George ignored her. Beads of sweat glistened on his forehead. "Got yourself a floozy?"

Dad pushed him.

Uncle George shoved him back.

Dad lost his balance and fell on the ground. He grabbed Uncle George's legs, pulling him down too. They rolled around like two kids play wrestling, only they were grown men, and they weren't playing.

I raced out of the dugout with my new bat in hand. A group of fathers charged down from the bleachers and tore them apart.

I thrashed the Louisville Slugger over and over again on a wood post until it broke. The skin on my hands was splintered and torn, and hurt like hell.

"Look what he did to his bat," Rocky shouted.

"No way you can count on a kid like that," said Frank.

A patrol car cruising by screeched to a halt. The cop rolled down his window. "What's going on here?"

The fathers let go of Dad and Uncle George.

"Everything's okay," Uncle George said. "My brother-in-law just got a little excited."

Dad held up his fists. "I'll show you who's excited, you son-of-a—"

The officer hightailed it over to my father. "You need to come with me, sir."

Dad's tone suddenly sounded sheepish. "I'm sorry for the disturbance, sir. You see—"

"Just follow me out of this ballpark," said the cop. "If I see you here again, I'll haul you off to the station."

Dad tucked his shirt back in his pants and rubbed his neck.

As he left the park, he caught sight of my broken bat and frowned at me.

The president of the PTA sat above the dugout with the other mothers. "I've heard the creep's moved out of the house," she said loud enough for everyone to hear.

"Poor Marion," said another mother, patting her shellacked hairdo. "What's she gonna do?"

How dare she gossip about my mother? I wanted to tell her to shut up. But instead, I snatched up my glove and ran toward the parking lot.

Bobby chased after me and grabbed my shirt from behind. "Don't be a quitter, Marshall."

"Leave me alone," I said wrenching my jersey out of his fingers.

"We need you," yelled Bobby.

Hot tears blurred my vision. I ran off, ignoring his pleas. I could hardly see in front of me.

"Wait," yelled Coach Lee. "Marshall, please."

I stopped running and stood rooted to the spot. Five teammates scrambled out of the dugout and raced toward me. Rocky and Frank were part of the crowd.

"Please don't go," said Rocky. We can't beat Jamaica without you."

"What are we gonna do for a right fielder?" said Frank.

"All we got is Bernie Jackson," Rocky said. Bernie had only been selected because his father was the commissioner of the Flushing league. Never expecting a chance to play, he'd left town with his family for the Jersey Shore.

While I just wanted to disappear, I hadn't realized how much they were counting on me. "Okay," I said hesitantly, "I'll play."

Bobby placed his arm around my shoulders and I returned with him to the dugout.

The umpire hollered, "Play ball."

The Jamaica pitcher, a short, stocky Puerto Rican guy who looked like he had no neck, wiped sweat from his brow with the sleeve of his shirt. Then he wound up his arm and threw the first pitch.

Mike swung and missed for strike one. Two more fastballs and Mike struck out.

Rocky stepped up to the plate and took some practice swings. The pitcher threw a fastball down the middle. Rocky smacked the ball hard and bolted from the plate to first base.

The game continued for the next hour. While we played our best, we just couldn't score. Inning after inning, we left one or two players on base. During the bottom of the fourth, we ended the inning with the bases loaded.

But we managed a tight defense. After five-and-a-half innings, we were tied, zero-to-zero. As we sprinted from the field to the dugout, a small streak of lightning flashed off in the distance. Coach Lee told Bobby to get on deck.

The umpire looked up at the darkening sky, paused and arched his back.

"It's not raining yet," yelled the Jamaica coach, a skinny Puerto Rican guy with a pencil thin mustache. "Let's get this game finished."

The umpire checked the sky again and said, "Play ball.

The announcer held up the bullhorn to his lips. "Batting for Flushing, Bobby Cechinni."

The clouds grew darker. A few drops splashed on my arm. My cousin stepped into the batter box. Uncle George whistled and all the Flushing kids and parents cheered. "Go, Bobby."

"Marshall, get on deck," Coach Lee shouted.

I grabbed my old bat and took a few practice swings. The pitcher threw one in at Bobby.

He hit the ball to left field for a stand-up double just as rain splattered on the field. The Jamaica coach and Coach Lee approached the umpire and stood in a huddle. The rain slowed down to a mere drizzle.

The umpire scratched his head. "Okay, play ball."

I entered the batter box and dug my cleat into the dirt. My hands were covered with so many painful red blisters I could barely hold the bat. I wanted to quit but I was Flushing's last chance.

The pitcher came out of his windup and the ball fired toward me. The Flushing crowd shouted my name, "MARSHALL, MARSHALL!"

I hit a slow grounder to the second baseman who fumbled the ball as I motored to first base. Bobby ran full speed to third. The second baseman threw the ball to the first baseman, who dropped it.

I was out of breath and safe at first, as Bobby rounded third and headed for home. The first baseman picked up the ball and sent it high and wide to the catcher who tagged Bobby just as he slid across home plate. The umpire threw both hands out flat. "Safe."

The Jamaica coach raced over to him. "Are you blind? That kid was out."

"Don't you second guess me Burt!" shouted the umpire.

Coach Lee rushed up to them. My teammates ran out of the dugout. They cheered and surrounded Bobby at the plate.

The Jamaica team got their last time at bat. Three strikeouts and they were done.

Lightning sparkled in the sky like fireworks. A rumble of thunder followed with a downpour that quickly turned the field to a muddy mess.

"Game over," said the umpire.

"We won," said Rocky.

One of the Jamaica players came behind him. Water dripped down his face. "You didn't win, Jerkface, Bobby was out."

"I was safe," Bobby shouted slicking his wet hair back.

The Jamaica player moved his face next to Bobby's and clenched his fists. "You're full of shit."

I moved protectively next to my cousin.

Bobby held up his fists and the kid punched him in the stomach.

A free-for-all exploded in the downpour, and we all joined in the muddy fight.

Within seconds, the fathers and coaches took hold of us and broke up the brawl. Uncle George grabbed both me and Bobby and pushed us toward the Yellow Cab where Aunt Ethel sat waiting. We were soaking wet and splattered with mud.

Dad's Galaxie pulled up next to the cab and he rolled down the window. His eyes were bloodshot. "Get outta their stinkin' car, Marshall, and drive home with your father."

"From the looks of your dad," Uncle George said, "he's had a whole lot to drink."

"Come have a pizza with us," Aunt Ethel pleaded.

I felt torn. Should I go with my father?

"I don't have all day," Dad shouted. "Get your bag and get

outta the car."

"I'm…going with them for a pizza."

He looked at me with a wounded expression then hit the gas and zoomed off.

MARSHALL

SHEETS OF RAIN fell as Uncle George veered the Yellow Cab into the driveway of our house.

When I got inside, I shouted, "Ma, you there?"

She didn't answer.

I bounded up to her bedroom, where she lay in bed propped up on pillows with a glass of wine in her hand. A half-empty bottle sat on her nightstand. "How's my boy? You look drenched."

"It's okay. We won the first All-Stars game."

"Why didn't you wake me?"

"Me and Aunt Ethel, I mean…Aunt Ethel and I thought you needed the rest."

My mother slipped out from under the covers and sat on the edge of the bed. "Con Edison called. Your father didn't pay the electric bill. I put them off for a few days."

"I got some money if you need it."

"You *have* money."

"I pulled out a five and some singles from my jacket pocket.

She arched an eyebrow. "Where did you get that?"

"I've been running errands for our neighbors."

"You put that money away somewhere safe. I can take care of us."

"But you've never worked."

"You're wrong. I used to be a dancer. Not quite a star, but I worked in a nice place on the Lower East Side. People used to say I was quite good." She slid off the bed, turned on the radio and switched the dial until she found some jazz. Then she started kicking her legs, twirling around and leaping in the air while snapping her fingers to the beat of the music.

We both laughed. "There you go. You can get a job dancing," I said.

My mother glanced at herself in the full-length mirror next to the dresser. "But I'm not young and pretty anymore."

"You're real pretty, Ma. If you'd comb your hair, and maybe put some lipstick on."

"You think so?"

"Are you kidding? You're the prettiest lady in the neighborhood."

"That's such a sweet thing to say."

I moved closer and hugged her. Thank God. It appeared she was feeling better. "Why don't you take a hot bath and fix yourself up? I'll treat you to the late movie. What do you say?"

"I don't know…"

"Please, Ma. You haven't been out of here since the baby…

"Okay, it's a date."

"How long will it take you to get dressed?"

She moved toward the bed and before I knew it, she burrowed herself back under the covers. "Tomorrow, honey. I need to sleep now."

I ran downstairs and grabbed the canvas bag with my baseball equipment from the closet and went outside. The rain had slowed to a mere drizzle as I sat on the steps of the porch and hugged my knees to my chest.

Who cared about baseball anymore? It was just a stupid game. All the things I used to care about were going away. Images of my mother baking cookies, watching the Yankees on television with Dad, playing catch at Hudson Park ran through my head. My throat burned and my eyes stung with tears. For a moment I stood there, uncertain what to do. Then I stood up, seized the canvas bag, and stumbled over to the trashcan.

ROGER

I STEPPED OUTSIDE and fished out a pack of cigarettes from my shirt pocket. Before I could light up, I noticed the kid next door had taken the metal cover off a garbage can in front of his house and was tossing his baseball glove inside. "Hey, Marshall."

He turned beet-red and quickly retrieved his glove from the trash, placing it in a canvas bag. "Ah, hi, Rog."

"Why don't you come over?"

He leaped down the steps and joined me on the porch. His hair was disheveled and his face was drawn as he stood there wordlessly, blinking back tears.

"What's wrong?"

"My dad moved out."

I wanted to throw my arms around him but I resisted. "I'm sorry."

"I don't care about baseball anymore."

"Don't you ever stop caring about baseball," I said. "It's the one thing that will help you deal with your father taking a hike."

He shrugged.

Come on inside. Big Julie brought over a tub of ice cream.

Johnny Cash's hit, "I Walk the Line" blared from the stereo. It had been over a week since Mick collapsed in the locker room. He and Whitey both sat on the couch in the living room with a tall, slender girl in their laps. According to Mickey, one of them was married to some famous Spanish racecar driver.

I pushed Marshall toward the kitchen where Big Julie was dishing out bowls of Breyers Vanilla ice cream. He handed a bowl to Marshall.

Just then Mick shouted from the living room. "Get your asses over here, now."

"I'm not interested in joining your little party," I hollered.

"It's the BIG announcement," Mickey said. The music from the stereo was replaced by the voice of Jim McKay an announcer for ABC's "The Wide World of Sports" on the television.

Jules, Marshall, and I drifted into the living room and stood in front of the TV console. Jim McKay sat behind a sports desk in a suit. He adjusted his headset. "While the M&M boys are drawing record crowds everywhere they go, Commissioner Ford Frick gave us plenty to talk about today."

Big Julie moved closer to Mick. "What's he yapping about?"

"Shhh, just listen," Mick said.

The station cut to an interview with Ford Frick, the Commissioner of Baseball. "A player who hits more than 60 home runs during his team's first 154 games will be recognized as having established a new record. However, if the player does not hit more than 60 until *after* 154 games, there would have to be some distinctive mark in the record book to show that Babe Ruth's record was set under the 154-game schedule, and the other total was compiled while the 162-game schedule was in effect."

Big Julie shook his head. "So the creep finally did it. Doesn't surprise me."

"Why's that?" said Whitey.

"Cause he was great buddies with Ruth. It's now almost impossible for Mick or Roger to get full credit for breaking his record."

"I don't get it," said the model perched on Mick's lap.

"What it means, sweetheart," Mick said, "is that if my buddy Roger over there or I don't break the record by our 154th game, we'll forever have a little asterisk in front of our name in *The Book of Baseball Records*."

Jules shook his head. "It would demean your accomplishment."

My throat tightened up so much I could hardly swallow. The home run race now seemed pointless. I felt like a prisoner in my pinstripe uniform. When I'd spoken to Pat earlier, she said Kevin just took his first steps. I sure wish I'd been there to see it.

"It's just not fair," Marshall said.

"This whole race is cursed. A no-win situation," said Mick.

The kid scratched his head. "What if Mickey hit 61 homers in 154 games and then you hit 62 in the next eight games? Would you be the homerun champ with 62? Or would Mick have set the all-time record with 61?"

We all laughed. "You'd have to be a rocket scientist to answer that one, Marshall," I said.

"A season is a season for Christ, ah, Christmas sakes," Big Julie said.

"Marshall is sharp as a tack," Mick said. "He's figured out Frick has opened up a can of worms with his ruling."

It felt awkward standing in the living room with Whitey and Mick sitting with girls on their laps. I couldn't imagine what poor Marshall thought of the scenario. "Let's go sit out on the porch. It's nice and cool out there.

Jules piped in. "Sounds like a plan to me."

The three of us stepped outside. Jules said his goodbyes and took off in his Lincoln. Marshall and I sat quietly in lawn chairs, listening to the crickets and watching the fireflies glow around us.

After a spell Marshall said, "I saw you smack the ball over the fence in Baltimore the other night on TV."

"Did you now?"

"*You're* gonna be the one to break the record, Rog. I just know it."

"You want to hear something funny, son? I don't care if I win the race anymore."

"Why?"

"Heck, the crowds are all rooting for Mick. That's okay, mind you. But they make me feel like two cents every time I go to bat."

"What's their problem?"

"I just don't fit in around here," I said. "They don't like country boys."

"They're all stupid if you ask me. The fans and the reporters."

"I'd sure like to just go home to my family in Kansas City."

Marshall's eyebrows inched up. "What about the Babe's record?"

"That's just a dream now. It's a terrible sacrifice sometimes just to play baseball."

"Now that my dad is gone, baseball doesn't seem the same for me either."

"My mama used to go away sometimes and I wanted to quit baseball too. But the more I played, the easier it was to get through the pain."

Marshall frowned. "My mother is too sick to get out of bed. And my father got in a fight at my game. Baseball used to be my life. Now, I just don't care."

"Your father's behavior is inexcusable. But the last thing you should do is give up on baseball."

Marshall looked me square in the eye. "You either."

I laughed. "Okay, sport, let's make a deal. We'll both stick with it."

We shook on it. I reached in my pocket, pulled out two Yankees' tickets, and handed them to him.

Marshall's examined them and his eyes lit up. "Wow! These are like right behind the dugout. We always sit in the bleachers. How can I thank you?"

"Well, I'm counting on you to come cheer me on."

"You bet I will. Better get back now." A grinning Marshall bounced down the porch steps clasping the tickets in his hand.

I felt a sense of mental calmness. Through all the insanity of the home run race, dealing with the hostile press and the booing fans, Marshall was my one saving grace. Maybe even my divine purpose for being here.

MARSHALL

AS I HEADED HOME, I slipped the Yankee tickets in my pocket. This summer, the one I thought would be the best time of my life, had turned into one big roller coaster ride. Thank God for Roger. I don't know what I would have done without him.

When I got home, I yelled up the staircase. "Ma, you need anything?"

No answer.

"Ma?" I ran up the stairs to her room.

She lay in her bed still as stone. Her lips were a pale shade of blue. A prescription bottle and an empty wine bottle lay on the floor.

"Ma!" I yelled again.

She still didn't move an eyelash.

It was stupid of me to have left her alone. I felt a bitter taste in my mouth and a cold sweat wash over my whole body. Had my mother taken her own life? No, no, she wouldn't do that. Not to me. My hands were shaking. I inhaled, then slapped her face with the palm of my hand. Not really hard, but not soft either.

Her eyes popped open and soon her lips parted. "Marshall!"

I let my breath out. "Thank God you're okay."

She placed her hand up to her cheek, which was red from my slap. "What's the matter with you?"

"I thought you were—"

"Were what?"

"Dead!"

"Why in heaven would you think that?"

I pointed at the prescription bottle. "You weren't moving."

"I'm sorry I scared you. I took some pills for my headache. I must have fallen asleep."

I didn't mention the empty wine bottle. "I'm just glad you're okay."

"Why don't we catch that late show tonight?"

"You're serious?"

"Of course. Go downstairs and I'll get dressed lickity-split."

Was this a sign that my mother was finally returning to the living? A half hour later, we sat together on the worn vinyl seats of the uptown bus, headed to the movie theater. A cool night breeze sifted in through the open bus windows.

My mother patted my hand "It's such a lovely night. I'm glad you got me out of the house." She looked like a different person dressed up in a pleated skirt and her favorite blue sweater. Dad had bought it for her last Christmas and she'd made a big deal about it when she unwrapped the package. Her dirty tangled hair was now washed, combed, and swept into a kind of bun. She had cut some bangs that did a good job of covering the big scar on her forehead.

We got off at Main Street and walked two blocks to the theatre. The marquee read:

THE ABSENT-MINDED PROFESSOR
Starring Fred McMurray

I escorted Ma to the ticket booth. Of all people, Mr. Gelaro got in line behind us. He wore a straw hat and a sports jacket that looked a size too big for him. "Well, hello, Marion, and, ah, Marshall."

"Nice to see you, Mr. Gelaro," Ma said.

"Please call me Lou. Haven't seen you around much lately."

"Marshall's been running most of my errands these days."

Mr. Gelaro glanced at me. "He's a good boy."

"He certainly is," my mother said. "I haven't been feeling up to snuff, as they say."

"Well, you look lovely tonight." Mr. Gelaro's eyes glowed. "Do you mind if I join you and Marshall? I hate to go to the movies by myself. Ever since Eve died, well I've had to. I rarely go at all."

"It would be our pleasure, Mr. Gelaro," my mother said.

"Lou."

Ma beamed. "Lou."

When we reached the ticket counter, Mr. Gelaro insisted on paying. Ma argued with him for a while, but finally let him hand the cashier the money.

As we entered the theatre, I saw Laila with the same two girlfriends from the baseball game.

She smiled and waved at me.

"I'll be right back," I told my mother, and headed over to Laila and her friends. I still hadn't washed the spot on my face where she'd kissed me earlier.

Laila touched my arm. "Wanna sit with us, Marshall?"

I worried about leaving my mother, but she looked like her old self as she stood by the refreshment stand chatting with Mr. Gelaro. He'd just bought them a big tub of popcorn.

I ran up to her and asked if she minded if I sat with some friends.

When she saw the three girls, she smiled and told me to meet her in the front of the theatre after the film ended.

I sat between Laila and her red-haired girlfriend. Laila kept passing me her popcorn. Sometimes our fingers touched as we reached in the tub at the same time. Halfway through the movie, Laila took my hand in hers.

My fingers felt like marshmallows in a campfire. I whispered, "You wanna be my girl?"

She licked salt off her lips, then moved her wet mouth toward my ear. "Sure I do."

I don't remember much of the movie, just the feel of Laila's small hand in mine.

An hour and a half later, I met my mother and Mr. Gelaro in front of the theatre. She had a big smile on her face. I guess I did too.

Mike Bernstein and another kid from my All-Star team left the theater together. Mike bounced a Spaldeen. "Wish I could get hold of some of that flubber."

My mother turned to Mr. Gelaro. "I just love that Fred McMurray."

"He's always good," Mr. Gelaro agreed. "Can I treat you and Marshall to an ice cream or something?"

I smiled at my mother. "That would be great."

She looked at her watch. "It's kind of late."

"Please, Ma." The thought of ice cream was so much better than going home and watching her become all weepy again.

"Come on, Marion," said Mr. Gelaro. "I'll open the store and teach Marshall how to make one of my super-duper sundaes."

My mother tilted her head as she decided. "Well, okay." Then, suddenly, she frowned. "Oh, dear. I must have left my sweater in the movie theater."

"I'll get it for you. No sweat," I said.

"No, sweetie. I know exactly where it is. I'll be right back."
She dashed back inside the building as people were lining up
for the next show.

I stood staring at some ants crisscrossing the sidewalk and
tried to think of something to say to Mr. Gelaro. When I looked
up, I saw my father walking with some lady on his arm. She had
funny plucked eyebrows and her hair resembled a beehive. Her
dress was so low-cut her boobies looked like they might pop
out. The woman was laughing at something dad had said, like
he was the funniest guy in the world.

Just then, Dad caught sight of me and Mr. Gelaro, standing
on the corner. His forehead wrinkled. "Hello, Marshall."

I stood silently and glared at him.

"I'd like you to meet Miss Fowler."

"I don't wanna meet her."

"Now don't be rude, boy."

Miss Fowler touched Dad's arm. "It's okay, Edmond."

"No, it's not," Dad said.

Mr. Gelaro interrupted. "He has every right in the world to
be rude, Edmund."

"You stay out of it, Gelaro," Dad said.

"Your wife is coming out of the theater any minute. I sug-
gest you hightail it out of here."

Dad squinted, then gripped Miss Fowler's hand. "Let's go,
Gloria." As they paraded off, he spun back around. "I'll call you
soon, Marshall."

Ma arrived with a big smile holding up her blue sweater.
"I'm so glad I found it. This is my favorite." She looked down
the street and the smile vanished from her face. "Edmund!"

"Don't, Ma!"

Dad and Miss Fowler picked up the pace and crossed the intersection.

"At least have the decency to face me," Ma shrieked.

My father stopped walking and turned to her. "What do you want, Marion?"

"I want to meet your...your girlfriend."

Dad pushed Miss Fowler forward. "Keep walking."

I grabbed my mother's arm. "Let him go, Ma."

She charged over to Miss Fowler ignoring my advice. "You're nothing but a home-wrecker."

I raced after her.

"Don't you talk to her like that," Dad said.

Ma's jaw dropped. "Talk to her?"

Miss Fowler's face and neck reddened. "I didn't mean for this to happen."

Dad took Miss Fowler's arm. "Let's go, Gloria." They rushed off.

Ma stood planted in the middle of the street oblivious to the sound of cars honking at her.

I grabbed her arm. "Please, let's just go home."

We returned back to the sidewalk where Mr. Gelaro stood awkwardly. He patted her hand. "Can I, ah, give you a lift home?"

Ma jerked her hand away like she'd been stung by a wasp. "Leave us alone, Lou. Find yourself your own family."

Mr. Gelaro eyes watered up, then he tipped his straw hat, and scurried down the street to his station wagon.

My mother and I headed toward the bus stop.

There was an old guy already there, with a face like an old catcher's mitt, and a faded tattoo of a ship on his forearm. Not the kind of guy you want to stand next to while waiting for the bus, but my mother was so mad she didn't even notice. She just barged right over to the bench and sat down.

I snuck a look at him.

He grinned back, showing a gap where his front tooth used to be. "S'cuse me, ma'am. You know when the C bus is s'posed to be here?"

She glared at him like he'd just asked her to give him her purse, grabbed my hand, and dragged me three blocks to the next bus stop. It was as though something snapped inside her, broke like a tree limb in a storm and couldn't be fixed. When we arrived home, she headed up the stairs into her room and slammed the door.

I spent the next few hours playing with my baseball card collection. It was well after midnight. I couldn't sleep and didn't see any sense in trying.

Suddenly, my mother appeared, her mouth all pinched up like an old apple core. "Go to bed this instant." She snapped off the light in my room. "Just because your father's not here anymore, doesn't mean there aren't rules around here, young man."

"Sure, Ma." Her mood swings confused me. I got into bed and pulled the covers over my head, feeling frightened and alone.

MARSHALL

AS THE SUMMER DAYS passed, my mother barely left her room. In the mornings I'd knock on her door with buttered toast and a mug of coffee, and she'd say something weird like, "Is that you, Edmund?" When I'd remind her it was *me, Mar-*

shall, she'd respond, "Give me a minute, son, and I'll make you breakfast." Then she'd go back to sleep.

I was afraid to leave her alone, terrified of what I might find when I got home. Without making excuses, I stopped going to baseball practice, and only left the house to run a quick errand for Roger and Mick, or buy us groceries at Mr. Gelaro's. I used what money I earned and he let me buy the rest on credit.

Early Saturday evening, Bobby stopped by the house and banged on the door.

I was surprised and so happy to see anyone that I practically hugged him as I opened the screen door and invited him inside.

Instead of coming in the house, he stayed on the porch with his feet planted wide apart. A vein in his neck bulged out as he stood there silently.

"What's wrong?"

"What's wrong! You missed our second All-Star game. Coach Lee had to play efin Bernie Jackson in your place."

Bernie, son of Commissioner Jackson, wore coke-bottle glasses and couldn't see a hippopotamus if it was kissing distance from him. "So, we lost?"

"Whaddaya think? It didn't take long for Forest Hills to figure out alls they needed to do was hit the ball to right field. Fly balls, grounders, it didn't matter. Bernie fumbled them all."

A lump formed in my throat. "I'm really, really sorry."

"Everyone's pissed off at you. Thought you should know that." He huffed off down the street.

When I delivered a bowl of SpaghettiOs to my mother a few minutes later, she flung it against the wall and screamed,

"Get out!"

"Why are you acting like this, Ma?"

Her face turned the color of the tomato sauce on the wall. "Don't you get it? I can't stand for you to see me like this." She pulled the covers over her head.

My whole body shuddered. Should I call Aunt Ethel? Dad always said that our family's problems were nobody's business but ours. One time, he'd caught my mother talking on the phone to my aunt about how a check bounced at Con Ed. He'd grabbed the receiver right out of her hand and slammed it back on the phone.

To hell with him. I raced downstairs, grabbed the phone from the kitchen wall, and dialed Aunt Ethel's number. I hated to bother my aunt since she worked the graveyard shift in a hat factory. When I explained what was going on with Ma she said she'd come right over.

"Tomorrow's fine," I said. "She's already asleep." Money was tight and my aunt couldn't afford to miss a night of work. I wondered if there was such a thing as "good lying." Maybe I'd ask Roger about it.

The next morning, Aunt Ethel and Bobby showed up at the front door. She gave me a warm hug while Bobby looked at me icily. "You shouldn't have to deal with this yourself," my aunt said. "I've told my boss I need some time off."

Bobby blinked. "Are you gonna practice today?"

"I can't leave Ma. She's still sick."

"Geeze, Marshall. My mom's gonna take care of her now. If we lose the next game, we're out of the All-Star tournament. Double elimination."

"I know the rules. It's just—"

"It's okay, Marshall," Aunt Ethel said. "A break will do you some good."

Even with my aunt at the house, I was too frightened to leave Ma. She was all I had left. "I can't go, Bobby. I'm sorry."

"Didn't you hear what my mom said?" He opened the screen door and stormed outside.

"Ya know…" I began then stopped. How could I explain what it felt like to have a father who had checked out and a mother whose antenna didn't pick up all the channels anymore? I barely understood it myself.

Aunt Ethel patted my head. "I'll talk to Bobby. But honestly, you should just go."

"You're right. Let me just say goodbye."

As we climbed the staircase and entered my mother's darkened bedroom, the sound of loud snoring filled the air. Aunt Ethel pulled open the curtains and gathered up three empty wine bottles and soiled tissues from the floor.

"Ma, look who's here."

My mother opened her eyes, then squinted as patches of yellow sunlight landed on her face.

"Rise and shine, Marion," Aunt Ethel said.

"Who are you, Little Mary Sunshine?" Ma snarled. "Close the damn drapes."

Aunt Ethel forced a smile. "I came to cheer my little sister up."

My mother covered her head with a pillow. "Leave me alone."

Aunt Ethel grabbed the pillow from her.

"Who the hell do you think you are?"

"Insult me all you want, Marion, but I'm not gonna leave

until you're human again."

Ma pulled the quilt over her head. Aunt Ethel peeled the covers completely off the bed. My mother remained curled up like a little baby on the flowered sheets. Then suddenly, she bolted up ramrod straight and glared at Aunt Ethel with red-veined eyes.

My aunt bent down and touched her cheek. "You need to move on." She pointed at me. "For him."

Ma pushed Aunt Ethel away from her.

Aunt Ethel lost her balance and fell on the floor. Her eyes pleaded with me. "Leave the room, Marshall. NOW!

I barreled down the stairs in a major panic. My heart hammered in my chest. No denying my mother was losing it. Would she be like this forever? And what was going to happen to me?

A few seconds later, Aunt Ethel appeared behind me. "I know you're scared, Marshall, but your mother is going to be okay."

"Is she crazy?"

"No, of course not. Your mother's having what they call a nervous breakdown. It's an illness like the chicken pox, only you can't *see* her spots. Best you don't repeat those words to your father or anyone outside the family. Do you understand?"

"Yes, ma'am. But are you sure she'll get better?"

"I've known your mother her whole life. She's a strong woman."

"But *when* will she be okay?"

Drops of sweat formed on my aunt's forehead and dripped down her face. "It's just gonna take some time. I honestly think it best you leave me alone with her right now."

I grabbed my canvas bag of baseball equipment from the

closet and went out to the porch. Tears dripped down my neck and stained my T-shirt. I recalled what my father had said one time when I'd run home from the third grade, sobbing. Some older kids had knocked me down, stolen my lunch box, and left me on the ground with a bruised lip. "Grow up, son. Only girls and babies cry."

Things were bad enough. I was glad he wasn't around to see me now.

CHAPTER NINE

The Divorce

August 1, 1961

WASHINGTON — *The Administration's fall-out shelter plan could save at least ten to fifteen million lives in case of a nuclear attack, Defense Secretary Robert S. McNamara said today. (8)*

ROGER

Awarm summer breeze kicked up some dust as I stepped outside for some fresh air. The sound of whimpering came from next door. It was Marshall on the front porch holding his knees. I slammed our screen door to give him time to compose himself. "Mr. Marshman." I lit up a cigarette and stubbed it out, remembering the promise I made to Pat to quit.

He wiped his face with the end of his T-shirt. "Hey, Rog, great game yesterday." His voice sounded hoarse.

He was talking about the ballgame I'd given him tickets for. "How come you weren't there?"

"You knew?"

"I looked up at the seats and some other jokers had taken them."

Marsh looked down at his knees. "I, ah, heard the game on the radio. I'm sorry I wasted the tickets. It's just—"

"You don't have to explain, son."

Marshall joined me on the porch. "I don't want you to think I'm not grateful. You see, things at home are still kind of a mess. I can't leave my mother alone right now."

"I understand more than you know."

"I thought about giving the tickets to my cousin, Bobby, and his father. But I couldn't stand for them to go while I sat home. That's pretty bad, huh?"

"Any kid who stays home to take care of his mother is okay in my book. Family first. I hope my kids grow up to be just like ya."

He smiled. "Really?"

"You're my man." The two of us just sat there for a spell, staring out at the powder-blue sky. There was something about the boy that tugged at my heart. So many things that reminded me of my own childhood. "Ya know, my parents had a rocky marriage, too. Many a night my brother, Rudy, and I hid under the bed while Mama and Daddy went at it. Sometimes we held our ears and sang "Jingle Bells."

He let out his breath. "I thought I was the only one whose parents were always fighting."

"There are lots of married folks who just don't get along." In the silence that followed, images from childhood rose from the depths of my memory, ones I'd tried so hard to forget. Mama always pointed out the worst in people. Especially my daddy. I often didn't want to go home after baseball practice fearful of the never-ending quarrels that escalated as I grew older. Often she'd huff out of the house and we wouldn't see her for days. Sometimes weeks. Rumors spread around Fargo that she had a string of boyfriends. But if anyone said something to me about it, I'd smack 'em in the mouth. Same with Rudy. When he was barely thirteen he punched a grown man's lights out for calling her a tramp. Sadly, after years of turbulent times together, my parents got a divorce.

Pat was very different from my mother. I loved her throaty laugh and the fact she hated gossip. She had a calming effect on me whenever we were together. When I married Pat, I swore we would raise our kids in a house full of laughs and love. My only regret was my baseball career that forced me to be away so much of the time.

I looked down at Marshall who was still brooding. "I'll get you some tickets to another game when things are better, okay?"

"That would be really swell."

It was the least I could do for him. If only I could take him home to Kansas City and make him a part of our family.

MARSHALL

ROGER HAD TO get ready for the second game in a series with Chicago, so I walked back home, made myself a peanut-butter-and-jelly sandwich, and poured a large glass of milk. I was free to go to practice but was anxious what Coach Lee and my teammates would say after I'd missed the game. It was hard enough dealing with my mother. When I finished my sandwich, I went upstairs and stood quietly in the open door of my mother's bedroom.

Aunt Ethel was sitting on the bed. "Did you know Marshall missed one of his All-Star games?"

Ma sat up. "Why would he do that?"

"He felt he had to stay home with *you*, Marion."

"I-I had no idea."

"What happened to my sister, the fighter? I remember you hit Heidi Rufus in the nose for telling the whole school I stuffed my brassiere with socks."

My mother grinned. I hadn't seen a hint of a smile on her face since the night we saw Dad with Miss Fowler. "She retaliated by sticking my braids in the ink bottle."

Aunt Ethel's eyes lit up. "And you stuffed them in her mouth, ink and all."

Both of them started laughing. My mother produced this high-pitched giggle I'd never heard before. Aunt Ethel had more of a deep belly laugh. Both sounded wonderful to me.

I cleared my throat and entered the room. "Are you okay now, Ma?"

She held out her arms. "Come give me a big hug."

As I hugged her, she ran her hands through my hair like I was a little boy. But I didn't mind.

"When's your next game?"

"He's got practice right now," Aunt Ethel said.

"You hurry up and get to Hudson's Park before it's too late."

My aunt winked at me. I looked back at my mother. "Are you sure?"

"If your aunt won't let *me* quit, then I'm not going to let you. Now scoot. And there's something I want to tell you before you go."

I swallowed.

"It isn't your fault that your father left, honey."

I blinked back tears. "I'm sorry I told him to go."

"He would have gone anyway. It had nothing to do with you."

Aunt Ethel nodded in agreement. I hugged my mother again. Then Aunt Ethel joined in. Tears ran down all of our faces.

I breathed a sigh of relief, grateful for my aunt helping out. "I'll be back in a few hours."

"Take your time." Aunt Ethel reached in her purse, retrieved a dollar, and handed it to me. "You and Bobby buy yourself some ice cream cones after practice."

I headed downstairs, grabbed my baseball bag, and ran down the street to the bus stop. For the first time in a while, I was excited at the prospect of playing baseball again. But would Coach Lee let me back on the team?

MARSHALL

WHEN THE BUS stopped at Hudson Park, the doors shot open and I walked to the exit. But then I just stood there blocking the door, unable to step outside, or return to my seat. Who was I kidding? No way Coach Lee would allow me to return. I'd be lucky if Rocky and Frank didn't come after me with their fists. Hell, who could blame them?

The bus driver peered at me through his rear view mirror. "Are you getting off or not, kid? I can't wait around all day."

"Uh…sorry." I raced through open door and down the

street to Hudson Park.

A few parents and Uncle George chatted in the bleachers. When he saw me on the field, he jogged over and placed his hand on my shoulder. "Go out there and knock 'em dead. They need you."

I flashed on how Dad loved to poke fun of Uncle George's grammar and often called him a "scabby cabbie." Aunt Ethel once told me that my uncle had dropped out of school in the ninth grade to help support his family after his own father had died of a heart attack.

My uncle looked down at me. "Marshall?"

"Yes, Sir."

"What are you waiting for?"

"I bet they're still pissed at me."

"If you don't go out there, you'll never know."

"I-I'm afraid."

"Tell me something. What do you have to lose?"

I shrugged. "Nothing, I guess."

"Well, go on then."

I ran to the dugout where Coach stood with his clipboard. The players were out in the field throwing the ball around. He slid his reading glasses down his nose and peered down at me. "How are you, Marshall?"

"I'm just real sorry about missing the game, but I—"

"Your uncle told me why you've been gone, son. Family first, happens to be my motto." He removed his baseball cap. "On the other hand, we don't have the luxury of you missing another game. Now, head out to right field and tell Bernie you're taking over."

"I won't disappoint you, sir."

As I walked out on the field, Bobby shot me a thumbs up from behind home plate. Rocky spat on the ground when I passed him on the field, while Frank examined his glove like I didn't exist.

When I told Bernie what Coach Lee had said, he threw his hat on the ground and stormed off the field. Then he turned back around and squinted at me through his thick glasses. "We'll see what my dad has to say about this."

During practice, I threw hard, made every catch, and smacked each ball Coach Lee threw to me. After an hour or so, Coach Lee signaled for us to head in from the field and reminded us to be prepared for the upcoming game with Rockaway.

Rocky collided into me. I shot him an angry look, but part of me thought I deserved it. While we stood listening to Coach Lee's last minute pep talk, Frank deliberately stepped on my foot.

"Ow!" I wanted to stomp on his foot right back but I knew it would just start a big ruckus. So, I let it pass and a strange calm settled over me as I thought about what Roger had said about resisting his impulse to lash out at the Yankee fans booing him. If Roger could deal with that, I could deal with this.

"Are you with us, Marshall?" Coach Lee glared at me daydreaming. "Your teammates want to know whether you're gonna stick around and fill that big hole out there in right field or let them down again."

I gazed at each of my team members standing around me on the field. Then I looked Coach Lee in the eye. "I'm back and you can count on me, sir."

MARSHALL

THE NEXT FEW DAYS, my mother acted more like her old self. She awoke each morning, got dressed, and made me a big breakfast. When I offered to shop for groceries at Gelaro's like I'd been doing the past few weeks, she insisted on going herself. Thursday evening, she even showed up at our All-Star game with Rockaway.

For six innings we played our best game, but so did Rockaway. Three players from the Jamaica team showed up and started heckling our pitcher, Freddy Silverstein. They booed him every time he wound up for a pitch. During a time out, one of the Jamaica kids with a crusty scar on his cheek moved on the field and hocked up a loogie that hit Freddie in the neck.

Coach Lee called a time out, headed to the pitcher's mound with his handkerchief, and wiped the loogie off of Freddy's neck. Coach whispered something in his ear and Freddy nodded.

The umpire pointed at Scarface. "If you do something like that again, you're outta the park."

"Yes, sir," Scarface said.

As Freddie wound up again, one of the other Jamaica players gave him the finger.

Visibly shaken, Freddy walked the next two batters.

At the bottom of the seventh inning, the score was tied. Freddy struck out the first two Rockaway batters ignoring the taunts of the guys from Jamaica. Rockaway's third hitter, a skinny kid with a sunburned nose, smacked a ball over Rocky's head at shortstop and raced to second base for a double.

Then a wiry black kid with a silver front tooth entered the

batter box. He looked tough as he held the bat back, and took a few practice swings.

Freddy cracked his chewing gum, went into the windup, and threw a strike on the outside corner. On the next pitch, the sun sparkled off the kid's tooth and CRACK, he whacked a sharp ground ball that sailed through Rocky's legs into the outfield.

The runner came home winning the game for Rockaway.

Double elimination. Our team was done. Freddy and Mike had tears running down their cheeks. Bobby kept punching his hand into his catcher's mitt.

The Jamaica players cheered with the Rockaway parents as we scrambled off the field. They wove their way through the bleachers and gathered behind our dugout. Now there were five of them. "You guys deserved to lose," shouted Scarface. He was built like a Mack truck.

His chubby friend poked him in the side. "Shoot, we woulda beat these guys easy. Maybe gone all the way to Cooperstown if it weren't for you Flushing cheaters."

"You guys stink," piped in another Jamaica player. "Tonight just proved what everyone already knew."

Coach Lee walked up to the five of them mouthing off at us. "I'm sick of you kids saying that crap. Why don't you put your money where your big mouths are?"

"Whaddaya mean?" said Scarface.

"My boys challenge you to prove once and for all who's the better team. You have your coach call me and we'll arrange a rematch game." Coach Lee pulled out a slip of paper and a stubby pencil, scribbled down his phone number, and handed it to Scarface.

We cheered and formed a half circle around the coach. The

new challenge gave us another chance to end the season with a win. We may have been defeated by Rockaway, but we would all be there together to beat Jamaica once and for all. Rocky Romano even gave me a hug. I'd finally earned his forgiveness and it stunned me so much I couldn't speak.

As a team, we headed to our parents' cars with a new hope that balanced the pain of defeat.

Uncle George drove us home in the Yellow Cab. My mother sat in the back seat with me and Bobby. Uncle George switched on the radio. "Let's check out the Yanks."

Mel Allen: "The M&M boys are knotted at thirty-six home runs a piece after Roger Maris poled a round-tripper in the first inning of their double header in Boston. Mickey Mantle came back with a homer in the second game."

"One of those guys is gonna break the record," Aunt Ethel said.

Bobby whistled. "Sure hope it's Mickey."

Uncle George peered at me through the rearview mirror. "Who are you rooting for, Marsh?"

"The Mick, who else?" Bobby answered for me.

I smiled. "Nope. Roger's now my man."

"No sh—"

"Bobby!" Aunt Ethel's eyebrows flew up.

"Sorry, Mom." He wrinkled his nose at me. "Why would you root for the country bumpkin?"

"He may be from the country, but he's not a bumpkin. And he's the one's gonna win."

"Five dollars says he don't," Bobby said.

"You're on," I said.

When we reached our house, a white car was parked in our driveway. Bobby pointed at it. "Isn't that your father's Galaxie?"

My mother bit her lower lip.

Aunt Ethel tapped Uncle George's shoulder.

Bobby leaned forward with his head between Uncle George and Aunt Ethel and peered through the windshield. "Wow, that is his car."

"Shhh," Aunt Ethel said, then turned to my mother. "Do you want us to come inside?"

"No, I'd rather face him myself."

Bobby asked the question on everybody's mind. "Do you think he's come back for good?"

Aunt Ethel glared at him. "You shush now, son."

My mother grasped my arm as we got out of the cab. She wobbled unsteadily up the path.

I couldn't ignore the part of me that still wanted my father back, but reminded myself not to get my hopes up. Another part of me wished he'd just go away and leave us alone.

Uncle George rolled down the window. "You call us if you need anything. Anything at all."

Dad stepped out of his car, dressed in a navy suit. He patted my head then turned to face my mother. "Hello, Marion. We need to talk."

MARSHALL

WHEN WE WERE all in the living room, Dad gave me a stiff hug. He held a big manila envelope in one hand, which made it all the more awkward. "How you been, son?"

I didn't know how to respond. Should I say, "Just great," or "You just missed me play another game," or maybe, "We got eliminated from the All-Star contest but I'm sure you don't give a damn?" I ended up with, "I'm fine, thank you."

"Glad to hear that. Your mother and I need a little privacy while we talk. Maybe you could go to your room for a while."

My mother looked at me with a weak smile. "We'll call you when we're done, sweetheart."

I headed up the staircase and wondered if he wanted to be alone with my mother so they could kiss and make up. If I were to judge by the starry-eyed look on my mother's face, I'd say that's what she expected. But I had a sinking feeling in my gut.

When I reached the top of the stairs, I figured out why Dad had come home. Two green-plaid suitcases stood next to my parents' bedroom. He'd already come inside the house and pulled the valises out from the attic. I ran back downstairs. After all, whatever my parents were discussing would affect me too.

Neither of them seemed to notice me standing there. My mother was dabbing her eyes with a tissue. "I don't believe in divorce. The church says—"

"Contesting this will only cost us both a lot of money."

"What happened to 'until death do us part?' You made a solemn vow to God."

"Don't give me any religious crap, Marion. I'm done." He held some papers and tapped them with his hand. "This is a fair deal, here. I've left you the house and all the furniture."

"What about your son?"

They both glanced over at me.

Dad blinked. "I plan to have Marshall visit on weekends."

"What a loser you are, Edmond. How could I have not seen

that fifteen years ago?"

"Have you looked in the mirror lately? You're only what, thirty-five, thirty-six? Shoot, you look like you're closing in on fifty."

"How can you be so mean?" I shouted.

He ignored me and bolted up the stairs returning with the plaid suitcases. He set them down to turn the doorknob, turned around and looked at me. For a moment, he froze in place and ran his hand through his hair. Was there a chance he might change his mind? His eyes clouded over. "Come here, boy."

I did as told.

He gave me a limp hug.

I started to say something, anything. But what *could* I say? Beg him not to leave? Part of me felt a sense of relief. I was tired of him yelling at my mother all the time. Tired of waiting and wondering if he'd come home, hoping he'd play catch or show up at my games. I'd been disappointed plenty by my father. My head ached just thinking about it all.

"I'll call you real soon." As his car pulled away from the curb, I slammed the front door so hard the living room windows rattled. I didn't care, even if they broke.

BIG JULIE

THE MIAMI NEWS HELD a contest asking readers to predict who would hit more home runs, Roger or Mickey. Home runs seemed to be on everyone's mind. *Newsweek* was one of many magazines that had the M&M Boys on their cover that summer. The two posed together so often for pictures that Mickey said,

"I'm beginning to feel like a Siamese twin." (9)

One morning in early August, me and Bob Cerv were cooking up some bacon and fried eggs in the kitchen. Roger walked in wearing a pair of boxer shorts. That guy would wake up from the dead if he smelled food cooking. I filled up a plate and handed it to him.

Bob pointed at Roger's face. "Where'd you get those spots?"

"What spots?" Roger asked. He had a rash all over his face and neck. There was even one on the back of his head where a patch of hair had fallen out.

After he finished eating, I drove him to a dermatologist. The doc gave him some ointment. "You need to stay out of pressure situations, Mr. Maris." Either the guy lived on the moon, or he didn't have a clue what it was like being hounded day and night by the press.

When we arrived back at the duplex an hour later, Bob looked relieved. "Your mother-in-law just called. Pat's in labor."

Roger's eyebrows rode up to his crew cut. "For how long?"

"Sorry, I didn't think to ask."

Roger turned to me. "Can you give me a lift to La Guardia?"

"I'll call the airlines while you pack."

"Jesus, Jules. Pat pops those babies out in the time I can run the bases. We have to leave now!"

Roger didn't even pack a suitcase. He kept telling me to step on it as we drove down Cross Island Expressway to the airport. The rush hour traffic made it impossible to do much more than a crawl. I tried a few alternate routes I knew of, but the traffic wasn't any better.

"I hate New York," Roger said. "All these people living so

close to each other like a bunch of rats."

I glanced over at him and noted the number of pinkish-red spots on his face had easily doubled.

A major thunderstorm blew in as we approached the terminal door, walked inside, and picked up the ticket at the American Airlines counter that Selma had reserved for him.

Roger sat in a plastic chair at the gate wearing sunglasses and a Red Sox cap for two hours before the airport reopened and he could board his flight.

I tried to keep him calm. Miraculously, no one recognized him. Maybe it was the glasses and Red Sox cap, or perhaps no one wanted to go near a guy with red spots all over him. He looked like a damn leper. We headed to an airport bar where we each threw down a couple of shots of Jack Daniel's. Roger was three sheets to the wind by the time we heard the boarding announcement over the intercom. "Last call for flight 3434 to Kansas City."

He headed in the opposite direction of the gate.

"Where you going? The gate's the other way," I said.

"I just got to speak to Pat. Tell them not to leave without me."

"They don't hold planes," I shouted. "Even for big shots like you." But of course, he didn't listen to me.

The American Airline clerk was closing the door as Roger blasted into sight. "It's a boy," he beamed. "Randy Maris is twenty-four minutes old and Pat is already talking about wanting a girl next time."

Roger waved to me as he walked through the gate. The proud papa had a big grin on his boyish face. I hadn't seen even a slim smile in weeks.

CHAPTER TEN

Spiral Down

August 5, 1961

Berlin Crisis: At the close of the meeting in Moscow, the Warsaw Pact nations announced that they had agreed unanimously to sign a separate peace treaty with East Germany, the objective of ending the occupation of American, British and French troops in Berlin. That day, the number of East Germans fleeing into West Berlin had reached 1,500 or "one per minute." (10)

MARSHALL

The following night, I sat on the couch in my pajamas listening to the theme song of *The Andy Griffith Show*. My mother was slumped on a big stuffed chair dressed in her ratty robe. She didn't even smile at the joke about Aunt Bee's pickles, which Barney referred to as "kerosene cucumbers," or hum along like she always did to the Maxwell House Instant Coffee commercial.

I might as well have been sitting there alone. My mother used to talk to me and laugh at the jokes on the TV. Would she ever be her old self? When the commercial ended, I noticed the sky lit up with flashes of lightning. Claps of thunder were followed by the sound of a major downpour. The electricity flickered off for a few seconds, then came back on.

My mother stood and gazed out the window. "Marshall, better close the car windows."

Should I tell her that Dad had taken the car? Better not. Pretending to follow her instructions, I opened the front door and stepped outside on the porch. To my shock, a woman stood there blue-lipped with water dripping down her coat. Her hair stuck to her head in clumps. Streaks of black makeup ran down her face.

"Who are you?" I said.

"Um, hi. Not sure you remember me. I'm Miss Fowler."

I grabbed the railing to steady myself. "What do you want?" The lady standing there bore little resemblance to the one with a beehive hairdo I'd seen with my dad a few weeks ago.

My mother appeared at the door. "It's okay, Marshall.

Drops of water trickled down Miss Fowler's cheeks. She gazed up at my mother. "I gotta talk to you."

"Talk!"

"Out here?"

I shivered at the thought of what my mother might do or say to this woman.

She turned to me. "Go upstairs, sweetheart, and do some homework."

"I don't have homework, Ma. School doesn't start for another month."

"I guess it doesn't matter if you hear what this floozy has to say." She opened the door and invited Miss Fowler into the hallway.

Water from her clothing pooled into dark spots on the rug as she removed her coat and draped it over her arm. She wore a black dress that clung to her curvy body. "I'll get right to the point," she said. "I want to marry Edmond. I-I *have* to marry him."

My mother glared at her. I had no idea what she planned to do. Would she punch Miss Fowler in her gut, or throw her out the door?

After a few moments, my mother spoke in a soft, calm voice. "If I understand you correctly, Miss Fowler—"

"I think you do. I'm having Edmond's child."

My mother's face puffed up. My God, what was she going to do? To my surprise, instead of lashing out at Miss Fowler, my mother began laughing. Not, "ha, ha, ha, ha," but loud bursts of throaty sounds like the hyenas at the Bronx zoo.

Should I call Aunt Ethel before she went totally nuts? Was she getting ready to attack Miss Fowler like some wild animal?

"Ma, please don't do anything crazy!" I shouted.

She suddenly went silent.

Miss Fowler arched her eyebrows at me, as though asking for guidance.

After a short pause, my mother said in a very normal voice, "Let me have your coat." She draped the wet coat on a chair and pointed at the living room coach. "Have a seat."

Ma joined Miss Fowler on the couch. As she sat down, creepy-sounding giggles bust out of her again.

"What could possibly be funny about this situation?" Miss Fowler said.

"Judging from how you look, Edmond impregnated us about the same time."

"That's ridiculous. He said he hadn't been with you in years."

"Ha. That's what they all say, I guess. It doesn't really matter anymore. I lost the baby."

Miss Fowler squeezed her eyes shut. "I-I'm so sorry. I don't know what to say."

My mother smiled. She looked more normal than she had in weeks. "I do. My boy no longer has a father. Don't be surprised if your child ends up the same way."

Miss Fowler's lashes were wet. "He lied to me, didn't he?"

"You think he only lies to me?" Ma picked up the divorce papers that had been sitting on the coffee table ever since Dad brought them over. Then she turned to Miss Fowler. "Got a pen?"

Miss Fowler opened her big leather purse, took out a ballpoint pen, and handed it to my mother.

She signed the papers and handed them to Miss Fowler. "He's all yours, honey."

MARSHALL

LATER THAT NIGHT, I awoke to the sounds of loud music. At first I thought it must be coming from next door. But when I rolled out of bed and stumbled down the stairs, I found my mother gyrating around the living room to some jazz music playing on the phonograph. She was stuffed into a sequined cocktail dress that was way too small for her. Her hair was teased in a beehive hairdo similar to Miss Fowler's at the movie theatre. Ruby-red lipstick coated her lips, and blue stuff was smeared on her eyelids. She barely looked like the mother I knew.

She wobbled unsteadily on three-inch high heels that clicked on the wood floor as she danced to jazz music blaring from the phonograph. She would stop every so often to take a slug of wine straight from the bottle.

I closed my eyes then reopened them, watching this stranger prancing around, hoping it was a dream. So much for my mother's sanity returning.

"What do you think?" she said when she saw me standing there. "I wore this dress when I worked at the Riviera Club. Gosh, that seems like a hundred years ago."

"Why are you dressed like that, Ma?"

She stopped dancing and plopped down on the couch, out-of-breath. "I want to look good when your father comes home."

"I want you to act normal," I shouted.

She pawed at the sequins on her dress then got up and continued gyrating around the room.

I finally understood. My mother's battery was not fully charged. She was still sick like Aunt Ethel had talked to me about. An illness like the measles or the mumps. I placed my arm around her shoulders and softened my voice. "He's not coming home, Ma."

She knitted her brows together. "When I glanced in the mirror tonight, I realized why your dad left. I look like a hag." She hiked her dress above her knees. "I still have nice legs though. Don't you think?"

I flinched. "Go to sleep, Ma."

"Who needs sleep? I want to dance until dawn." Her voice was low and throaty like her favorite actress, Lauren Bacall.

"Wait until your dad sees me all dolled up like this."

"No offense. You look like a floozy. Do you want to be like Miss Fowler?"

"Don't you see? That's what your father finds attractive. Yes, I want to look like her if that's what it takes to get him to come back home."

I swallowed. "You're scaring me, Ma."

MARSHALL

WHEN I AWOKE the next morning, the smell of bacon and coffee filled the air. I rushed down the staircase thrilled to find my mother turning over scrambled eggs with a spatula. She still looked white as the eggshells on the counter, but she'd dressed in a in a navy skirt and a red blouse with a big bow.

"Ready for breakfast?" she said.

"Sure."

The *New York Daily News* lay on the kitchen table opened to the classified section. A number of ads had been circled in red pen. "I'm going to look for a job today," my mother said.

"What kind of job?"

She smiled. "Don't worry, not a dancer."

I gave her a big hug.

"After breakfast, I want you to go to Bobby's house. Aunt Ethel is expecting you. And she's making your favorite dinner, too."

I had a fun day with my cousin. We traded baseball cards most of the morning. Aunt Ethel brought us tuna sandwiches for lunch. Then we piled into Uncle George's cab and he drove us to Hudson Park. "No catch, good try," he'd say, if me or Bobby missed a fly ball. On the drive home, he told us how much better players we were than he had been as a kid. "We just played stickball on White Plains Blvd. Spent half the time dodging cars driving down the street. But we had fun."

Once again, I thought about the contrast of my father bragging about how great a player he'd been growing up. I always felt like I could never compete with his accomplishments.

That night, Aunt Ethel served her legendary pot roast and roasted potatoes. She'd been runner up for her recipe in a Betty Crocker contest a couple years back. Got her picture in the *Ladies' Home Journal* and everything.

She handed me a big plate of food. "Your mother seems so much better today."

"She is," I said, but wasn't sure if she'd be all crazy again tomorrow. It was hard to count on anything these days.

"Signing the papers was a good thing," Uncle George said.

Aunt Ethel frowned at him. "Probably best not to talk about that."

After dinner, my uncle drove me home. "It looks pretty dark in there," he said. "I'll wait until you get inside."

After picking up the key from under the mat and opening the screen door, I waved at him.

Every room in the house was pitch dark. I headed into the kitchen and snapped on the light switch but the florescent bulbs did not come on.

"Marshall, is that you? I'm in here," Ma said.

As I stumbled in the dark from the kitchen to the living room, I banged my knee on a footstool. Two scented candles provided a dim, flickering light. I found Ma on the sofa.

"What's going on?"

"Guess your father didn't pay the electric bill," she said.

"I got some money. How much do we owe?"

"It's not just the electric bill. He hasn't paid the mortgage either. I spent the whole day out looking for a job. No one wants to hire a washed up old bag like me. I can't even type."

I plopped down next to her on the sofa. "What are we gonna do?"

Before she could answer, someone knocked on the door. My mother grabbed my hand. "I hope it isn't that Fowler woman again."

As soon as I opened the front door, Uncle George, Aunt Ethel, and Bobby rushed into the hallway. "Something didn't seem right when I dropped you off. We decided to take a little family ride and check on both of you."

"Why are you sitting in the dark?" Bobby asked.

"My dad didn't pay the bill."

Aunt Ethel's eyes widened. "That son-of-a—"

"Now, Ethel," Uncle George said.

"Don't 'Now Ethel' me. Look what he's done to my baby sister."

"Me and Ethel can help you through this," Uncle George said.

My mother shook her head. "No, way. Money is tight for you guys, too."

"We'll figure it out," Uncle George said.

Aunt Ethel squeezed his hand.

The next couple of nights we sat around with candles my mother picked up at Woolworths. Aunt Ethel and Uncle George took home most of the food in the refrigerator so it wouldn't spoil. I ate dry Wheaties without milk for breakfast, and peanut-butter-and-jelly for dinner. Mother said to pretend we were living in the pioneer days. I couldn't believe how much I missed the TV.

A few days later, the lights returned. Uncle George had worked two double Yellow Cab shifts to come up with the money for Con Ed.

I finally understood what Roger meant about putting family first. My uncle had the concept down, too. My dad, on the other hand, played ball by a different set of rules.

MARSHALL

I DIDN'T SLEEP that well anymore. Often, I was still awake when the sun filtered through my blinds. A few days after the lights returned, I awoke to the sound of the phone ringing. I rolled out of bed and stumbled down the stairs hoping it was Dad. A part of me, still hated him for what he'd done to my mother. But I was worried how we were gonna make it without him. My mother complained about all the bills. While Dad had given her the house, she couldn't pay the mortgage. The mail scattered on the kitchen table was full of unopened bills.

As I picked up the phone in the kitchen, I hoped my father had finally realized he'd made a big mistake. I wanted my old life back.

"Hey, Marsh, it's me."

My mood shifted from hopeful to annoyed at the sound of Bobby's voice. "Why you calling so early?"

He laughed. "Early? It's after eleven o'clock."

I glanced at the clock on the wall above the sink. It was nearly eleven-fifteen. "So what do you want?"

"Geez, what did I do? You sound pissed off."

"I'm sorry. It was a rough night. "

"With your mother?"

"Yeah."

"I thought she was better."

"Is that why you called?"

"No, I called because they set a date for the rematch game with Jamaica. Pop just got off the phone with Coach Lee. Word's spreading all around Queens."

I'd completely forgotten about the rematch. I already felt my stomach knotting up at the thought of playing again. "When?"

"Not until next month. But we're gonna start practicing right away."

I felt sick to my stomach. "I don't know if I can play."

"Sure you can. My dad said he'd help you with batting practice. Since yours is, ah—"

"Gone."

Bobby cleared his throat. "Yeah."

I didn't really want to talk about my parents' split. It made it all too real. "I gotta go."

"Why don't you come over so we can throw the ball around?"

"I don't feel like it, okay?" I shouted.

"Heck, you don't have to yell at me."

"I'm sorry. Just can't talk right now." After I hung up the phone, I ate a bowl of Wheaties. I felt crummy for being so mean to Bobby, and thought about calling him back. Instead, I prepared a bowl of Cornflakes for my mother's breakfast.

When I got upstairs, I pushed the door to her bedroom open. It was dark in the room so I pulled open the curtains. White sunshine filled the room with light. My mother's bed looked like it hadn't been slept in.

"Ma?" I ran into the bathroom and pulled open the shower curtain. No Ma. I spun around and raced back into her bedroom and looked in the closet.

The phone rang.

I kneeled down and peeked under the bed. Nothing but dust bunnies. Where could she be? We only had two bedrooms and she wasn't in mine. I checked again to make sure she hadn't gone in my room while I was talking with Bobby.

The phone kept on ringing.

I finally leaped down the stairs and grabbed the receiver.

"Hello, Marshall," said the voice on the other end. "It's Dad."

"Dad? It's been a while—"

"Yeah, I'm sorry about that. But, ah, there's been a kind of accident."

"What kind of accident?"

"Your mother. She came to work and made a really bad scene in front of Mr. Brooks and everyone in the office. Then she walked outside and stole the car."

"Whose car?"

"*My* car," he said.

"The Galaxie?"

"That's the one."

"It's not stealing if you take your own car."

"It *used* to be the family car. It's mine now. I was very generous with your mother."

I sputtered, "Where's Ma now?"

"That's why I'm calling, son. She had a car accident."

"Oh, Jesus. Is she gonna be okay?"

"She's fine. Got a few scratches is all. But she banged up the car pretty bad backing out of the parking lot."

"Are you gonna bring her home?"

"Umm, not today. She's at the hospital."

"Huh? You said she just had a few scratches."

After a pause, "She's spending some time at Bellevue."

"You took her to the loony bin?"

"She was screaming when the police got there. I didn't have any say about it."

"You didn't try to stop them?"

"There's no easy way to say this, son. Your mother's gone wacko."

My hand shook so badly the receiver fell to the ground. I listened to his voice shout my name through the receiver, as it dangled on its cord.

"Marshall. Marshall. MARSHALL! Answer me, boy."

CHAPTER ELEVEN

Bellevue

August 11, 1961

WASHINGTON — *President Kennedy said today that he would make a "most critical" and probably "decisive" judgment this month of the Soviet Union's willingness to arrange a well-policed ban on nuclear testing. (11)*

MARSHALL

My mother lay still as a painting in the hospital bed. I placed my hand over her mouth and felt a faint breath on my palm. Aunt Ethel dabbed at her eyes with a tissue.

I blinked back my own tears as a fat nurse entered the room and took my mother's blood pressure. "Excuse me, ma'am, is she gonna be okay?"

The nurse's eyes twitched. "Sure, kid. She's gonna be just fine." She craned her neck in Uncle George's direction. "It may be best for the kid to wait out in the visiting area."

"His imagination would only be worse," Uncle George said. I loved my uncle for standing up for me once again.

The nurse shrugged. "We gave her some sedatives."

Just then, my mother's eyes popped open. She gaped up at the ceiling and seemed to be unaware of us. I grabbed her hand. "It's me, Ma. I came to take you home."

She rolled her red-rimmed eyes at me. "I'm so…sssorry, bubby." Her words were jumbled like she had marbles in her mouth.

My aunt squeezed her other hand. "I'm here, too, Marion."

"Get Marshall out of here, Ethel," Ma said.

"I wanna be with you," I cried.

"I'll be home soon," she whispered. "Go stay with your father."

My father wanted me about as much as a pet gorilla. I'd tried to call him back at work but he hadn't answered his phone. He was probably too busy with Miss Fowler. It wouldn't do any good to share my feelings with my mother. Not now.

A tall man with a giant handlebar mustache entered the room with a clipboard in his hand. He glared at us like we were Martians. "We don't allow children in here."

"Sorry," Aunt Ethel said. "No one stopped us when we took him up in the elevator."

The nurse at the front desk had been preoccupied with a magazine and didn't notice Uncle George sneak me by when we'd arrived.

"Doctor, my son wants to know when I'm going home," my mother said.

He shuffled some papers. "Possibly a few weeks, maybe a month, depending on your progress."

Ma's eyes filled with tears.

"I can take care of her." It was all I could do to keep from crying myself.

"I'm sorry. She's going to have to stay here for a while," the doctor said. He put his arm around my shoulders. "It will all be okay."

I kissed her goodbye tasting the salty tears on her cheek. Then, feeling numb, I left the room with my aunt and uncle. As we stood by the elevator, the doctor suddenly appeared and asked Aunt Ethel to speak to him in his office. Me and Uncle George walked back to the waiting area.

Someone flew past us dressed in a hospital gown with her saggy behind in full view. I shaded my eyes with the palm of my hand and thought about one thing. I had to get my mother out of this place. And soon!

"She's had a nervous breakdown, right?" Uncle George asked my aunt on the ride home."

Aunt Ethel shook her head. "It's somewhat more complicated. The doctor said she has this thing called Schizophreniform disorder. It's a short-term type of schizophrenia.

"But it's temporary?"

"Yes, thank God. The doctor says with proper treatment, Marion will get better. We all know what the catalyst was."

I squinted at her. "I don't understand."

"Remember we talked about mental illness, honey?"

"Yes, it's like the chicken pox or measles, only there's no spots."

"The doctor says what your mother has distorts the way she thinks and acts. Sometimes she can't tell what is real from what is imagined."

"This all seems so extreme," Uncle George said. "I mean, don't people deal with death, divorce, crises every day."

"According to the doctor, my sister's been a victim of mental abuse for a very long time."

What did that mean? On the other hand, I didn't want to ask any more questions fearful of what the answers might be.

MARSHALL

I MOVED SOME of my clothes and stuff into Aunt Ethel and Uncle George's house, and said a prayer. "Please, God, I need you to make Ma better soon. I promise to be good. I'll even go to church every Sunday. Well, if that would help."

The next morning after breakfast, Bobby and I helped Aunt Ethel clip piles of freshly washed sheets to the clothesline with wooden pins. When we got done, and wet sheets were flapping in the August breeze, she suggested we take the bus to Woolworth's. "There's a big sale on school supplies. Everything's half-off."

I didn't hear from my mother for a week. Then she gained what she described as "phone privileges," and called every night at exactly eight o'clock. I'd sit around the kitchen after dinner, helping Uncle George do the dishes, and wait for the telephone to ring.

My mother wanted me to tell her every last detail of my day. What time I woke up, what I ate for each meal, who I played with, what we did. Sometimes I got annoyed at all her questions. "What do you care if I ate a bologna sandwich for lunch?" I asked one night.

"I don't want to miss anything else in your life. I've already missed cooking for you, making sure you take a bath, and all your baseball games this summer. And if I don't get out soon…" She cleared her throat. "I might miss sending you off on your first day of junior high school." At this point, she blew her nose. "I'm sorry, Marshall."

"It's not your fault. Aunt Ethel has explained it all." When I'd ask her about her own day, she'd say little other than she liked the cherry Jell-O they served every night at dinner. Before we hung up, she'd always remind me to help Aunt Ethel and Uncle George with chores, and remember to say my prayers. She sounded a little better each time we spoke. A little less sad.

Uncle George was always bone tired when he got home at night. According to Bobby, he suffered from something called herniated disks, which meant he was in pain all the time. But he never complained, not once, although he might groan when he plunged full speed for a ball during our evening catches. Each night, he and Aunt Ethel held hands on the couch while they watched *The CBS News with Walter Cronkite*. My aunt left for work at the factory right after she served dinner.

I slept on the top bunk bed in Bobby's room, and we'd stay up late with flashlights reading Marvel comic books. In some ways, I felt a sense of relief no longer having to endure my parents' fights. Was it wrong for me to feel happier with my aunt and uncle? At least three times a day, I made a point to mosey by Laila's grandma's house, but I never saw Laila in the front yard. I was too shy to knock on the door.

On Labor Day weekend, Uncle George drove me home to pick up more clothes and some school supplies I had left over from sixth grade. Junior high would be starting on Wednesday. He pulled a note off the front door that said had the word FORECLOSURE on it in caps. When I asked him what that meant he said nothing to worry about. But his face looked white.

There weren't any cars parked next door, since the Yankees were en route to Detroit. I sure missed hanging out with Roger and Mickey and hoped they didn't think I'd deserted them. When we arrived back at my uncle and aunt's house, a shiny blue car crept up behind us and parked across the street. It looked like Dad's Ford Galaxie only in a royal-blue color.

My heart revved up when the driver killed the engine, stepped out on the street, and waved. He wore an oversized red shirt with painted palm trees all over it. "Hey, buddy. Come give your old dad a hug."

As Dad crossed the street, Uncle George gritted his teeth. I took a deep breath. Seeing my father made me all mixed up. Was it possible to love him and hate him at the same time? I couldn't move toward him or away from him.

Dad looked wounded. "What's the matter with you?"

"Nothing." When he came up to me, I gave him a limp hug. He pulled me closer. "That's my boy. You like my new car?"

I shrugged.

"They couldn't salvage the White Diamond after your mother wrecked it. I'm calling this one The Sapphire."

Bobby and Aunt Ethel came outside. My aunt shot Dad a penetrating look. "Nice of you to visit your son."

"I came to bring him home with me."

My aunt spread her fingers out in a fan against her chest. "You've moved back into the house?"

"Of course not. The house belongs to Marion. And just so you know, I caught up on the mortgage. She hadn't made a payment for two months and the bank was ready to foreclose. Four hundred bucks."

Aunt Ethel angled closer to him. "You're such a sport, Edmund."

"Well it wasn't easy coming up with the dough. Thanks to Marion's little episode at Kraftworks, I got fired."

"So how you gonna support everybody?" Aunt Ethel said. "Miss Fowler, Marshall, the new baby."

I'm moving upstate to Binghamton. Miss Fowler's uncle has offered me a great job opportunity. Not that it's any of your business."

Uncle George scratched his head. "You got a house? A room for Marshall?"

Dad stepped so close to Uncle George, it looked like their noses rubbed together.

My uncle glared at him with ice-blue eyes.

"Please don't fight," I shouted.

"Don't worry." Uncle George stepped back. "That won't ever happen again."

"Get your stuff together, son," Dad said.

I swallowed. "I…don't know. I should wait until Ma gets home. She needs me to take care of her."

"I spoke with the head shrink at Bellevue," Dad said. "It could be weeks, maybe months."

"He can stay right here until she's released," Aunt Ethel said.

Dad grabbed my hand and glared at my aunt. "You don't have legal rights."

"But he's happy here," Uncle George said. "He feels secure."

Dad let go of my hand. "He'll be happy upstate. I'll make

sure of that."

"What about school?" I said.

"And the Jamaica game?" Bobby added.

"We'll sort that all out." He pointed to the house. "Go inside and get your bags together so we can get a move on. It's a long drive to Binghamton."

Aunt Ethel, Uncle George, Bobby and I froze like chess pieces on a board waiting for our next move. No one budged or spoke.

Then the phone rang.

Aunt Ethel raced inside. A minute later, she shouted through the screen door, "It's Marion. And she wants to talk to you, Edmund."

It was only noon. My mother never called this early. I thanked my lucky stars. Surely, she would tell my dad I didn't have to go with him. We all went inside the house.

Dad talked to her for a few minutes, then handed me the phone.

My mother cleared her throat a couple of times. "Everything's going to be okay," she finally said. "Go upstate with your father for now. I'll be home really soon."

"I don't wanna go with him," I moaned. "Can't I stay here?"

"Be a good boy, Marshall," she said. Then the phone went dead.

With no other choice, I packed my clothes in my baseball duffle bag and hugged everyone before heading outside where my dad waited for me in his new Galaxie.

Tears streamed down my aunt's cheeks. "This isn't right."

"Why can't he just stay with us?" Bobby asked.

Uncle George stuffed a twenty-dollar bill into my pocket

and then looked up at Bobby. "It's against the law."

I tried to hand the money back to him.

"Take it," Uncle George said. "You may need it."

CHAPTER TWELVE

Bingo

September 3, 1961

JERUSALEM (Israeli Sector), Sept 2— More than two weeks after the general election in Israel there is still no prospect today of a new coalition Government to rule the country. (12)

MARSHALL

On the drive upstate, sweat dripped down Dad's neck, fusing into dark stains on the collar of his Hawaiian shirt. He talked about what a swell place it was in Bingo.

"Bingo?"

"Binghamton. Your new home, son. We can go fishing in the Susquehanna River."

"But you don't like fishing."

"Miss Fowler, you can call her Gloria now, will take good care of you when I'm at work. And she's got twin boys a little older than you."

"She's got kids?" I'm not sure why this information surprised me so much.

Dad's eyes twitched. "I didn't know…"

"She never told you about her boys?"

"There's a little girl, too."

Dad sure didn't know a whole lot about Miss Fowler. "Will I have my own room?"

"I, ah, dunno. Won't it be nice to have brothers? You've always wanted one."

Hot tears prickled my eyelids as I thought about the baby my mother lost. How dare he even bring that topic up?

Dad switched on the radio just in time for the Yankee game.

Mel Allen: "34,065 excited fans have poured through the turn-stiles of Cleveland Municipal Stadium, to catch the M&M Boys today."

Later:

Mel Allen: "That ball is soaring halfway up the distant left field bleachers at least 425 feet. The Cleveland fans are going wild. Number 42 for Roger Maris!"

After the game, Dad placed his freckled hand over mine. "Give Binghamton a try. I've decided to coach your Little League team next spring. Now won't that be nice?"

Dad had never shown any interest in coaching before. What if I didn't play good and embarrassed him again? He'd resent being the coach and…

"I thought you'd be thrilled."

"Yeah, sure."

"I want you living with me," he said. "I feel outnumbered."

"Huh?"

"Gloria has her kids, why shouldn't I have you?"

"What about Ma?"

"Your mother's sick. You'll be happier up in Bingo. We're gonna be one big family."

I slumped down into the new Galaxie's soft leather seat.

The highway stretched ahead of us for miles. I stared out the window at winding curves, covered bridges, and canoes in the waters below. Some of the leaves on the trees had already turned burnt-orange and gold.

Hours later a sign appeared: UNIVERSITY OF BINGHAMTON NEXT EXIT.

"That's where I could have played ball," Dad said shaking his head. "But I turned down the scholarship to take care of you and your mother."

I'd heard the story many times but I'd never given it much thought. But now I felt like someone had just poured a bucket of ice water over my head. "You mean if I hadn't been born, you would have played college ball?"

"That's not what a meant, boy. I wouldn't trade you"…His voice trailed off as he turned off the highway at the next exit. We drove down a long winding road to a tree-lined street and pulled into the driveway of a two-story house with big white shutters.

Dad cut the engine and we stepped out of the car.

Miss Fowler rushed out from the house dressed in a Muumuu and a pink apron. Her stomach looked like an inflated balloon was inside. She hugged Dad and planted a gushy kiss on his lips. Then she walked up to me with a big grin on her face. "Welcome to your new home, Marshall."

I looked down at my black high-top sneakers. My mother had bought them for me right before the end of sixth grade. "I've got a home in Queens."

She placed her arm around my shoulders. "Come inside. We cooked a nice pot roast and an apple pie for you two."

A blonde boy, with ears so big, I couldn't help think about Dumbo, sprinted down the stairs and gave me the once over. We stood about the same size. "You ain't gonna sleep in our room," he said.

"Now, Darren," Miss Fowler said. "Be nice to Marshall. He's your new brother."

"He ain't no brother to me," Darren said.

Another boy almost identical to Darren but a few inches taller, leaped down the steps and landed next to him. "To me neither," he said in greeting.

Miss Fowler pulled a pack of Winstons from her apron pocket. "Be polite now, Billy." She lit up a cigarette and inhaled. "Let's everyone go to the kitchen for dinner. Granny and I have been cooking all day."

The kitchen smelled of pot roast, apples, and cinnamon. We all gathered around a long pine table. A small girl with brick-red hair sat eating Cheerios in a high chair. She giggled as she slipped some to the shaggy mutt under the table.

An old woman mashing up potatoes stood by the stove. She had boney legs and a huge potbelly that bulged out from her scrawny frame. Miss Fowler placed her arm around the old lady's shoulder. "Sit down and let me serve everyone, Mama."

The old woman sat in the empty seat next to me, and placed her wrinkled hand on mine. "You can call me Granny, like you wa*th* one of my own." She spoke with a lisp and some spit landed on my cheek.

I didn't dare wipe it off, but gave her my best fake smile.

"Cat got your tongue?" Billy said.

I clenched my jaw and said nothing.

Darren glared at Miss Fowler. "Where he gonna sleep?"

"You boys need to be nice to Marshall," she said.

Darren belched. "We don't want nobody else in the house. Bad 'nough we're gettin' another baby."

Dad cleared his throat. "You're all going to have a great time together, boys."

That ended the conversation. During the rest of dinner, all you could hear were forks and knives clanging, and Granny and Miss Fowler shuffling around the kitchen with platters of food. When Miss Fowler shoveled some mashed potatoes on my plate, I noticed a diamond ring sparkle on her finger.

I looked at Dad and whispered, "You married her?"

"Of course," Dad said. "Why else would I be here?"

Miss Fowler. "Your dad…and me would like you to be a part of the family."

The reality of the whole arrangement sunk in. I suddenly felt sick and raced to the bathroom where I leaned over the toilet and tried to throw up. Anything to relieve the horrible nausea. But no matter how much I gagged, nothing came out.

I stood by the sink and threw cold water over my face. No way would my life ever be the same. My parents were never getting back together. But worse than that, with my mother at Bellevue, I was stuck up here in Bingoland with Billy and Darren, Granny and Miss Fowler. They didn't want me here anymore than I wanted to be. How much worse could life get?

CHAPTER THIRTEEN

The Race Heats Up

September 7, 1961

Roger Maris shocked the world by wasting a time up at bat bunting against the Cleveland Indians. (13)

BIG JULIE

No one could fathom why Roger bunted in a game against Cleveland, missing an opportunity to hit one out of the park. But they didn't know Roger like I did.

After the game, I tried to move in closer, but the reporters swarmed around him like a bunch of locusts.

Roger shielded his eyes as the endless flashbulbs blinded him. Poor guy looked like a trapped animal.

Billy Herring, a big bald *New York Daily News* reporter with a bushy mustache and hair sprouting from his ears, asked Roger what they all were wondering. "Why the hell did you bunt that ball?"

Roger looked composed as he tried to give an honest response to the question. "I knew I could score Tony Kubek. I saw that Bubba Phillips was playing at third base, but on the right side, Vic Power and Johnny Temple were real deep. All I had to do was drag the ball in their direction, and I'd beat it out. They gave me the in, and I took it."

Herring scratched his bald head. "But why'd you lay down a bunt at such a crucial time in the home run race?"

I could tell by his tight-lipped expression that Roger was trying his best to keep his composure. But his chin quivered and his face burned red. "I was trying to win the game, you stupid jackass!"

There were times it paid to be a big, paunchy guy. I curled my lip at the bunch of them and shoved my way through the crowd. "Get the heck outta here. Can't you see he's had enough?"

The reporters scurried off with their big new story. After everyone cleared out, Roger sat on the bench, too exhausted to move.

I rubbed his shoulders. "Are you okay, kiddo?"

"I dunno. I'm real tired of it all."

"They don't get you, Rog."

He scratched his head and another patch of hair fell out. "I plain don't care anymore, Jules. I want to go home."

"You don't mean that. Houk needs to get you some protection. This is not right."

"I'm serious. I'm thinking about packing up the convertible and leaving for Kansas City tonight."

The next day, I arrived at the duplex without any newspapers. I usually took *The Times* and at least one other New York paper along with a dozen fresh bagels. Still concerned about keeping his identity a secret, Roger and Mick never chanced going to the local newsstands themselves.

When I entered the living room, Roger was sprawled out on the couch listening to the radio. The announcer was reciting some print headlines I'd seen earlier.

SPORTS ANNOUNCER: "Here's a quote from this morning's *Daily News,* 'Roger Maris curses out reporter for asking about bunt.' And *The New York Times* printed this: 'Country boy, Roger Maris, uses profanity.'"

"I'm calling the radio station," Roger said.

"It will only make it worse. Like everything else, this will blow over," I said. But there was something in his eyes, a deep pained look that made me concerned.

"Maybe. But in the meantime, I don't want my kids to think bad of me."

I searched my brain for something to cheer him up. His kids were all under five and would be clueless to this type of scuttlebutt. But the headlines reached deep into the core of his integrity. "How 'bout we take in a movie?"

"I don't know."

"We can invite Marshall to come with us."

"Ya know, I'm worried about him. I haven't seen hide nor hair of him in over a week. No lights on in the house either."

"Can't remember the last time I've seen his dad's Galaxie.'" Bob added.

"The guy deserted his family," Roger said. "That kid deserves a heck of a lot better than that."

"As do you, Rog."

BIG JULIE

TWO DAYS LATER, the Yankees threw a Whitey Ford Day celebration. After the festivities, the fans who stayed for the whole game got their money's worth as the Yanks scored four runs in the ninth inning, notching a fourth straight victory, 8-7 over the Indians.

Roger hit his 56th homer off Cleveland pitcher, Mudcat Grant. As the reporters encircled Rog and Mickey after the game, it took some thunder out of Whitey's event. This time, I elbowed my way next to Rog, ready to pounce on any reporter who dared to antagonize him.

A small guy with horn-rimmed glasses and slicked-back hair from the *Newsday,* got the first question, which he directed at Mickey. "What method of attack do you think is best to break a home run hitting slump?"

Like always, Mickey turned on the charm. "I don't know, I've never had a slump."

We all broke out laughing. Then Billy Herring, the same bald reporter that got Roger's goat over the bunt, aimed another question at the Mick. "The pennant is a shoe-in. We all know why the fans are coming now. But is it fair to you, Mick, with Roger batting third—"

There was a hushed silence for a moment then Mickey literally pushed Herring aside. "If you want me to duke it out with my buddy, Roger, you jerk, it ain't gonna happen." He nudged his way through the crowd and left the room.

All the reporters trailed behind him except Billy Herring, who focused his attention on my guy. "So Rog, what's gonna happen tomorrow in Chicago?"

It was just Billy, Roger, and me left standing in the room. Roger gave him the finger, then headed to the showers.

Billy clenched his fist then barreled toward the door. "You'll pay for that one, buddy."

I burst out laughing. "And who will believe you?" With no one else but Rog and me as witnesses, old Billy would have a hard time proving what happened. We'd declare him a liar and he'd have to retract the story. Reporters hated that.

On the plane to Chicago, Roger stared out the window and was quieter than usual. I sat next to him, reading a copy of *Life Magazine*.

When a stewardess came by with our dinner, Roger said he wasn't hungry. Now if you knew Roger Maris, there was never a time he wasn't hungry. He loved his food and could eat with the best of us. One night in Chicago, Mickey introduced him to crab legs, and he ate as much as all of us put together. And that's saying a lot when you include me in the equation.

"What's wrong with you, Rog?" I asked.

"I need to see my family. I can't go on anymore if I don't."

I knew how much he suffered being away from Pat and the kids. When his son, Randy, was born, Houk only allowed him to stay in Kansas City for a couple of days. Hell, if I was separated from Selma and Danny, I wouldn't be any good to nobody.

"Hang in there, bud," I said. "I'll make it happen. Maybe we can bring them all to Chicago."

"No way Houk will go for that."

"I promise, Rog, I'll work something out."

It was the same scene in Chicago. Before the game, the reporters clustered around Mick and Roger in the Comiskey locker room. I stood next to Roger as he did his best to ignore the chaos by playing his favorite labyrinth game on a large oak table. He told me his daddy had got him started on the game that consisted of steel balls rolling through a maze in a wood box.

A short reporter, in a tan sports jacket too big for him, tapped Roger's shoulder. "So Rog, what's your biggest worry today?"

"Ya really want to know?"

He pulled out his pen. "Of course."

"How I'm gonna fly Pat and the kids to New York for the World Series."

"Do you fool around on the road, Roger?"

Roger's face turned crimson. "I'm a married man."

Another reporter standing behind him said, "I'm a married man myself, but I fool around on the road."

All the guys laughed.

Roger picked up the labyrinth game and headed to a john stall.

"You can't hide in there forever, Rog," yelled the obnoxious reporter who'd said he cheated on the road.

"Come on, bud," said the one in the tan sports jacket. "Give us a break. We need something to write about."

"Don't act like a hick, Rog, talk to us," said the first jerk. He reached in his pocket and pulled out a set of keys with something dangling on the end. Before I realized what was happening, he'd unscrewed the hinges from the stall door. It fell and shattered a section of the tile floor.

Roger stood up and a metal ball flew out and rolled on the floor. He looked like a caged tiger who'd just been released. But to my surprise instead of taking a swing at the reporters, he just stood there silently eyeballing them.

I put my arm around each of the assholes and escorted them out of the bathroom. "If you ever pull this bullshit again, I'll bash your fucking heads together. You hear me?"

Houk was gonna have to get Roger's family out here soon, or the slugger was toast.

ROGER

IN MID-SEPTEMBER we flew to Detroit for a three game series with the Tigers. When we arrived at the local Holiday Inn, I stood in line behind Tony Kubek, Bobby Richardson, Bob Cerv, and Yogi Berra at the reservations desk. Each one of them checked in and then ambled over to the elevator with their luggage. Bob waved his key at me and said he'd catch me later at dinner.

I stepped up to the desk and inquired about my reservation. The clerk, a young man with a raspy voice and bad skin, looked through the roster and couldn't find my name on the list. We all used pseudonyms at hotels to avoid a stampede. I generally went by Rudolph Perkovich, my father's first name, and my mother's maiden name.

"There's got to be a mistake," I said. "You checked in all my teammates."

When the young clerk looked up at me, his eyes snapped out like two ping-pong balls. "Are you…Oh my God, you're Roger Maris!" He examined the entries in his book of reservations and rubbed some zits on his chin. "I'm sorry Mr. Maris,

I don't see a reservation. But I could—"

Just then, Big Julie sidled up next to me out of breath. "Come with me, Roger. You're not staying here."

"What are you talking about? Why wouldn't I want to be with the team?"

"I promise you won't be disappointed where I've set you up." He shuffled me out the door to the parking lot then opened the passenger door of his rental car.

Fifteen minutes later, we arrived in downtown Detroit in front of this swanky hotel with views overlooking a beautiful park with big trees, water fountains, and bronze statues.

"Why spend the money on a joint like this?"

Jules gave the car keys to the parking attendant. "Trust me."

We entered the spotless marble-floored lobby. Crystal chandeliers sparkled on the ceiling. A woman with white-blonde hair, and a curvaceous body that reminded me of Marilyn Monroe, hung on the arm of a gentleman in a white tuxedo.

A tall man with a big mustache, dressed in a gray-pinstriped suit greeted us. "Welcome to the Statler Hilton, Mr. Maris. I'm Edward Steck, manager of this joint. If you need anything, you just ask for me at the desk."

I looked at Jules. "What's going on?"

He just grinned.

Mr. Steck escorted us to a glass elevator. When the elevator doors slid open on the top floor, I could hear children's laughter. *My* children's laughter!

The suite Jules had reserved for Pat and the kids was nothing short of fantastic. A huge platter of cheese and crackers, and a bowl of fresh fruit sat on a coffee table in the large living area that looked out on the park. Pat and I had a private "boudoir" and there was another bedroom for Roger, Jr., Kevin, and baby Randy. My eldest, Susan, slept in a small alcove off the living room.

Pat greeted me with a warm hug. We started to kiss just as the kids raced up to us squealing with delight when they saw me. I hugged each one in turn. Evidently, they were as surprised to see me, as I was to see them. Pat had kept it all a secret.

I barely recognized Randy, who'd nearly doubled in size since the last time I'd seen him. Roger Jr., had shot up a few inches, and Susan chattered endlessly about her ballet school.

Jules stood around with a sheepish smile on his face. Evidently, not only had he made all the arrangements, but he'd picked my family up at the airport and brought them to the hotel.

Roger, Jr. tugged on my hand. "Daddy, come see roof."

I looked at Pat." What's he saying?"

She smiled. "He wants you to go up on the roof of the hotel."

Everyone, including Mr. Steck and Jules, climbed a short stairwell to the hotel roof. It had a garden and playground complete with tricycles, hobby horses, swings, and a canopied sandbox. Mr. Steck explained that the hotel occupancy had been declining in Detroit so he decided to make the Statler more kid-friendly.

It was the perfect place for my family. "You outdid yourself this time, bud," I said to Jules.

His eyes sparkled green-gold in the sunlight, but for once he didn't say a word.

BIG JULIE

IT HAD TAKEN some persuading to get Ralph Houk to fund the plane tickets from Kansas City to Detroit and the pricey Statler Hilton hotel bill for Pat and the kids. Yankee management didn't generally encourage the players' wives to come out the road, as it was considered a distraction. But it paid off big time for Ralph, just like I said it would.

The next day, with his family watching, Roger banged one against the roof over 400 feet from the plate.

Phil Rizzuto: "There's number 57 off the top of the deck. And the ballgame is tied up two and two. Al Kaline, Detroit's right fielder, picked up the home run ball that bounced back on field and tossed it to the Yankee dugout so Roger could keep it."

That afternoon a writer asked Roger, "Don't you think it was a nice gesture for Kaline to get the ball for you?"

"I appreciate it," Roger said. "But I guess anyone would have done it."

All he meant was that he would have done it too, but the press characterized him as ungrateful.

September 16, 1961 – *New York Daily Post*
EMBITTERED YANKEE SLUGGER HITS HIS FIFTY-SEVENTH
HURLING INSULTS TO DETROIT OUTFIELDER

The following day, I sat behind the team dugout with Pat and the kids, holding little Randy on my lap. It was the top of the twelfth inning, a tie ball game. Shortstop Tony Kubek held second base for us as the Detroit crowd applauded Roger in the batter box.

Roger winked at Pat and the kids and prepared to hit. Then something high over the ball field caught his attention. A long and elegant, V-shaped pattern of Canadian geese glided over the right-center field grandstand.

Roger stepped outside the batter box and took off his helmet. For a prolonged moment, his gaze followed the beautiful formation of geese. All eyes in the packed Tiger Stadium were on Roger. Pat had a big smile on her face. The baby clasped his little fingers on my chunky ones and cooed.

We were all antsy as we waited while Roger fit his helmet on his head and stepped back in the batter box. There were two balls and one strike. Then on the fourth pitch, CRACK...the ball launched into a high trajectory towards the very same distant spot where Roger had admired the geese.

Phil Rizzuto: "There's the drive that might carry all the way. Man, he hit that one and the photographers are happy they finally saw him. Roger Maris' fifty-eighth homer of the year. And look at his teammates congratulating him."

Unlike the usual scenario in Yankee stadium, everyone in Detroit stood and applauded him. Me, Pat and the kids squealed and shouted until our voices were hoarse. "Go Roger! Go Daddy!"

I couldn't have been happier, if I'd smashed the ball myself. My man, Roger, was now on track to break the record. What a day!

CHAPTER FOURTEEN

The Runaway

September 20, 1961

I imagine when this is all done someone will write a story about the month-long excruciating pressure. (14)

MARSHALL

O ver the next few weeks, things did get worse. A lot worse. Miss Fowler, rather Gloria, enrolled me in Binghamton Junior High School. I made no friends and sat by myself most days with a peanut butter-and-grape-jelly sandwich, and a carton of milk. Darren and Billy had spread rumors around school that I had lice in my hair so no one came anywhere near me.

Dad had found an old army cot at the Goodwill, and carried it up the staircase to the second floor. Then he shimmied it up the wood ladder to the tiny attic where Darren and Billy slept in bunk beds. The room was about half the size of my bedroom in Queens. I couldn't blame the boys for not wanting another kid sharing it. The cot took up the space they'd used to play board games like Parcheesi, Monopoly, and Risk. Now they had to drag their stuff down to the living room or kitchen.

The attic was far enough away from Dad and Gloria that they couldn't hear anything going on up there. After I'd fallen asleep that first night, I woke up a few hours later and felt like I couldn't breathe. My nostrils were all plugged up with something. I hurried down the attic ladder to the bathroom, stuck a finger up each nostril, and dug out some gooey stuff that was yellow, pink, and blue. The brothers had plugged up my nose with Play-Doh.

When I climbed back up the ladder to the attic, Darren and Billy were laughing so hard they had tears streaming down their cheeks. "Bet you can't guess which one of us did that to ya," said Darren. "Ha, ha, ha."

"Real funny," I said. "My father's gonna whip your butt for that."

"Your dad ain't gonna do squat," said Billy. "Cause he'd have to answer to our mother who'd rip him a good one."

Well, I didn't say anything to my father, but over the next few weeks they kept doing all kinds of mean things to me. They'd poke me with their forks under the kitchen table at dinner, hide my homework after I'd finished it, put bubble gum in my hair, steal all my underwear so I'd have to wear my pants without any.

I was afraid to fall asleep at night and would force myself to stay awake until both Darren and Billy were out cold. I'd even get up and check their eyes with a flashlight, before I'd allow myself to close my own.

My father went to work in their Uncle Herman's carpet-cleaning business. He said the company had sounded much more successful than an old Chevy van with a built in hose and an industrial-sized carpet cleaner. According to Dad, Uncle

Herman had misrepresented the whole operation. He'd been led to think he'd come to manage a team of employees and land big commercial accounts, not dress in overalls and spend his days spot cleaning cat pee out of old ladies' carpets.

For some reason, my mother didn't call me. I kept asking Dad when I could go home. He mumbled something about her therapist said that talking to me upset my mother, but I didn't believe him.

One night, I snuck downstairs and dialed Aunt Ethel and Uncle George's number. Uncle George picked up the phone and said hello in a groggy voice.

"It's me, Marshall," I whispered.

"How are you?" Uncle George said.

Then a hand grabbed the phone from me and placed it back on the hook. "Don't you never use*th* my phone without permi*th*ion," said Granny.

"I-I'm sorry," I said.

"Money don't grow on trees around here, ya know."

"Yes, ma'am."

Turned out Granny owned the house and was not so happy that Miss Fowler kept bringing home all these babies. The old lady often threatened the bunch of us that we'd have to move out if everyone didn't do their share of chores. Wash the floors, vacuum, clean the bathroom, wash the dishes, dust the furniture, hang up the laundry. Her upper lip would quiver as she barked orders at us.

Darren and Billy had me doing their chores whenever they could get away with it, which was most of the time unless my father was around.

Dad volunteered to coach Little League like he'd promised.

But it didn't start until the spring and I doubted I could survive "the torture chamber" that long. I had been upstate for a few weeks but it felt like a few years.

One chilly fall morning, I awoke feeling like something was crawling up my leg. I pulled the covers off and screamed at the top of my lungs at a scaly green snake slithering in my bed.

The brothers woke up with big grins on their faces. "Ha, ha, ha, ha, ha." Darren laughed so hard he fell out of the upper bunk. "Fuck!" He grabbed his ankle. "I think it's sprained." Tears filled his eyes. "It's all your fault, Marshall. Wait till I tell Granny."

That was the last straw. I grabbed a towel, wrapped the snake in it, and carried it down the ladder to Dad and Miss Fowler's room. No one was in there but Granny. "They's gone to the hospital," she said. "Appears like that baby's coming early. Maybe too early."

I opened the contents of the towel and she screamed.

"This is what your grandsons left in my bed."

"Well, get ridda the *th*ucker, and don't ya make no more trouble."

Me make trouble? Was she nuts? I left the snake slithering in a trashcan, then headed down the road to catch the school bus.

The Fowler boys pointed at me and began laughing with a few of their friends.

When the bus stopped and the doors slid open, instead of stepping on, I took off down the street and reentered the house through the back door.

Granny sat in the kitchen reading the advertisements in the newspaper as I tiptoed up the stairs and climbed the ladder to the attic. I threw my clothes in my duffle bag and made sure the twenty-dollar bill Uncle George had given me was still stuffed in my Little League pants pocket where I'd hid it.

Seven hours later, I stepped off the Greyhound bus in Flushing.

MICKEY

WHEN I RETURNED from Detroit, my knees and my right arm felt like someone had banged them with a sledge hammer. And if that wasn't bad enough, I'd caught a miserable cold I couldn't shake. A buddy of mine found some quack who gave me a shot in the hip that was 'sposed to "cure everything." Well, things went from bad to worse. The shot created an abscess the size of Oklahoma that was oozing with puss and blood.

Back in Queens the next day, Rog was in better spirits than I'd seen him in a while. He and Big Julie stood around putting golf balls into a tin cup on the carpet. Bob sat on the couch eating a bowl of cornflakes, while I nursed a vodka and tonic. Ray Price's *San Antonio Rose* filled the living room.

Then the doorbell rang.

"Hell, you think the press finally found this place?" Roger said.

I shrugged. "You guys expecting someone?"

"Maybe we shouldn't answer," Roger said, but Bob had already got up and opened the door.

We were all relieved when it turned out to be the kid from next door.

"Where you been, Marshall?" Roger said. "We haven't seen

you in weeks."

The kid frowned. "I had to go upstate with my dad. Does anyone need anything from Gelaro's?"

"Can you get me a new arm?" I said, then sneezed four or five times in a row.

"You should let Marshall get you something for that cold," Roger said.

"Heck, I went to this new doc the other day and he gave me the cure."

Roger patted the kid's shoulder. "We don't need anything right now. Take a seat. Or you can have a shot at putting if ya want."

"Yesiree," I said. "You can help me cream these guys at golf."

Marshall sat down on the sofa next to Cerv, while I putted the golf ball right into the cup.

I handed the club to Bob who missed a ridiculously easy putt, then flung the club like it was some big deal.

We all made fun of him. The boy even laughed. He always seemed so serious whenever he came over the house. But he was a good kid. Kept his mouth shut all summer while we were here in the duplex. I smiled at him. "I guess Little League's over for you by now."

He pulled off his Yankee cap and wiped his brow. "Well sorta. The All-Stars are done, but there's a rematch game with the Jamaica All-Star team."

"Why's there a rematch game?" Big Julie said.

"They're telling everyone the only reason we beat them was the game got rained out."

"Sounds like a bunch of sore losers to me," Roger said.

Marshall looked solemn. "They've been bad mouthing us all over Queens."

I looked him square in the eye. "Just do your best, 'cause that's all you can do. Mutt used to always say that."

"Who's Mutt?" Roger piped in.

"My daddy. He started me playing baseball by the time I could walk. Named me after his favorite Hall of Fame catcher, Mickey Cochrane."

Marshall's eyes lit up. "Your father sounds like a neat guy. He must be real proud of you."

My eyes misted up as I thought about my daddy. "I loved Mutt more than anyone. He died after my first World Series."

Roger looked puzzled. "How old was he?"

"Only thirty-nine. Grandpa Charlie and my uncles all died young. Heck, I probably will too."

"You might consider changing your lifestyle," Roger said.

"We all can't be the picture of perfection like you, Rog."

"Yeah, I'm a saint. I came this close to punching out one of those reporters yesterday."

Big Julie rubbed the back of his neck. "You gotta keep it together, bud."

Roger held up his beer bottle like it was a microphone and tilted it toward me. "So tell me, Mickey, do you think the ball's livelier now?"

"No, but the girls are."

Roger punched me playfully in the stomach.

I winced and he backed off. He had no idea how much pain I was in.

"What's wrong with ya, Mick?"

I lifted up my shirt, lowered my pants a bit, and tore off a bloody bandage, revealing the huge abscess in my hip.

Everyone gasped.

The room began to spin. Big Julie and Roger picked me up and carried me to the couch. "I'll be okay," I whispered. But I knew I was in big trouble.

ROGER

BY THE TIME Jule's doctor friend arrived, Mickey was burning up with fever. One part of me was mad as hell at him for taking such bad care of himself. The other part was truly frightened for him. The gaping hole in his hip was no joke. To be completely truthful, I didn't want Mickey to drop out of the home run race. I couldn't handle chasing the Babe's record on my own.

The doctor recommended Mickey check into a hospital immediately. "No ifs, ands, or buts. If this infection has spread to your internal organs, well…"

The Mick turned on his infamous charm with a big smile. "Look, Doc, there's only a few games left. I'll play until I can't play no more. I gotta give it my best."

"This isn't a game, Mickey. You need an IV full of antibiotics." The doctor closed up his black bag and left the room. We followed him outside. Jules pulled some bills from his wallet and handed them to him. "This should cover the house call. I can't thank you enough for coming."

The doctor's face lacked color. "I can't keep patching him up, Jules. This is beyond my capability."

Big Julie shrugged. "He ain't gonna listen to me."

He glanced over at me. "Have you spoken to him?"

"Till I'm blue in the face. Mickey listens to no one but Mickey."

The doctor swallowed. "I'm going to say this once, and once only. If he doesn't check into a hospital in the next twenty-four hours, you'll be carrying him out in a coffin."

ROGER

WHEN JULES PICKED me up two days later, I told him that even with nine games left, I doubted I'd be able to tie, let alone beat the record by the end of the season.

He wagged his chunky finger at me. "Don't prove those assholes right."

"I'm just so tired, and frankly, I don't give a damn."

"Who do ya think you are? Clark Gable?"

I cracked a smile. "It's 'frankly, *my dear*, I don't give a damn.'" *Gone With the Wind* was Pat's favorite movie of all time.

"'Frankly, my dear,' I do."

"You got some big bucks riding on me, Jules?"

"That's not fair, and you know it. For the record, I have no money riding on you. Well, if you don't count my bet with Mick."

"You have a bet with Mick?"

"It was the only way I could get him to agree to move to Flushing. But I wouldn't dream of taking his money when *you* win the race. Lord knows I've been tempted to pony up some real action, but I didn't wanna jinx nothin'."

I had hit Jules below the belt with that comment. He was

very sensitive about his former life as a bookie and gambler. "I had no right to say that. Please accept my apology."

He waved his hand with a shooing motion. "I don't give two shits if you break the record, Roger. But give it your best shot or you'll always regret it."

I nodded.

"That's my *boychick*." He wheeled the Lincoln down Seventh Avenue and peeled into a parking lot. Then we hit the street to the Stage Deli for baloney and eggs.

Later that afternoon as I pulled into the driveway, I tooted my horn at Marshall. He was throwing a Spaldeen against the wall of his house. "Mr. Marshman. How's it going?"

"Good. Are you ready for the Oriole game tonight?"

"How 'bout you come to Baltimore with me?"

"Serious?"

"I've decided to drive the convertible down there. Houk thinks I'm nuts, but it will relax me."

"Wow! Sure. Am I gonna see you hit number 59?"

I smiled. "Now don't you start putting pressure on me. I got enough with everybody else."

Marshall opened the passenger door of the convertible and sat down in the bucket seat.

"You need to tell your mother where you're going. We won't get home until very late tonight."

I watched as the kid ran inside the house and was back out in less than a minute. He'd gone from a clean-cut, muscular young boy in early summer to a skinny and haggard looking one. I hadn't seen the father's car around in weeks. I sure would have liked to give that jerk a piece of my mind.

MARSHALL

WE DROVE TO Baltimore in Roger's red convertible with the top down. Someday, when I became a famous ballplayer like him, I imagined people would talk about how Roger Maris and Marshall Elliot had driven together to Memorial Stadium the night Roger broke the Babe's record. This was the 154th game of the season and Roger needed to hit three home runs to beat Ruth's record in the same amount of games as Babe.

"I hope the press will leave me alone once this game is over," Roger said as we cruised down the Jersey Turnpike. "If I break the record in the next eight games, Frick says it won't really count."

Country music blared from Roger's stereo. He turned up the volume when *Walking After Midnight* by his favorite singer, Patsy Cline, came on and then he sang off-key at the top of his lungs.

The next few hours on the road went by quickly with Roger doing most of the talking. He asked me about my parents. I told him about Dad getting remarried and moving upstate but omitted the fact that my mother was at Bellevue. I didn't want him to think she was crazy. It was hard for me to understand that my mother had "mental issues," let alone speak about them. Plus if Roger put 1+1 together, (Dad in Bingo and Ma at Bellevue), he would come to the realization that I was living at the house by myself.

Roger spoke about his hopes and dreams for his family. He wanted his kids to get a good education. He'd already started a college fund for each of them. "I was stupid not to go when I had a full ride to play football at the University of Oklahoma."

"Football? Wow!"

He shrugged. "My life would have certainly been different."

"But you wouldn't be a Yankee."

He shrugged. "But I'd be home with my family right now. Little Kevin said, "Da Da," on the phone to me yesterday. My biggest fear is my boy doesn't recognize me next time I see him."

Classic Roger. His biggest fear was not breaking Babe's record, but his kid not remembering him. To think that I'd been gone for three days and my father didn't even notice I was missing.

By the time we reached the Baltimore city limits, Roger was chatting about retirement. "Pat and I want to move to Florida. She's tired of the cold winters of the Midwest."

When we arrived at Memorial Stadium, he drove to a special area designated for the players. He handed his car keys to the young parking attendant whose shiny black hair was greased back in a ducktail. Roger slipped him a ten-dollar-bill and looked the kid in the eye. "You take good care of her, you hear?"

Big Julie introduced me to Yogi Berra and a couple of other players while I waited for Roger to change for the game in the locker room. Mickey waved at me. He had taken the train down from New York with the team. His face dripped with sweat from a fever, and he couldn't walk without leaning on someone.

I dawdled along the bleachers to my seat, my shoes crunching the broken shells of roasted peanuts. A few minutes later as I stood for the national anthem, I thought about what an amazing summer it had been. If it wasn't for my father, I'd be on the top of the world.

During the next two hours the Oriole stands filled up, and Yankee sportscaster, Phil Rizzuto, cleared his throat in the press box.

Phil Rizzuto: "Good evening, ladies and gentleman. I'm here at Memorial Stadium where 21,000 or so baseball fans attending the Yankee-Oriole game hold their breath as the game is about to begin. The Oriole fans are hopeful they get to see slugger Roger Maris hit his fifty-ninth home run before the end of the night."

The fans booed when it was announced that Mickey wouldn't be playing. If they only knew how much pain he was in. The first time Roger came up to bat against the Oriole's pitcher, Milt Papas, he smacked a ball clear into his sweet spot.

Phil Rizzuto: "Ah gee. That ball but is caught in the teeth of the wind and headed straight to the center fielder."

By the third inning, the score was 2-0, Baltimore, with two outs, as Roger came up to bat again.

Phil Rizzuto: "Here's the first pitch. Low, ball one. Pappas is ready with the windup, inside, ball two. Two and one. There's one, it's going, it's going it is gone! And the Yankees are claiming number fifty-nine for Roger Maris. And so he becomes the second man in history to ever reach that total, surpassing Jimmy Fox and Hank Greenburg."

I cheered so loud my throat hurt. As he predicted, Roger did not break Babe's record that night. When the game was over, I sat in my seat waiting for him as Memorial Stadium emptied out. Soon, there was no one there, but me and the guys sweeping up the peanut shells and trash. Had he forgotten about me after everything that had happened? No way. I had to remind myself that Roger wasn't my dad.

Big Julie showed up as the lights in the stadium went out. "Roger sends his sincere apologies. The press are still badgering him in the dressing room."

"But he said they'd leave him alone now that he didn't break the record in 154 games."

"Wishful thinking on Roger's part. Despite Frick's 154-game rule, Roger is still a big story. They'll hound him to the bitter end."

"That won't make him happy."

"Hell, don't I know it? They're all over him now like a cheap suit."

"So when will he be done?"

"Who knows? He suggested you take the train back to New York with me."

After the two-hour train-ride to Penn Station, Big Julie rode the subway with me one stop to Times Square where he placed me on the Queens-bound 7 train to Flushing. It was well after 2 a.m. before I reached the house. When I entered the dark rooms, it felt especially eerie. I snapped on the light switches in every room, but it still was creepy. There was nothing but static on the TV, and I began to feel really scared as I thought about what was going to happen to me. When would my mother get better and come home? Would Dad force me to live upstate with that horrible Miss Fowler and her family?

Suddenly, the phone rang. I was real tempted to answer it, but I reminded myself that if anyone found out I was there, I'd get shipped back to Bingo.

For the next few hours, RING, RING, RING.

Should I take it off the hook? But then whoever was calling would know someone was at the house. Instead, I went to my bedroom, burrowed myself under the covers, and placed the pillow over my head. After twelve or thirteen rings there'd be a pause, then it'd start all over again.

I'd been home by myself for three days. Was it possible that Dad finally noticed I was gone?

Big Julie

ALL THE REPORTERS yapped about after the game was how Roger had failed to break the record in 154 games.

Roger responded courteously. "Commissioner Frick makes the rules. If all I'm entitled to is an asterisk, then so be it."

It was a gracious response but the press reacted with venom.

September 21, 1961 – *Miami Sun*
"MARIS FAILS TO BREAK BABE RUTH'S RECORD OF 60
HOMERS IN 154 GAMES"

September 21, 1961 – *Milwaukee Journal*
"NO REGRET HERE. IF THE RECORD IS TO BE BROKEN,
IT SHOULD BE DONE BY SOMEONE OF GREATER BASE-

BALL STATURE AND GREATER COLOR AND PUBLIC AP-
PEAL. MARIS IS COLORLESS. HE IS NOT MORE THAN A
GOOD BI-LEAGUE PLAYER…THERE JUST ISN'T ANY-
THING DEEPLY HEROIC ABOUT THE MAN."

MARSHALL

THE NEXT MORNING, I stood on the porch watching the rain
form puddles in the potholes in the road. I felt sure that it had
been Dad calling over and over during the night. Maybe it was
a mistake not to answer the phone. Maybe he really was freaked
out when he discovered I was gone from Miss Fowler's house.
I considered calling him back, but didn't want to risk the possibility of ending up back in the Bingo torture chamber.

I heard the squeal of the screen door open at the duplex
next door, and was surprised to see Mickey with a beer in his
hand. It was early even for him to be drinking. His face and
shirt were drenched. At first, I thought he'd been out in the
rain. But when I walked next door, I realized he was in trouble.
Sweat streamed down his face, and his whole body was trem-
bling. "You don't look too hot, Mr. Mantle."

"I don't feel too hot, kid."

"Can I get you anything? A bottle of aspirin, or maybe
some Vicks Vapor Rub? My mother smears that on me when
I'm sick."

"My wife's coming in from Dallas. She'll take care of me.
I'm s'posed to pick her up at Penn Station at two. You could
do me a favor."

"Whatever you need, sir."

Mickey took a twenty from his wallet. "Take a cab to Penn and meet my wife's train. Her name's Merlyn. Bring her back here." He scribbled down her train information and pulled out a snapshot of an attractive woman in an evening gown. "Take this so you'll recognize her." Just then, his knee gave out and he fell to the ground. "Geez!"

"Let me help you up."

Leaning on me, Mickey hobbled back inside the house to the couch. He began coughing uncontrollably.

I wrapped a blanket around him, then ran next door to get some cough syrup.

When I returned a few minutes later with a bottle of Ma's Vicks Formula 44, sweat was dripping down Mick's face, yet he was shivering.

I felt his head with my hand like Ma did when I was sick. He was burning up. Could someone die of a high fever? I had to do something. "Mick, I'm calling an ambulance."

A hand suddenly emerged from under the covers and grabbed my wrist. "Please...don't do that. I beg you." His words were interspersed with coughing. "Get Merlyn. She'll know what to do." Then he squeezed my hand and closed his eyes.

I felt torn about leaving him, but did as he said. A few hours later, I returned with Mickey's wife, a pretty blonde lady about my mother's age.

"Oh my God, look at him!" she said, when we entered the living room.

Blood was draining through his pants to the blankets.

"Call an ambulance, young man!"

Mickey opened his eyes. "No, no for crissakes, don't do that.

It will be in all the papers."

Merlyn raised her voice. "You need to check in to a hospital, Mick, or you're gonna die here in this hovel."

"I'm not arguing. You can drive me to Lenox after we go to the game."

"Are you crazy? You can't do that. I won't let you."

Mickey tried to step out of bed and collapsed on the floor. This time she shouted at me, "Call an ambulance, now!"

I dialed zero for the operator, and she connected me to the hospital. When I got back into the room, Mickey was barely conscious.

Merlyn sat on the floor, mopping his forehead with a bed sheet she'd soaked in cold water. "I love ya, you old coot."

He squeezed her hand and whispered in a hoarse voice, "I love ya too, honey. You think there's still a shot for us?"

With all the booze and babes, did he really still love his wife? It didn't make any sense to me. All I could think about was the possibility that Dad still loved my mother. And whether I even wanted him to.

CHAPTER FIFTEEN

The End of the Race

September 22, 1961

At 3:45 a.m., Antonio Abertondo arrived in Dover and became the first person to swim across the English Channel, and right back again, resting for only ten minutes between crossings. (15)

MICKEY

I don't remember the ambulance ride or my arrival at the hospital. I was scorched with fever, yet I shivered. Hot and cold…flushed, freezing, roasted…burning up.

The sunset permeates the Oklahoma sky with a blaze of gold, pink, and vibrant purple. The pain is gone. I'm twelve years old, with a shock of white sandy hair, and a lean, hard body.

My daddy throws a bucket of balls to me in the side-yard of our small clapboard house. Granddaddy stands behind him chewing a wad of tobacco. Both of them are stooped over from years of working in the Commerce coal mines. Granddaddy can barely walk and leans on a cane.

"Try hitting left-handed for a change," Daddy says.

I wrinkle my nose. "How am I s'posed to hit lefty?"

"Get on the right side of the plate, put your left hand on top, right hand on bottom, right elbow up."

Granddaddy laughs, then coughs. Daddy pitches to me.

I swing and miss the ball at least ten times. It feels awkward hitting lefty and I switch the bat back to my right side.

"I ain't gonna pitch no more to your good side," Daddy says.

"Well, I'm no good as a lefty."

"Neither was yer Daddy, were ya, Mutt?" Granddaddy says.

Daddy winks at Granddaddy, then looks me in the eye. "You listen up, boy. Most fellas can hit righty. A few are born natural lefties. But if you want to be the best of 'em all, you need to hit both ways."

"I can't do it. I'll never be a switch hitter."

Mutt sighs. "Don't ever give up unless you've given it your best shot, son. Can you honestly say you've done that?"

"I, ah, guess I could hit another bucket of balls."

I swing at ball after ball in the bucket until the sun has set and a smattering of stars fill the sky.

"Have you given it your best now?" Mutt says.

"Yes, sir."

He smiles. "Okay, then you have nothing to feel bad about. We'll try again tomorrow."

When I awoke, Merlyn and the kid were standing next to my bed. "How long you two been here?"

Merlyn clasped my hand. "About ten hours. I told Marshall to go home, but he refused. He's been a big comfort to me."

"Thanks, kid," I said.

Merlyn shook her head. "At one point, the doctors thought you might not make it."

"Hell, you can't kill the Mick off that easy."

"But the race is over," Merlyn said. "You can't play."

I swallowed. "Yeah, I guess."

"You gave it your best," Marshall said.

It was like Mutt was speaking to me through the kid. I suddenly felt like a big weight had been lifted from my shoulders. "I sure did."

I told Merlyn to call a cab to take the kid home then check herself into the Ritz.

Marshall scribbled down his phone number, and handed it to me. "Call me if you need anything, Mick." Then he turned to Merlyn. "You can call me, too, Mrs. Mantle."

"You're such a sweet boy," she said. "Your parents must be so proud of you."

His mouth formed a tight line. "Sure they are."

CHAPTER SIXTEEN

Homecoming

September 26, 1961

KENNEDY WARNS U.N. OF ATOMIC WAR PERIL (16)

MARSHALL

The house felt hollow, like the air had been sucked out of it. Yet I was more relieved than scared to stay all by myself the last few days. Anything was better than the Bingo torture chamber. I dared not contact Aunt Ethel and Uncle George, or even Bobby. I couldn't chance that I'd end up back in Bingo. Dad and Miss Fowler were probably too busy with the new baby to miss me. It hurt that Dad had made no effort to call me.

That night, I sat watching *Leave It To Beaver* in my pajamas eating a Stouffers fried chicken TV dinner I'd bought at Gelaro's. Beaver's older brother Wally had girl troubles and went to his dad for some advice. As the dad tried to explain what he knew about the female sex, they discovered eight-year-old Beaver hiding behind the couch. "I wanna know about girls, too," he said.

This brought big bursts of laughter from the studio audience, but I had to blink back the tears.

Then the mother walked into the room. "What's all this about girls?" she said with a big grin. "Why doesn't anyone ask me?"

Watching the Cleaver family made me feel even worse. Why couldn't my parents be like them? Would Ward leave his family for another one? Would June ever find herself in the looney bin? No, of course not.

With only a few dollars left from the Uncle George's twenty, I couldn't stay in the house alone much longer. And then, there was the matter of the seventh grade. Technically, I was playing hooky. If the truant officer found out, I could be in big trouble.

The longer I stayed alone, the harder it was for me to do anything. A couple more days passed and I didn't even get out of my pajamas. I sat and watched TV all day. Game shows mostly. I felt paralyzed.

One night, I glanced out the window at hundreds of bright stars and the eyes of the man in the moon. He gazed back at me with a slim smile. "Please help me," I said to my imaginary friend in the sky. Or was I speaking with God? Something I'd never been much good at. I didn't even know what to wish for.

The sound of the front door deadbolt jarred me from my prayer. I leaped from the couch and ran into the entry where Ma stood with her suitcase. Her eyebrows shot up. "My God! What are you doing here?"

"I hated it in Binghamton. I'm not going back."

She stretched out her arms to me. "You won't have to, I'm home for good." Tears filled our eyes as we hugged.

"Are you really all better?" I had to know the truth.

I'm okay, honey. I'll have a weekly appointment with Dr. Vidor for a few months. But I feel great."

A few seconds later, Aunt Ethel walked inside carrying sacks of groceries. "Marshall! I thought you were up in Binghamton with your dad."

After another round of tearful hugs and explanations, we all went to the kitchen and unpacked the paper bags. As my mother and aunt cooked up a batch of fried chicken and mashed potatoes, I sat at the table with a renewed belief in miracles.

Ma handed me a plate of food and I ate every last bite. It felt like I hadn't eaten in weeks.

"I have some great news," Ma said.

I thought about Dad's news and decided it best I didn't mention it to her.

"When Aunt Ethel and I were shopping at Mr. Gelaro's, he offered me a job."

"Wow, that's terrific."

"I mean it's not a lot of money, but I think we can manage. Your dad paid the mortgage last month, but from now on it's up to me. Things are going to be tight and you'll have to be alone after school for a few hours."

Ha, if she only knew.

"He can come home with Bobby," Aunt Ethel said. She smiled at me. "You still are our favorite nephew."

My mother smiled. "Perfect."

My aunt cleared the dishes from the table and began rinsing them.

"Leave them," Mother said. "Go home to your family."

"Are you gonna be okay?"

"I'm great. Never felt better."

Aunt Ethel kissed the top of my head, waved at Ma, and strolled out the door.

Then, the phone rang.

Ma picked up the receiver. "Edmund?" She spoke in a velvety voice that I didn't recognize. They talked for a while.

What was he saying to her? He had to know that I'd run away from Binghamton. Would my parents be angry at me for staying alone at the house? Would my father make me go back upstate?

After Ma hung up the phone, the color in her cheeks paled. "Your Dad has a new baby boy."

"Please don't get all sad on me, Ma."

"No, no, I won't sweetie. I promise. It's just…"

I knew she was thinking about the baby she'd lost. Our baby.

I swallowed. "Did he say I had to go back upstate with him?"

"Actually, he said something about him moving back to Queens."

I couldn't imagine that Miss Fowler and those nasty kids of hers had left Bingo to move down here. Could he be here by himself? That made no sense either. He had a new baby to think about.

MARSHALL

IN THE MORNING, my mother dressed in a navy skirt and a crisp white blouse. It was her first day of work at Gelaro's Market and she wanted to make a good impression. It was also my first day at Edward Bleeker Junior High School.

After registering in the office, I walked down the hall to my new locker, and tried the combination scrawled on a piece of paper the school secretary had given me. After four or five unsuccessful tries, I kicked the metal door a few times.

Rocky Romano poked me in the ribs. "Need some help?"

The small hairs on the nape of my neck stood at attention as I braced myself for a showdown.

Frank Caruso emerged on my other side and shoved my shoulder. "Where you been?"

No escaping the two of them. "I, ah, had to go upstate." They were the last two people I wanted to talk to about my parents' split. Were they gonna pummel me again? My leg muscles tightened in anticipation of making a run for it.

"Well, are you playing or not? You've missed a lot of practices," Rocky said.

"We need you in right field," Frank added.

The Jamaica game. I'd totally forgotten about it. "Yeah, sure I'd like to play."

"It's Sunday at three o'clock. You think you might get your ass to a couple of practices? We got one after school today," Frank said.

"I'll be there." There was nothing I'd like better.

"See you then," Frank said. The two disappeared down the hall without looking back. One last spin of the knob, and my locker finally opened.

Later that morning as I sat by myself in the cafeteria, someone tapped my back.

I spun back around ready for anything. A fight if need be.

From Frank and Rocky's expressions, I wasn't sure they'd been mad or glad to see me.

To my surprise, Bobby sat down next to me. I thought he was still mad. "Glad to see you, Cuz."

"Is everyone on the team angry at me?"

"We've just been freaked out that we didn't have enough good players to beat Jamaica. I hear there's lotsa money riding on us losing."

"That means we have to win."

He grinned. "And now that you're back, we've got a shot."

"I'm real rusty. Haven't hit in weeks."

"You got five days to get in shape. You can come to the batting cage with me and Pop."

"I don't have any money for the cage."

"Don't worry. My father always has cash when you need it."

I thought about what Ma said about Dad coming back to Flushing, but knew it best not to count on anything when it came to him.

Big Julie

THE STANDS FILLED up at Yankee Stadium as sportscaster Mel Allen sat down in the press box.

Mel Allen: "Good evening ladies and gentleman. I'm here at Yankee stadium where baseball fans attending the Yankee-Oriole game hold their breath as the game is about to begin. While the Yankees have already clinched the pennant, the fans are hopeful they get to see slugger, Roger Maris hit his sixtieth home run before the end of the night."

The Yankees took their places in the field. Roger ran out to center field in Mickey's normal position. Everyone in the stands stood as the national anthem played. By the third inning the score was two-zero Baltimore, with two outs, as Roger came up to bat. The first pitch was a foul ball.

My stomach filled with butterflies.

Then–CRACK–Roger smacked that ball and no one in the stands doubted that this was the one.

Mel Allen: "There it is, they say it's fair. Number sixty into the third deck in right field!"

The crowd roared. We all stood and watched Roger trot around the bases. Mel Allen's voice was choked.

Mel Allen: "How about that, folks, there's a standing ovation. A standing ovation for Roger Maris. And they're asking him to come out of the dugout. That is most unusual. There he is!"

Roger stepped out from the dugout, took off his cap, waved it at the fans, and raced right back inside. It didn't take but a second before one of the other announcers in the stadium got behind the mike.

Unidentified Sports Announcer: "This comes at game 159 and is not considered tying Babe Ruth's record made in 154 games. But it's a great night for the twenty-seven-year-old Maris."

Why did he have to come on and say that? Couldn't they

just give Roger one full moment of glory?

Four more days went by with no more home runs for Roger. Heck, He swung at bad pitches, hit grounders and pop-ups, and had lost his groove.

There were two more games left for Roger to hit one homer to break the Babe's record. To everyone's shock, Roger asked Houk if he could take the first game against Boston off. He said he was exhausted, which was true, but he also wanted to attend my Danny's Bar Mitzvah. Pat was flying in from Kansas City for the event.

Houk said yes, but I don't believe for a minute he took Roger seriously.

MARSHALL

THE NEXT COUPLE of days, I worked hard to catch up with schoolwork. I went to the batting cage with Bobby after school, followed by an All-Star practice. All the Flushing kids were psyched to prove once and for all that we'd beat Jamaica fair and square.

Laila sat with her friends during my practices at Hudson Park. She'd cheer whenever I smacked a good hit to the outfield or made a tough catch. I was so busy with school and baseball I barely thought about my father much at all.

My mother had lost a bunch of weight and bought some new clothes for work. She came home every day bursting with stories about things she had accomplished during the day. "What a mess Mr. Gelaro's books were. He hadn't kept them up since his wife died. But I have them all organized now." She seemed really happy again. Maybe even happier than she used to be because she didn't have to worry about Dad always getting mad at her.

One day she arrived home and said, "Some lady came in today and wanted to fix Lou up on a date with her widowed sister. He told her, no thank you."

"Who's Lou?" I said, as I grabbed a couple of oatmeal cookies and poured myself a glass of milk to go with them.

"Mr. Gelaro, of course. Anyway, he turned to me after she'd left and asked if *I* wanted to go out on a date with him Saturday night. After your game, of course."

I nearly dropped my glass of milk on the floor. "What did you tell him?" Ma and Mr. Gelaro? I'd never thought about my mother with anyone besides my father.

She smiled. "I told him I'd ask you."

"Me? Why'd you do that?"

"Because if it bothers you, son, I won't go. You've had enough turmoil in your life the last few months."

"It doesn't bother me," I said, even though it did feel a little weird.

"I'm glad that—"

A loud knock on the front door halted our discussion. We both made a beeline to the entry. My mother pulled the front door open but kept the latch on the screen door in place.

There before us stood Dad, dressed all spiffy in his gray-pinstriped business suit. He held a bouquet of yellow roses in his hand. "Can I come in, Marion?"

My mother unlatched the hook on the screen door, and Dad tousled my hair as he stepped inside the house. "How's my favorite boy?"

Was he here to take me back to Bingo? I glared at him. "From what I hear, you got yourself a new baby boy."

He placed his hand on my shoulder. "No one could ever take your place."

"Yeah, right. I ran away from Bingo and you didn't even notice your *favorite* boy was gone."

"So that's why you're mad at me?"

"Jesus, Dad. Why don't you just leave us alone?"

"Listen to me. After the baby came, I drove straight down here to see if Brooks would give me my old job back. Gloria never said one word to me about you being missing."

That made sense, but I still wasn't letting him off the hook. He handed my mother the flowers, then eyeballed her from head to toe and whistled. "You look great."

The rims of her eyes grew shiny. "I'll get a vase."

"I'm serious. Did you go on some kinda diet? And your hair. Very flattering."

"What do you want, Edmond? Let me guess. You and Miss Fowler would like to move into the house."

"You couldn't be more wrong." He took her hand. "I do want to move back into the house, but not with Miss Fowler. I want to be with *you* and Marshall. I-I want to get back together."

"What? Are you crazy?" She pulled her hand from his grip. "From what I've heard, the ink wasn't dry on our divorce papers before you married that woman. And now there's a child."

I couldn't believe my ears. Dad wanted to come back home after everything that had happened?

"I made a big mistake," he said. "I never should have left you. She tricked me into thinking—"

"Thinking what?"

Dad shook his head. "Son, perhaps you should go to your room."

"He's staying right here!" My mother's tone had an air of authority like Sergeant Bilko.

Dad held up his hand like a stop sign. "Okay, he stays."

My mother folded her arms. "You were saying?"

"Here's the gist of it. I was downright miserable in Binghamton. Heck, everything Gloria had told me was a lie. The whole time she was at Kraftworks, not a word to anyone about kids. Not a photo on her desk or nothin'. The great management opportunity to work in her uncle's business was nothing but a van with carpet-cleaning equipment. And then, there was her bitchy mother, and worst of all…" Dad let out his breath.

"And worst of all?" my mother said.

"I can't be sure the baby is even mine."

My mother's eyes almost popped out of her head.

"When I stopped by the office to apply for my old job, I went for a beer with George Greeley. Turns out, Miss Fowler was humping more than just me. That baby could belong to any of a number of fellows."

Ma gawked at him. "I don't believe it."

"A few weeks ago, *you* were the one calling her a floozy."

"A woman who fools around with someone else's husband is a floozy in my book."

"Don't you see? You were right about her. And I'm not taking responsibility for that scrawny baby and the lot of those other brats. She tricked me into getting married. Ruined my whole life."

"You're sick, Edmund."

"I understand this is a shock. I'm gonna make it all up to

you. You can't deny that Marshall needs a father."

"Yes, he does," Ma said. "And I hope someday I find one for him. Now get the hell out of here."

Dad moved toward the front door. "I'll, ah, give you a few days to think about it." He turned to me. "When's that rematch game you've been talking about?"

"Sunday afternoon, three-thirty."

"I'll be there rooting for you." He pulled out a pen and a slip of paper, scribbled his new address and phone number on it, and handed it to me. "Call me anytime you need me." Then he pushed open the front door and walked out to his blue Galaxie. The screech of tires filled my ears as he peeled out of the driveway.

My mother and I sat at the kitchen table without speaking for a long time. Finally, I broke the silence. "You're not gonna let Dad come home, are you?"

I honestly didn't know what I wanted her answer to be. My mother was just about her old self again, and we were doing okay. It was true Miss Fowler had tricked Dad, but he had no right to cheat on my mother in the first place. If Ma let him come back and he hurt her again, she'd never survive. It wasn't worth that risk to have our family together again. We'd never be like the Cleavers. But the one thing I wanted, the one thing I still needed, was for my dad to show up at my game.

CHAPTER SEVENTEEN

The Bar Mitzvah

September 29, 1961

President Gamal Abdel Nasser said tonight that the United Arab Republic was in "grave danger" as a result of an army revolt in Damascus early in the day. (17)

MARSHALL

My hero Mickey was lucky to be alive. When I arrived at the hospital with Mrs. Mantle that night, a team of doctors and nurses raced up to us and attached Mick to an I.V. full of antibiotics. Things were touch and go all that night. Mrs. Mantle held his hand and prayed. I made coffee runs to the cafeteria and kept the press from entering the room. They all thought I was Mick Jr. I didn't tell them anything different.

The next few days I stopped by the hospital after All-Star practice to see if Mickey needed anything. On Saturday morning, Mick called me to bring over a radio so he could listen to the Yankee game in the afternoon. He looked a whole lot better as he lay in bed reading the newspaper. His wife sat in a chair reading *Life Magazine.*

Suddenly, the door snapped open, and Big Julie appeared. He was dressed in a grey pinstriped suit and held a big bouquet of flowers, which he handed to Mrs. Mantle.

Mickey smiled. "Who died?"

"Whaddaya talking about?" Big Julie said. "How you feeling?"

"Between the suit and those flowers, you look like you're headed to a funeral, is all. Did ya think I was kicking the bucket?"

Big Julie chuckled. "It's my kid's Bar Mitzvah."

"Well, what are you doing here, then?" Mickey said.

"It's over now. He made me real proud. But there's still the reception tonight. I was on the way to pick up my tuxedo and thought I'd stop by to see if you need anything."

"Merlyn's got it all under control. Go get your monkey suit and have a good time."

"Are you sure?"

Mrs. Mantle pointed at me. "Marshall's been running errands for us. He is one special little boy. We invited him to listen to the game with us."

"I wouldn't miss Roger breaking the record for anything," Mickey said. He seemed to have come to terms with the fact he'd lost the chance himself.

Just then, Roger ambled into the room dressed in a suit identical to Big Julie's. "You won't see it today."

Mickey's eyebrows flew up. "What the—?"

"I took the day off to attend Danny's Bar Mitzvah."

"You're shitting me," Mickey said.

"Do I look like I'm shitting you?"

"Hell, I've never seen you in a decent suit before. What happened to the seersucker jacket?"

Jules burst out laughing. "I bought him the suit yesterday."

I couldn't believe he was going to miss the game today. "There's three games left for you to break the record and you're missing one to go to—"

Roger patted my head. "I promised Big Julie I'd be there, and I'm going."

"I've begged him to renege and go to the game, but he won't," Big Julie said.

"I don't go back on a promise." He turned to me. "You come too, Marshall. You'll have a ball."

I shrugged. "Sure. If Roger and Mick aren't playing today, who cares about the Yankee game?"

"I'm afraid that's what the rest of New York is gonna think, too," Big Julie said.

"Houk's gonna blow a gasket," Mickey said. "The irony of it all. I've handed you the opportunity to break the record on a platter, and you'd rather go to a Bar Mitzvah? Hell, you ain't even Jewish."

We were all laughing when the phone rang. Big Julie picked up the receiver. "How'd you know where to find him?"

ROGER

"GET YOUR ASS to the stadium," Houk roared into the phone receiver. "The crowds are going ballistic. They all came to see you break the record."

I was baffled. "But you said I could have the day off."

"Hell, Roger. I never thought you'd actually do it. What kind of idiot—"

"This kind of idiot," I shouted, and hung up the phone. "Let's go, Jules."

"Houk's gonna kill you," Jules said.

"I don't care anymore."

Mickey shook his head. "I'll give you this much. You got some *cojones*."

An hour later, I entered the Waldorf Astoria with Big Julie, Marshall, and Pat on my arm. My wife was glowing and gorgeous in a red silk dress she'd bought for the occasion. I felt smitten, like we were teenagers again, headed to a high school dance. Jules had reserved a room for us on the eighth floor after the reception. I couldn't wait for Pat and me to get the rare chance to be alone together.

"You're nuts, Rog," Jules said.

I smiled.

The concierge escorted us to a large reception hall filled with people, elaborate bouquets of flowers, and a food table the size of the Yankee outfield.

Jules nodded at different friends and relatives as we promenaded down the hall. Dressed in one of Danny's suits, he introduced Marshall to his son. "Make him feel like family, you hear?"

Danny smiled at Marshall. "Follow me." He led him to an area where teenagers were playing the limbo.

Jules glanced at his watch. "If we go now, Rog, I can have you there by the third inning."

I squeezed his chin. "And leave all this amazing food?"

"I'll wrap up a plate. You can eat it on the cab ride over. I don't want you to have any regrets."

I looked him dead in the eye. "I made my choice and I'm at peace with it. Now let's have some fun."

An old guy with a bushy white mustache and beard handed Jules a *yamalkah*, which he placed on his balding head. Jules had explained the significance of the little round hat at my first Shabbat dinner at his house. Most all the men in the room were wearing them now, so when the old man approached me, I, too, placed it on my head.

Couples danced to a band playing hits from the forties and fifties. Jules' wife Selma floated across the hall in a gold se-quined gown. She was a small, slender thing who'd attended Wellesley and came from an orthodox Jewish family in Long Island. Such a contrast to Jules. And she kept the big guy in line with the slightest wave of a finger.

Selma greeted me with a big hug. "Jules said you weren't going to make it. Something about missing a baseball game. I said, 'Baseball, *schmaseball*,' what's one game?"

I chuckled. "Baseball, *schmaseball*." Where does that compare to attending my first Bar Mitzvah?"

Jules cracked up laughing.

Selma introduced herself to Pat. "Roger's told me so much about you." She whisked my wife away to a group of women who greeted them with big smiles.

Big Julie filled my plate with food from the silver serving dishes on the table. Little hot dogs on tiny buns, Swedish meat-balls, egg rolls, antipasto, salami on crackers, fruit bowls, a noo-dle dish called *kasha vanakas*, chicken wings, a variety of breads and tiny bagels, cookies, pastries, gefilte fish, and more. Much more. Selma had served me many of the Jewish delicacies at their Friday night dinners.

I stuffed myself with the delicious food until I couldn't eat another bite. A man with flutes of champagne on a tray kept replacing my empty glass. Jules introduced me to his elderly parents who still ran a hot dog stand in the Bronx, his twin sister who worked in advertising, and a number of other relatives and friends.

Danny appeared with his shirt hanging out the back of his dress pants. "I can't believe you're here, Mr. Maris. It means the world to me."

Before long, a small crowd of people surrounded us. A couple of them asked for my autograph.

"Not here, not today," Big Julie said.

"It's okay," I said grabbing a cocktail napkin from a boy about the size of Marshall. Ten people immediately lined up behind him.

Jules shouted, "Please, everyone. Mr. Maris came to relax. Can you give him a break? He hasn't seen his wife in two months."

An old lady began to tap people's hands with her wood cane. "Two months! Let the poor *mensch* spend some time with his wife."

As the crowd dispersed, the band began to play *Moon River*. I grabbed Pat's hand and whisked her around the dance floor. When the song was over, I stepped up to the bandleader and whispered in his ear.

The bandleader adjusted the microphone. "Ladies and gentlemen," we have a special guest here tonight who would like to sing for you. May I introduce, Mr. Roger Maris."

The band started playing *Hava Naglila*.

Roger grabbed the microphone and began singing an off-key rendition of the song. Frank Sinatra he wasn't, but he looked like he was having the time of his life.

I glanced at Pat. "Has he ever done anything like this before?"

"Our Roger?" She laughed. "I have no idea what possessed him."

Men, women, and children alike lined in a circle and danced the traditional moves of the *hora*. Four kids lifted Danny on a chair and moved him in the middle of the circle. It warmed my heart to see Danny and Roger enjoying themselves. Both my son and my dear friend had suffered their share of ups and downs this past summer.

Soon Selma, Pat, and I joined my favorite Yankee on the stage. Roger waved his hand at Marshall, and he climbed up there with us. We all sang at the top of our lungs.

When the song was finished, Roger latched onto Pat's arm and turned to me. "This was really a lot of fun, Jules, but I think we'll say goodbye now."

I squinted. "*Whatsamatta* with you? You're gonna miss the best part."

Roger smiled. "Is the circus coming?"

"No, dinner, you *schmiggegie.*"

Roger pointed at the enormous table of food that busboys were currently cleaning off. "What was that?"

"Hors d'oeuvres, of course. We've got prime rib and lamb chops, and salmon." He looked over at Selma. "What else is there, honey?"

"Well, there's beef ribs, and chicken, and the side dishes, a dessert buffet and—"

Pat answered for Roger, well aware of his reputation for enjoying large amounts of good food. "Lead the way, Jules."

I took Selma's hand and pointed at the door of an adjoining room. "Follow, me." I still thought Roger was crazy to miss the game, and a shot at breaking the Babe's record. But words couldn't express how appreciative I was that he'd chosen to come to my son's Bar Mitzvah. We were an odd pair, Roger and me, but we had more important things in common than geography or religion.

BIG JULIE

ON SUNDAY THE press had a field day.

September 30, 1961 – *San Diego American Statesman*
WITH TWO GAMES LEFT TO BREAK BABE'S RECORD, ROGER MARIS TAKES THE DAY OFF TO ATTEND A BAR MITZVAH.

September 30, 1961 – *Chicago Daily Post*
ROGER MARIS MISSES CHANCE TO BREAK RUTH'S RECORD PREFERRING TO STUFF HIS FACE WITH FOOD AT A YIDDISH RECEPTION.

September 30, 1961 – *Denver Daily News*
"MARIS LOSES HIS MARBLES AS JEWISH FRIENDS CHEER
HIS OFF-KEY VERSION OF HAVAH NAGILA.

I had to wonder who'd provided the reporters with the inside information about the Bar Mitzvah. My sister, Doris, my cousin, Hymie? I guess it could have been any bellboy or waiter at the hotel.

Bottom line, Roger and Pat had a ball at the reception, Selma got lots of points for having a celebrity to the party, and Danny's friends all thought his Bar Mitzvah was the coolest ever.

By the time Selma and I got back to our Brooklyn apartment, I was beat and ready for bed. But before I could unlock my front door, someone tapped me on the shoulder.

"If he doesn't break the Babe's record on Monday," said a red-faced Houk, "I'm holding you singularly responsible, Jules."

CHAPTER EIGHTEEN

The Big Game

September 30, 1961

Maris Hitless as Yankees Beat Red Sox; Mantle to Leave Hospital Sunday. (18)
Mets name Casey Stengel as Manager for '62. (19)

MARSHALL

At 3:00 p.m. on Sunday, we lined up on the baseball field at Hudson Park and tossed the ball from player to player. At three-thirty, the Jamaica team arrived on the city bus. They looked bigger and tougher than I'd remembered.

Coach Lee and the Jamaica coach shook hands and chatted while the Ravens warmed up in the field. Soon the bleachers filled up with parents and all kinds of kids from school and the neighborhood. Some hoods from Jamaica climbed up to the top of the bleachers in leather jackets, greasy hair, and pointy boots.

Uncle George and Aunt Ethel and the other Flushing parents wore matching T-shirts that read FLUSHING ALL-STAR TEAM.

Laila sailed by the dugout with a couple of her girlfriends dressed in the same T-shirts. As she passed by, she blew me a kiss.

Rocky, who was sitting next to me, imitated the kiss at least five times. He poked Frank, who began blowing kisses too, and soon, half the team were doing it. At first, I felt embarrassed, then I began returning kisses back at them. Everyone cracked up laughing.

Coach Lee held his clipboard and worked up our batting order.

My uncle and aunt stopped by the dugout. "Good luck, you two."

Aunt Ethel hugged each of us then touched my arm. "Where's your mother? I called her but no one answered the phone."

"Mr. Gelaro got a stomach virus and she had to work. Dad's coming though," I said.

At the mention of my father, Aunt Ethel pursed her lips.

"This is sure gonna be one heck of a ballgame," Bobby said. Maybe he thought changing the subject would ease the tension.

Our team gathered around Coach Lee. "The key to beating these guys is we can't get behind early on." For the last time, the 1961 Flushing All-Star team stacked our hands, and chanted, "One-two-three, Flushing."

A few minutes later, we took our places on the baseball field. Brady Belk, our pitcher, threw some warm-up balls to Bobby.

The umpire walked onto the field. "Play ball."

The first batter for Jamaica, a tall, skinny kid with buckteeth that protruded over his lip like two fangs, stood at the plate and dug his cleat into the dirt. One, two, three, he struck out. He threw down his bat so hard it broke in two. I thought it was good luck for us to start the game with a strike out. Beat them early on, as Coach Lee had said.

The next two batters hit consecutive pop flies.

Yahoo! Great start. There were cheers in the stands from all of our parents as the designated announcer said, "After half an inning, no runs, no hits."

I scanned the bleachers for my dad and felt the usual pang of disappointment at his absence. It was still early. Maybe Brooks gave him his old job back and he had to work late. Maybe he got stuck in traffic. I'm not sure why I still cared.

We felt cocky, maybe too cocky, as we headed to the dugout. Rocky Romano was the first at bat. He winked at Frank and then CRACK, he ripped a double into left field. I cheered with the rest of my team until my voice felt hoarse.

Our second player struck out. Bobby headed to the batter's box and looked back at me nervously. I shot him a thumbs up, and walked on deck, I searched through the bleachers but still no sign of Dad. Forget him, I told myself. But for some reason, I just couldn't get him out of my mind.

Bobby hit a little flare that dropped in for a single.

Rocky bolted to third and then home base as the fans went wild.

"And the Flushing All-Stars take an early lead. 1 to 0 on Bobby Cechinni's single," said the announcer.

I headed to the plate and looked up at the bleachers. Laila was throwing me kisses with both hands. Aunt Ethel and Uncle George were chanting my name. "MARshall, MARshall!" But my dad…

I swung at the first high inside pitch and missed.

"Strike one," shouted the announcer.

The pitcher threw the ball again.

I hit a hard ground ball that sailed straight at the shortstop, who swiftly tossed it to the second baseman, who in turn, threw to first for a double play.

The announcer shouted, "Flushing retires scoring one run on two hits, no errors, with no one left on base."

My heart felt heavy. Once again, I had screwed up. I walked back to the dugout with my head down.

Coach Lee handed me my glove. "Don't worry, son, you hit the ball hard. It'll go through next time. We need you to focus on defense now."

"I'll try my best," I said. As I trotted back out on the field, I felt comforted that my dad hadn't arrived yet. I couldn't have stood to hear his commentary on my poor performance.

"That's the way to jump on them early, guys," Coach Lee shouted.

By the fourth inning, things had gone south. We were now down by three runs and I was 0 for 2 at the plate. And I no longer had any hope of my dad showing up for the game. What a fool I was to think he'd changed. Dad was all about Dad. He didn't care about me, or my mother. She was smart not to take him back.

As I stood out in right field, a sinking liner was hit to the left of me.

I dove into the foul line to save a run. The crowds cheered. I felt a little better.

"That ends four-and-a-half innings with a fantastic snag by

right-fielder, Marshall Elliot. The score remains Jamaica 5, Flushing 2."

As we ran out to the dugout, a huge Jamaica player shoved Bobby in passing.

My cousin whispered, "I'm gonna ignore that."

"It's probably a good idea." The kid was a good fifty pounds heavier than either of us. And he looked like someone had flattened his nose. Bobby and I headed to the on-deck circle.

The announcer shouted, "Catcher Bobby Cechinni leads off the bottom half of the inning for Flushing."

I whispered to Bobby, "I've gotta get a hit this time."

"Don't worry, I'll get on base and you can drive me in," Bobby said.

We slapped each other's hands and Bobby headed to the plate while I remained on deck. Bobby eyeballed the first pitch and chose not to swing.

"Ball one."

On the second pitch, Bobby hit a long drive to left center that had HOME RUN written all over it. The Flushing fans shouted and stomped their feet on the bleachers as Bobby rounded third base and headed for home plate. But a thrown ball to home plate forced him back to third base. Uncle George's whistle pierced through the cheers.

"A triple for Bobby Cechinni," said the announcer. "Now Flushing's right fielder, Marshall Elliot, steps up to the plate to bring him home."

I glanced in the bleachers one last time for Dad. Then I swung wildly at the first three pitches that came my way. One, two, three strikes, and I was out. I staggered to the dugout, trying to hold back the tears stinging my eyelids.

"Told you." The Jamaica catcher winked at their pitcher. "Elliot couldn't hit a giant balloon."

Uncle George bounded down from the bleachers and stopped me before I reached the dugout. "Don't worry about it, Marshall. Everyone strikes out at times."

"Not in the clutch," I said. "Not if you're a ballplayer that can be counted on."

"You'll hit one next time."

"It's not just that." The damn of tears finally burst. "My father said he'd come today."

Uncle George hugged me. "I know I can't make up for your father, but remember that *I'll* always be there for you, son."

I nodded and mouthed, "thanks." It wasn't that I didn't appreciate my uncle. He just wasn't Dad. Wiping my cheeks with my T-shirt, I entered the dugout and moved as far away from the other players as possible. I sat there sulking like a pathetic baby with my head between my knees.

At the bottom of the seventh inning, we were down by two, with one last chance to catch Jamaica. Barry McCue, our number nine hitter, ended up on base with a walk. The Jamaica pitcher looked tired as he wiped sweat from his brow with his arm.

Rocky, our one-hole leadoff hitter, laid down a sacrifice bunt, moving Barry to second base. He was followed by Frank who hit a bloop left of the pitcher, for a base hit. Runners on first and third. The Flushing fans cheered and waved their flags.

My cousin left the on-deck circle for the plate.

"Bobby Cechinni is up next for Flushing. He's two for two, with an RBI single and triple. So far, he's provided most of

Flushing's offense."

The Jamaica coach signaled to his pitcher to come out of the game.

The pitcher cocked his head to one side like he wasn't gonna move. "Who you got to relieve me?"

"Just come on out," shouted the coach.

The kid sailed past the coach and headed into their dugout.

An enormous kid I'd never seen before, raced out to the mound.

"Who the heck is that?" Coach Lee shouted. The boy was the size of my Uncle George.

The Jamaica coach walked over to Coach Lee. "Our new pitcher, Johnny Brock."

"You can't just add new kids to your lineup," Coach Lee said.

The umpire joined the two coaches and the three of them stood in a huddle.

"That kid isn't even on their team," Coach Lee said.

"'Sure he is. His family just moved in from the Bronx," the Jamaica coach said.

Coach Lee glared at the umpire. "He's not eligible for All-Stars."

The Jamaica coach had a smirk on his face. "This isn't All-Stars anymore. It's just a game for the kids."

The umpire shrugged. "He's got a point, Lee. There's no precedent, since technically this isn't a regular season game."

The three men disbanded, and moments later, the Little League announcer hollered, "Now pitching for Jamaica, Johnny Brock, the former Bronx Little League strikeout champion."

He threw some rapid practice pitches to their catcher, and

damn if he didn't throw that ball like a pro.

I got on deck as Bobby walked to the plate and dug in his cleats. He looked up at Uncle George, then back at me.

Brock threw three straight fastballs right down the pipe to Bobby and the umpire called him out.

"That's two down for Flushing."

I could barely breathe as I headed to the plate. Out of the corner of my eye, I saw a group of men descending down right field line toward our bleachers. As I passed Bobby heading back to the dugout, he said, "You gonna have to start your swing early."

"I can't do this."

He touched my hand. "Geez, at least give it a try."

The first pitch, a thigh-high fastball, whizzed by for strike one. I swallowed hard and took a few practice swings.

The next pitch down the middle was followed by a loud pop when it hit the catcher's mitt. One more bullet pitch for strike two.

If only I could disappear before my final defeat. Nothing in my life was working out. Not baseball, not my father, not having our family united again. I seriously considered walking off the field. But then, I saw Ma smiling at me.

The parents in the bleachers began to yell and scream at the top of their lungs. I'd never heard a crowd get so excited at a Little League game.

Johnny Brock threw in two more bullets, high and out, but I took wild swings at them. Fortunately, I managed to hit the ball with the tip of the bat resulting in foul balls.

A young kid shouted from the bleachers, "Oh my God, that's the M&M boys and the Yankee ball team!"

The whole Yankee team sat down with the Flushing parents in the bleachers. The crowd was out of control and the umpire called a time out.

Roger pushed his way through the throngs of fans to the backstop. "Hey bud, how's it going?"

I shrugged. "Not too good. I haven't had a hit all day."

He smiled. "All it takes is one. I know you have it in you."

"This is unbelievable," said the announcer. "The New York Yankees have come to our Little League game."

The next pitch came at me in slow motion. I swung at it with all the strength I could muster up. As the ball made contact with my bat, I heard that sweet CRACK.

As I ran to first base, I heard the announcer, "It's a well hit ball. Way back, *waaay back*. No one's gonna catch this one. It's a three run homer to win the game for Flushing."

My teammates greeted me at home plate, picked me up onto their shoulders, and carried me to the Yankee team.

Roger had a smile from ear-to-ear. "Way to go, Marshall."

Mickey limped his way through the crowd and patted my back. "See, you came through in the clutch."

"You got out of the hospital."

"Heck," Mick said, "I wouldn't miss this for the world."

My mother gave me a big hug. "That's my boy."

"I thought you had to work late."

"I closed Gelaro's Market early, jumped in a cab, and arrived just in time to see your hit. You should have heard me yelling at the driver to step on the gas. Good thing he knew your uncle."

"It means a lot to me that you made it, Ma."

Bobby muscled his way through the crowds. "The Yankees

are telling everyone they came to see you. What the heck is going on?"

"It's a long story. Roger and Mickey lived next door to us all summer."

Bobby drew his brows together. "And you didn't tell me?"

Roger stepped forward. "I made him swear he wouldn't tell anyone, not even you, son. I'm real proud of Marshall that he was able to keep his promise."

Mickey moved next to Roger. "For that, me and Roger would officially like Marshall to be known as the third M&M Boy. We're now the M&M&M Boys."

My teammates surrounded us. Most of them stood with their mouths literally open.

"Why don't you kids come over to our house for an ice cream party?" Mickey said.

The players from both teams had huge smiles as everybody followed our heroes off the Hudson Park baseball field. It no longer mattered who won or lost. We were now just a group of lucky kids who got a chance to hang out with our heroes.

"Pinch me," Rocky said.

Frank obliged and then slapped my back. "Glad we got to know you, Marshall,"

One Flushing father asked Roger. "Can the dads come too?"

Roger smiled. "Sure, why not?"

Aunt Ethel cleared her throat. "How about the mothers?"

"Of course, everyone's invited," shouted Whitey.

We all moved happily toward the parking lot. I was joking with Bobby when someone grabbed my arm. "Great game," Laila said.

Bobby winked at me and jogged up ahead of us.

"Thanks," I said. "You're welcome to come to the party."

A tear bubbled up in her eye. "I'd love to but I have to leave."

"What do you mean, leave?"

"My father's much better," she said. "He's coming home from the hospital tonight. Mother is picking me up on the way back to Long Island. She'll be here in an hour."

"You're moving?"

"I'm afraid so."

"That's terrible." My voice cracked. "I mean it's great that your father's better, but I'm, ah, really going to miss you."

"I'll miss you too." She handed me a piece of wadded up paper. "My phone number in West Meadow. Call me."

Next thing I knew, she kissed me. Not on my cheek like last time, but right on the lips.

I closed my eyes and kissed her back.

"Call me soon," she said, and raced off leaving me there with lips still puckered up.

Bobby turned back around and grinned. "Come on, Marshall. Everyone's waiting for you."

As I opened the back door to Uncle George's cab, I noticed the huge pitcher, Johnny Brock, standing alone with a scowl on his face.

"You're one heck of a pitcher," I said. "I wouldn't feel too bad."

"It's not that. I don't have a ride to the Yankee's house."

"Where are your parents?" Aunt Ethel said.

"Mom's probably passed out by now. I don't have a dad."

"Why don't you ride with us?" I said.

Johnny Brock smiled. "Gee, thanks."

MARSHALL

AFTER THE ICE CREAM party, word spread so quickly that crowds of people mobbed our street. Flashbulbs went off. Vans from all the major TV stations pulled up with the logos for ABC, CBS, and NBC painted on their doors. Mel Allen stepped out of the CBS van with a camera crew. A few minutes later, he stood on our front lawn speaking into a microphone.

Mel Allen: "We're told the M&M Boys lived in this very place all summer. Can you imagine? How the heck did they keep it a big secret?"

Mel glanced at me sitting on my porch still dressed in my Flushing All-Stars uniform.

Mel Allen: "Hey, kid, did ya know who was living next door to you the past few months? Can ya tell us where they've gone?"

I smiled at him, opened the screen door, and ducked inside the house. I'd kept my mouth shut all summer. No way would I betray my heroes now.

CHAPTER NINETEEN

It's Over

October 1, 1961

"Holy cow! He did it! 61 home runs! —Phil Rizzuto (20)

BIG JULIE

The Yankee stadium stands were half-empty except for the right-field bleachers, which were jammed with both kids and adults holding up gloves in hope of catching Roger's 61st ball.

Mickey's infection had flared up despite the antibiotics and he was forced back into the hospital. He called before the game started to say he'd be raising a glass of milk in toast to Roger from his bed. His wife, Merlyn, and their four boys were by his side.

Pat and the Maris children took their seats behind the dugout next to me, Danny, Mrs. Elliot, and Marshall. Selma decided she'd prefer to get her hair done than attend the ballgame, so we gave her ticket to Marshall's cousin, Bobby.

Marshall sat between his cousin and his mother. Following the Little League game, the M&M Boys had moved out of the duplex. While Marshall was disappointed, he understood the sacrifice they had made of losing their privacy in order to support him at the game.

In the forth inning, Roger stepped up to the plate.

Phil Rizzuto: "Here comes Roger Maris. They're standing up, waiting to see if Roger is going to hit number sixty-one. Here's the wind up…the pitch to Roger…way outside, ball one."

The crowd booed.

Phil Rizzuto: "The crowd is angry. Low, ball two. That one was in the dirt. And the boos get louder," Rizzuto said. "Two balls, no strikes on Roger Maris. Here's the windup… fastball… hit deep to the right…THIS COULD BE IT!…Holy Cow! He did it! 61 home runs. They're fighting for the ball out there. Holy cow! Another standing ovation for Roger Maris." (21)

With his head down, Roger rounded the bases and attempted to go straight into the dugout, but was blocked by a wall of his Yankee teammates who forced him back onto the field, where he humbly waved his cap to the ecstatic crowd.

I looked over and smiled at Marshall, the little boy who shared the summer's triumphs, frustrations, celebrations, and disappointments with his heroes, Roger Maris and Mickey Mantle. He jumped up and raised his fist as his popcorn spilled in the air.

CHAPTER TWENTY

Maris & Marshall

October 2, 1961

Baseball player Roger Maris of the New York Yankees hit his 61st home run in the last game of the season, against the Boston Red Sox, beating the 34-year-old record held by Babe Ruth. The homer was made at 1:46 pm at Yankee Stadium, off of Boston pitcher Tracy Stallard, in the game's fourth inning. (22)

MARSHALL

The night after Roger broke Babe's record there was a knock on our front door. I was up in my bedroom when Ma called me from the hallway. "Get down here, Marshall. There's someone who wants to speak with you."

Roger stood in the living room with his baseball cap in his hand. "We owe your son a lot for everything he did for us this summer." He handed her a wad of money wrapped up in a rubber band.

"I'm sorry, we can't accept this," Ma said.

"He earned it," Roger said. "Ya got yourself a very special boy, ma'am."

She smiled. "Don't I know it."

When Roger saw me, he wrapped his arms around me in a bear hug. "You did it," I said. "You broke the record."

"No way would it have happened without your help." He handed me a piece of paper with something scribbled on it. "This is Big Julie's phone number. If you need anything, you just call him. And he'll have some tickets for the World Series waiting for you."

I swallowed. "I'm gonna miss you."

"I'll miss ya, too." He took a deep breath. "You take care now."

Later that night, my mother and I were sitting on the porch drinking lemonade and enjoying the cool October breeze. I was feeling really happy for the first time in a long while.

Then Dad's blue Galaxie pulled into the driveway. He got out of the car, walked up to the porch, and patted my head. Then he sat down next to Ma on the stoop. "Have you had time to think about giving our marriage another try?"

"Nothing's changed." My mother stood. "And you missed your son's game again."

Dad looked sheepishly at me. "I can explain."

"I really don't care anymore." And it was true. I no longer wanted to hear his lame excuses. I'd learned to be happy without him.

Dad glanced at my mother. "What about our sacred vows? And doesn't the Bible talk about forgiveness?"

She pursed her lips. "Oh, please."

An old Chevy screeched to a stop in front of our house. Miss Fowler stepped out and stood on the front lawn. Her whole body was shaking. "So you're going back to *her*?"

"Go home, Gloria," Dad said.

"Not without you. You have a baby to support."

"You never mentioned there were three other mouths to feed," Dad said. "Four, counting your mother."

She peered at me sitting with my frothy lemonade. "Just one kiddo here. Guess you figured it's a better deal?"

"Dad shouted. "Go back to Bingo, please."

"Don't worry," my mother said. "I'm not taking him back."

Miss Fowler slid down to the ground and started to weep. In between sobs she looked up at my dad. "How can you do this to me?"

"Go with her, Edmond," Ma said. "That would be the right thing to do. You're married to *her*." Ma walked up to Miss Fowler, extended her hand, and helped her up.

After a few awkward moments of us all standing there, Dad said, "Okay, okay. Get in the car, Gloria. I'll follow you home."

My mother and I went back inside the house. I was proud of her for what she had done. And deep down, I knew we were better off without my father.

I never doubted the baby was my brother. Or maybe it was wishful thinking. I often wondered how he was doing. If he was smart, he wouldn't count on Dad for much. I hoped someday, I might be there for him if he ever got into a jam. Like Roger was for me that summer.

EPILOGUE

Roger's record stood for 37 years until 1998 when a couple of sluggers named Mark McGuire and Sammy Sosa dared to challenge his legacy.

Later, Barry Bonds would hit 73 home runs. Because of the steroid allegations surrounding McGwire, Sosa and Bonds, there has been serious discussion that Roger should still have the single-season record.

Since it took Roger 162 games to break Babe Ruth's record, many refused to give him the respect he deserved. He was given a slice of baseball immortality, but lost big patches of his hair and his love of the game along the way.

Chasing history will do that to you.

ROGER MARIS

9/10/1934 — 12/14/1985

EARLY YEARS

Roger Maris's father, Rudy Maris, worked for the Great Northern Railroad and the family moved to Fargo, North Dakota, in 1942 where Roger and his older brother, Rudy, grew up. Roger claimed his brother was the better athlete, but he was stricken with polio at eighteen, and never recovered his sports ability. Roger was recruited to play football for the University of Oklahoma but gave up his scholarship to pursue a career in baseball. He signed a $15,000 contract in 1957 to play for the Cleveland Indians.

CAREER HIGHLIGHTS

Many say that 1961 was a fluke, but Roger hit 39 homers and was the American League MVP while playing for the Yankees in 1960. Not too many players become back-to-back MVPs. Roger was a major league right fielder for twelve seasons on four teams from 1957-1968.

Maris appeared in seven World Series, five for the Yankees, and two with the Cardinals. He hit six World Series home runs and drove in eighteen World Series RBIs. He also played in seven All-Star games. Besides holding the single season home run record for thirty-seven years (from 1961-1998), Maris hit 275 career home runs. His fine defensive skills were often overlooked although he won the Gold Glove Award for outstanding defensive play.

MARRIAGE & FAMILY

Roger met his wife, the former Pat Carvell, at a basketball game in high school. He was a loyal family man, a religious Catholic who put family first. His greatest regret about his baseball career was the long forced separations from Pat his kids.

Roger's own childhood had been plagued by parents who had a rocky marriage. While he adored his mother, she had gained a reputation for fooling around on his father. When he chose Pat, he was looking for a stable woman who had the same old-fashioned family values as he did.

Together they ultimately would have six children, four boys and two girls, making a family that would serve as an unshakeable foundation for Maris during even the most tumultuous days of his subsequent career.

PERSONAL

Throughout Roger's baseball career, he suffered many physical injuries. His aggressive base running and fielding left him prone to getting hurt. In Maris' seven years with the Yankees, the team went to five World Series and won two. In 1963, Roger hit 23 home runs in only 90 games, a rate of 41 home runs per 162 games.

The press didn't let up on Roger after 1961. The pressure to repeat his home run performance made him a continued target of criticism. He often was called the "one season wonder." Ironically, his teammates had nothing but praise for Roger as a true team player who put winning above his own performance, time and time again. He was an outstanding outfielder.

Maris sustained a painful wrist injury in 1965. For two seasons he insisted it was real, yet the Yankees contended it was not. The injury sapped Maris' power and rendered him an average hitter. With so great a fall from his heights and ill-feeling with the Yankee medical staff souring his already problematic public image, Maris began to be portrayed as both lazy and an agitator by the press.

Knowing it wasn't true hurt Maris deeply, but just as in 1961, he struggled to show a sympathetic side to the fans. His days in New York clearly grew numbered and he was traded to the St. Louis Cardinals at the end of 1966 season. He played his two final years in St. Louis where he helped the Cardinals win back-to-back World Series, the first in 1967 against the Red Sox, and the second against the powerful Detroit Tigers of 1968.

Many players from the '67 Cardinal team have said that Maris' presence on that squad brought an awareness of winning and dedication to hard work that helped elevate them from talented pennant contenders to World Champions.

Roger wrote a semi-autobiographical novel with veteran reporter, Jim Ogle, called *Slugger in Right*. The protagonist, Bill Mack, was a right fielder who closely resembled Roger.

Despite all the controversy and criticism, Maris was awarded the 1961 Hickok Belt as the top professional athlete of the year. It is said, however, that the stress of pursuing the record was so great for Maris that his hair occasionally fell out in clumps during the season. Later, Maris even surmised that it might have been better all along had he not broken the record or even threatened it at all.

His wife, Pat Maris, said, "Roger's combination of shyness

and outspokenness confuses people who do not know him very well." (23)

Ford Frick, the commissioner, a onetime colleague of Babe Ruth, announced that any record would have to be set in 154 games.

"I never wanted all this hoopla. All I wanted is to be a good ball player and hit twenty-five or thirty homers, drive in a hundred runs, hit .280 and help my club win pennants. I just wanted to be one of the guys, an average player having a good season."
—Roger Maris (24)

RETIREMENT

After Roger retired from baseball, he owned and operated an Anheuser-Busch beer distributorship in Gainesville, Florida, with his brother Rudy. A relationship that started with a handshake between baseball legend Roger Maris, and the owner of the world's largest beer brewery ended with a settlement of a defamation lawsuit resulting from the brewery terminating its contract in 1997. Maris' relatives accused the brewer of defamation after company officials said the family's distributorship was deficient and sold repackaged, out-of-date beer. The beer giant agreed to pay at least $120 million in a confidential settlement.

For many years, Roger shunned old-timers' games, because he resented the criticism and controversy from his playing days and feared he would be booed. But when George Steinbrenner, a Cleveland shipping magnate, bought the Yankees in 1973, he became determined to bring Maris to Old-Timers' Day. Four years later, Roger agreed to appear on opening day, stipulating the Steinbrenner promise not to announce his appearance in advance. Only Steinbrenner, Mantle, and a handful club officials, knew there would be a special guest that day.

As some old footage of Roger Maris hitting his 61st home run appeared on the center field video screen, he and Mantle trotted out onto the field. Instead of the anticipated boos, a standing ovation roared through the stadium. An older, heavier Maris, who still wore his trade crewcut, waved to the crowd and feigned punching Mickey, reminding everyone of their perceived feud. Then he linked arms with his good friend and accepted the unexpected adulation from the crowd.

He appeared at a few more reunions later, and he remained close friends with Mantle, Whitey, Yogi Berra, Tony Kubek, and his other teammates from the time when the Yankees ruled the day.

Roger Maris died on December 14, 1985, of lymphoma cancer at the age of fifty-one.

Despite his extraordinary contributions to the game of baseball, Roger Maris has never been elected to The Baseball Hall of Fame.

Go to YouTube.com to see Roger hit his 61st home run
called by Red Barber
http://www.youtube.com/watch?v=4hSNO_PhSnI

MICKEY MANTLE

10/20/1931 — 08/13/1995

EARLY YEARS

Mickey Mantle was born in Spavinaw, Oklahoma. From a young age, Mickey was trained as a switch-hitter by his father, Mutt Mantle, who worked in local lead and zinc mines. The young Mickey would bat left-handed to his father, and right handed to his grandfather for hours every night. Mickey adored his father who had a powerful influence on his life. An all-around athlete at Commerce High School, Mickey played basketball and football, and received a football scholarship to the University of Oklahoma.

CAREER HIGHLIGHTS

Mickey began his career as a Yankee in 1951, eventually replacing Joe DiMaggio in center field. The New York fans initially booed the outsider from Oklahoma for daring to try to fill the big shoes of their local hero.

During his eighteen-year career with the Yankees, Mantle hit 536 home runs and was voted the American League's Most Valuable Player three times. He won the Triple Crown in 1956, leading in batting average, home runs, and runs batted in.

Mantle appeared in 19 All-Star games, and 12 World Series. He holds the record for most World Series home runs (18), RBIs (40), runs (42), walks (43), extra-base hits (26), and total bases (123). In 1974 he was elected into the National Hall of Fame, together with his best friend, Whitey Ford.

MARRIAGE & FAMILY

Like Roger Maris, Mickey met his wife, the former Merlyn Johnson, during high school. She was a cheerleader for rivaling Picher High School. Her sister introduced them, and Mickey took her on their first date in the family's 1947 Chevrolet Fleetline. According to Merlyn, Mick was so shy, he hardly spoke a word.

Mickey asked Merlyn to marry him at his father's urging. They had four sons, Billy, Danny, David, and Mickey Junior. While their marriage was stormy because of Mick's drinking and renowned womanizing, they remained legally married until Mickey's death in 1995. Separated in 1984, the two remained friends and held a special affection for each other.

Merlyn was forthright about Mickey's infidelity in *A Hero All His Life*: Merlyn had come to understand that her husband regarded marriage as "a party with added attractions." (25)

Merlyn and all four of their sons were treated for alcoholism at the Betty Ford clinic. Shortly after Mickey's death, she spoke of the negative impact that alcohol had over her family's life. "I was in there partying and doing the same thing as Mick. That was our life and I was part of it. I can't deny that. It ruins families." (26)

PERSONAL

Mickey's left ankle became infected with Osteomyelitis, a crippling disease, from getting kicked in the left shin during a practice game in his sophomore year in high school. The injury almost cost him his leg and was the cause of chronic pain for the rest of his life.

In the second game of the 1951 World Series, Willie Mays hit a fly ball toward Mickey in right center field. Mantle raced for the ball together with center fielder Joe DiMaggio. To get out of DiMaggio's way, Mantle tripped over an exposed sprinkler and severely injured his right knee. He played the rest of his career with a torn ACL. This was the first of many accumulated injuries. Applying thick wraps to both knees before games, he also had heat treatments for a right shoulder injury and supersonic treatments for pulled stomach muscles.

After Mickey received a 4F deferment from the army during the Korean War, a columnist questioned how a man could play professional baseball when he wasn't healthy enough to fight for his country. He was called a draft dodger, a coward, and even a "Commie."

Known for his hard drinking and womanizing, and plagued with painful injuries, Mantle persevered to leave one of the greatest baseball legacies of all time. Mickey's father, grandfather, and an uncle all died before the age of forty from Hodgkin's disease. "If I knew I was going to live this long, I'd have taken better care of myself." (27) Mickey was quoted around the time he received a controversial liver transplant in 1995. He died shortly after of a heart attack.

RETIREMENT

The kid from Oklahoma's big-city restaurant, *Mickey Mantle's* on Central Park South in NYC, did quite well, as did a number of Mantle's post-baseball life investments. He remained a popular public speaker, coach, and sports commentator. When his

alcoholism and final illness became public, some critics casti-
gated him. But for most people, he died a hero, if not a role
model, a player who was loved by his fellow players and admired
by millions.

BIG JULIE ISAACSON

(DOB: unknown)

Julie Isaacson was a Jewish Brooklyn-born wheeler-dealer known as "The Fixer." Julius or Big Julie as he preferred to be called, had an interesting and somewhat unusual career history. He had a reputation as someone who hung out with top sport celebrities. A union man, he held the position as president of the International Union of Doll, Toy, and Novelty Workers.

"A would-be pitcher who threw with such velocity that he could knock down a wall—but only if he didn't aim at it. Big Julie stood 6'3" and weighed well over two hundred pounds. A boxer, he later managed Ernie Terrell, when Terrell became heavyweight champion." (28)

Big Julie did meet Roger Maris at LaGuardia airport when Roger first arrived in the Big Apple. The infamous story of him chiding Roger over his seersucker suit and Pat Boone shoes is known to be true. The two became lifelong friends.

As the story goes, Big Julie was a good friend to have when you were falsely accused of getting someone pregnant. "Mickey had a problem," said Isaacson in 1958. "A girl was trying to shake him down. It wasn't his. We had the girl come over to the Edison. We met her there. Took her to the East River and told her she had two choices: Leave Mickey alone, or this." (29)

DISCUSSION QUESTIONS

1. How much of a person's character is shaped by the time in which he lives?

2. What characteristics do Roger, Big Julie, and Uncle George have in common?

3. Is Mickey Mantle really a bad guy? What are his redeeming qualities? What did you like and dislike about him?

4. What important lessons does Marshall learn by the end of the novel?

5. Why does Marshall's mother fall apart when his father walks out? What does she learn about herself by the end of the story?

6. This novel is about unlikely friendships. What besides baseball bonds Roger Maris, Mickey Mantle, and Marshall?

7. Is the Roger Maris in this story a believable character? What does he learn from Big Julie?

8. Who is your favorite character in the story and why?

9. What is the significance of Big Julie's character in the story?

10. Who is the real antagonist?

11. Baseball is often said to be a microcosm of life. Can you give examples of things that happened on and off the field in this book?

ACKNOWLEDGEMENTS

This book is dedicated to:

My wonderful father, William Resnick, a devoted Yankee fan since the days of Babe Ruth.

Jacob, Matthew, and Marshall whose Little League games inspired my understanding of how very important the game of baseball is to young boys. Even though I'm remembered as the mother who sat in the back of the bleachers reading a book, I did pay attention.

Rudy, an amazing Little League coach. At the end of every game, no matter how bad a kid's performance might have been, he always reminded him of something positive he had done during the game. He inspired good sportsmanship, confidence and a love of the game to all his teams, but especially to our three sons. I couldn't have chosen a better husband or father for my children.

And to the two loves of my life, Madison Elizabeth and Taylor Paige Chavez.

Special thanks to the cadre of authors who have bonded with me to mutually help each other through the maze of creating and marketing a work of fiction in the new frontier of the twenty-first century independent publishing world. Especially: Tosh McIntosh, Cynthia Stone, Brad Whittington, John J. Asher, and Susan Rockhold. Check out some of their wonderful novels online.

Above and beyond the call of duty:

Tosh McIntosh – for the time he spent on the eBook and print edition covers and the formatting of this novel for Kindle.

Kathy Sargent – for a great job on the print book formatting.

Rita Singer – the sister who never gets tired of reading and commenting on the endless revisions of all my writing projects.

Susan Rockhold – for a painstakingly excellent job of proof editing and critiquing.

Lidia Pabon – for her valuable time editing and the incredible find of mistakes no one else saw.

ALSO BY LARA REZNIK

The Girl From Long Guyland

MEMOIR MEETS THRILLER. Set against a 1969 psychedelic love-in backdrop, *The Girl From Long Guyland* is shared through the eyes of Laila Levin when decades later, an unsolved murder pulls her reluctantly into her past. A dramatic collision of then and now entwining family, marriage, profession and ethics.

http://www.amazon.com/The-Girl-From-Long-Guyland-ebook/dp/B00A45OYD0

"In Reznik's debut novel, a woman confronts long-buried secrets when an old college friend commits suicide ... While effective as a page-turner, the novel also tells a timeless, universal tale of a woman's journey toward self-acceptance. An exciting tale of past crimes and dangerous friendships."
—Kirkus Reviews

"Laila Levin is an I.T. executive in Austin, TX, with a happy marriage and a successful career. But her life is about to get much more complicated. Laila is forced to confront a dark part of her past that she never shared with her husband. ... Readers, particularly those who remember the late 1960s, will find this an entertaining read."
—Publishers Weekly

★★★★★ "I love a mystery and I love stories about the late 60's/early 70's and this book has both! Really fun read."
*—*Barbara Gaines, Executive Producer, *The Late Show with David Letterman*

★★★★★ "It's one of those books that takes two different time periods in a women's life and as the story unfolds weaves them together gradually in a very clever way. Reznik uses a great technique going back and forth constantly building suspense along the way . . . As someone who is selective about what I read, this book didn't disappoint. Great mystery and suspense. Add a star if you were a " flower child " from the sixties.
—Les Goodstein, Former President and COO of the *New York Daily News*

Screenplays by Lara Reznik:

The M&M Boys
Bagels & Salsa
Dance of Deception

Novels by Lara Reznik:

The Girl From Long Guyland
The M&M Boys

ABOUT THE AUTHOR

Lara Reznik grew up on Long Island in the fifties and sixties, attending many Yankee games with her father and Uncle Sol during her childhood. At ten years old, she saw Roger Maris hit his sixty-first home run.

In 1970, Lara left New York for the wild west of New Mexico in a Karmann Ghia that she jump-started cross-country. As an English major at the University of New Mexico, Laura studied under esteemed authors Rudolfo Anaya and Tony Hillerman. Ambidextrous from birth, she preferred her right-brained creative side, but discovered she could make a better living with her left-brain skills, so entered the I.T. field.

In 1995 she and her husband Rudy, and their three sons, relocated to Austin, TX, where she worked as an I.T. manager for a utility. Since that time, she's written and optioned three screen-plays and two novels.

After the breakout Amazon success of her first novel, *The Girl From Long Guyland,* Lara left her career in I.T. to write full time.

Visit the author at: www.larareznik.com
E-mail: Larareznik23@gmail.com

Footnotes

1. *"Affirmative Action,"* in *Encyclopedia of Black Studies* (Molefi K. Asante and Ama Mazama, eds.) (SAGE, 2005) p. 3

2. Peter Wyden, 1979. *Bay of Pigs — The Untold Story.* Pp. *220-222*

3. "Freedom Riders," WGBH American Experience," PBS.

4. Byline - Homer Bigart *"Adolf Eichmann Felt Like Pilate,"* The *New York Times,*

5. "Gun Kills Ernest Hemingway," Pittsburgh Post-Gazette, July 3, 1961, p. 1

6. Jae-Cheon Lim, *Kim Jong Il's Leadership of North Korea* (Taylor & Francis US, 2009) p. 47

7. Patsy Sims, *The Klan (University Press of Kentucky,* 1996) p. 94

8. Peter Braestrup, *Special to The New York Times.* August 1, 1961, p. 1

9. Harvey Frommer, Mickey Mantle, *Roger Maris: The 61ˢᵗ Home Run*, October 1, 1961, *http://www.travel-watch.com/rogermaris61sthomerun.htm*, 2014

10. *Satellites Plan E Reich Pact: "German-a-Minute Fleeing to West." Milwaukee Sentinel,* August 6, 1961 p.1

11. Byline: Max Frankel, Special to *The New York Times.* August 11, 1961, p. 1

12. Byline: *Lawrence Fellows Special to The New York Times.* September 3, 1961, p. 23

13. "Phil Rizzuto commenting on Yankee baseball, 1960-1961 (You Tube)

14. "Phil Rizzuto commenting on Yankee baseball, 1960-1961 (You Tube)

15. Conrad Wennerberg, *Wind, Waves, and Sunburn: A Brief History of Marathon Swimming (Breakaway Books, 1997) pp 64-65;* "He Swims Channel, And Swims Back!" *Miami News,* September 22, 1961

16. Front Page Headline, *The New York Times,* September 26, 1961

17. Byline: Jay Walz, *Special to The New York Times,* September 29, 1961, p. 1

18. Byline: John Drebinger, *Special to The New York Times,* September 30, 1961, p. 1

19. Byline: Bill Becker, *New York Times,* September 30, 1961 p. 2

20. Phil Rizzuto, commenting on Yankee baseball, October 1, 1961 (You Tube)

21. Phil Rizzuto commenting on Yankee baseball, October 1, 1961 (You Tube)

22. *"I'm The Only Man To Hit 61 Homers,"* *Miami News,* October 2, 1961, p. 1C

23. Tom Clavin and Danny Peary, *Roger Maris, Baseball's Reluctant Hero,* p. 76

24. Roger Maris, Baseball Almanac, *www.baseball-almanac.com/quotes/quomari.shtml*

25. Mickey E. Mantle, David Mantle, Dan Mantle, Merlyn Mantle, Travis Swords, Dorothy Schott, *A Hero All His Life: A Memoir by the Mantle Family p. 25*

26. Ibid, P. 131

27. Biography.com, *http://www.biography.com/people/mickey-mantle-9398023*

28. Jane Leavy, *The Last Boy, Mickey Mantle, And the End of America's Childhood.* p. 149

29. Ibid, p. 150

BIBLIOGRAPHY

1. Allen, Mel, commenting on Yankee baseball in 1960-1961 (You Tube)

2. *New York Times, Time Machine http://timesmachine.nytimes.com/browser,* 1961

3. Leavy, Jane, *The Last Boy, Mickey Mantle, And The End of America's Childhood,* Harper Perennial; Reprint edition, October 4, 2011.

4. Rizzuto, Phil commenting on Yankee baseball, 1960-1961 (You Tube)

5. Kubek, Tony, Pluto, Terry, *Sixty-One: The Team, the Record, the Men,* Fireside, April 1989

6. Clavin, Tom, Peary, Danny, *Roger Maris: Baseball's Reluctant Hero,* Touchstone, Reprint Edition, May 10, 2011

7. Mantle, Merlyn, Mantle, Mickey Jr., Mantle, David, Mantle, Dan, *A Hero All His Life: A Memoir by the Mantle Family,* HarperCollins 1st Edition, October, 1996

8. Rosenfeld, Harvey, *Still A Legend: The Story of Roger Maris,* iUniverse, September 10, 2002